We Need New Names

We Need New Names

189094921

This large print edition published in 2014 by
W F Howes Ltd
Unit 4, Rearsby Business Park, Gaddesby Lane,
Rearsby, Leicester LE7 4YH

1 3 5 7 9 10 8 6 4 2

First published in the United Kingdom in 2013
by Chatto & Windus

A CIP catalogue record for this book is available
from the British Library

ISBN 978 1 47125 846 6

Typeset by Palimpsest Book Production Limited,
Falkirk, Stirlingshire

Printed and bound in Great Britain
by TJ International Ltd, Padstow, Cornwall

For Za

CHAPTER 1

HITTING BUDAPEST

We are on our way to Budapest: Bastard and Chipo and Godknows and Sbho and Stina and me. We are going even though we are not allowed to cross Mzilikazi Road, even though Bastard is supposed to be watching his little sister Fraction, even though Mother would kill me dead if she found out; we are just going. There are guavas to steal in Budapest, and right now I'd rather die for guavas. We didn't eat this morning and my stomach feels like somebody just took a shovel and dug everything out.

Getting out of Paradise is not so hard since the mothers are busy with hair and talk, which is the only thing they ever do. They just glance at us when we file past the shacks and then look away. We don't have to worry about the men under the jacaranda either since their eyes never lift from the draughts. It's only the little kids who see us and try to follow, but Bastard just wallops the naked one at the front with a fist on his big head and they all turn back.

When we hit the bush we are already flying, scream-singing like the wheels in our voices will

1

make us go faster. Sbho leads: *Who discovered the way to India?* and the rest of us rejoin, *Vasco da Gama! Vasco da Gama! Vasco da Gama!* Bastard is at the front because he won country-game today and he thinks that makes him our president or something, and then myself and Godknows, Stina, Sbho, and finally Chipo, who used to outrun everybody in all of Paradise but not anymore because somebody made her pregnant.

After crossing Mzilikazi we cut through another bush, zip right along Hope Street for a while before we cruise past the big stadium with the glimmering benches we'll never sit on, and finally we hit Budapest. We have to stop once, though, for Chipo to sit down because of her stomach; sometimes when it gets painful she has to rest it.

When is she going to have the baby anyway? Bastard says. Bastard doesn't like it when we have to stop doing things because of Chipo's stomach. He even tried to get us not to play with her altogether.

She'll have it one day, I say, speaking for Chipo because she doesn't talk anymore. She is not mute-mute; it's just that when her stomach started showing, she stopped talking. But she still plays with us and does everything else, and if she really, really needs to say something she'll use her hands.

What's one day? On Thursday? Tomorrow? Next week?

Can't you see her stomach is still small? The baby has to grow.

A baby grows *outside* of the stomach, not inside. That's the whole reason they are born. So they grow into adults.

Well, it's not time yet. That's why it's still in a stomach.

Is it a boy or girl?

It's a boy. The first baby is supposed to be a boy.

But you're a girl, big head, and you're a first-born.

I said *supposed*, didn't I?

Just shut your kaka mouth, you, it's not even your stomach.

I think it's a girl. I put my hands on it all the time and I've never felt it kick, not even once.

Yes, boys kick and punch and butt their heads. That's all they are good at.

Does she want a boy?

No. Yes. Maybe. I don't know.

Where exactly does a baby come out of?

The same place it goes into the stomach.

How exactly does it get into the stomach?

First, Jesus's mother has to put it in there.

No, not Jesus's mother. A man has to put it in there, my cousin Musa told me. Well, she was really telling Enia, and I was there so I heard.

Then who put it inside her?

How can we know if she won't say?

Who put it in there, Chipo? Tell us, we won't tell.

Chipo looks at the sky. There's a tear in her one eye, but it's only a small one.

3

Then if a man put it in there, why doesn't he take it out?

Because it's women who give birth, you dunderhead. That's why they have breasts to suckle the baby and everything.

But Chipo's breasts are small. Like stones.

It doesn't matter. They'll grow when the baby comes. Let's go, can we go, Chipo? I say. Chipo doesn't reply, she just takes off, and we run after her. When we get right to the middle of Budapest we stop. This place is not like Paradise, it's like being in a different country altogether. A nice country where people who are not like us live. But then you don't see anything to show there are real people living here; even the air itself is empty: no delicious food cooking, no odors, no sounds. Just nothing.

Budapest is big, big houses with satellite dishes on the roofs and neat graveled yards or trimmed lawns, and the tall fences and the Durawalls and the flowers and the big trees heavy with fruit that's waiting for us since nobody around here seems to know what to do with it. It's the fruit that gives us courage, otherwise we wouldn't dare be here. I keep expecting the clean streets to spit and tell us to go back where we came from.

At first we used to steal from Stina's uncle, who now lives in Britain, but that was not stealing-stealing because it was Stina's uncle's tree and not a stranger's. There's a difference. But then we finished all the guavas in that tree so we have moved to the other houses as well. We have stolen from so many houses I cannot even count. It was Bastard who decided that we pick a street and stay on it until we have gone through all the houses. Then we go to the next street. This is so we don't confuse where we have been with where we are going. It's like a pattern, and Bastard says this way we can be better thieves.

Today we are starting a new street and so we are carefully scouting around. We are passing Chimurenga Street, where we've already harvested every guava tree, maybe like two-three weeks ago, when we see white curtains part and a face peer from a window of the cream home with the marble statue of the urinating naked boy with wings. We are standing and staring, looking to see what the face will do, when the window opens and a small, funny voice shouts for us to stop. We remain standing, not because the voice told us to stop, but because none of us has started to run, and also because the voice doesn't sound dangerous. Music pours out of the window onto the street; it's not kwaito, it's not dance-hall, it's not house, it's not anything we know.

A tall, thin woman opens the door and comes out of the house. The first thing we see is that she is eating something. She waves as she walks towards us, and already we can tell from the woman's thinness that we are not even going to run. We wait, so we can see what she is smiling for, or at. The woman stops by the gate; it's locked, and she didn't bring the keys to open it.

Jeez, I can't stand this awful heat, and the hard earth, how do you guys ever do it? the woman asks in her not-dangerous voice. She smiles, takes a bite of the thing in her hand. A pink camera dangles from her neck. We all look at the woman's feet peeking underneath her long skirt. They are clean and pretty feet, like a baby's. She is wiggling her toes, purple from nail polish. I don't remember my own feet ever looking like that; maybe when I was born.

Then there's the woman's red chewing mouth. I can tell from the cord thingies at the side of her neck and the way she smacks her big lips that whatever she is eating tastes really good. I look closely at her long hand, at the thing she is eating. It's flat, and the outer part is crusty. The top is creamish and looks fluffy and soft, and there are coin-like things on it, a deep pink, the color of burn wounds. I also see sprinkles of red and green and yellow, and finally the brown bumps that look like pimples.

Chipo points at the thing and keeps jabbing at the air in a way that says *What's that?* She rubs her stomach with her other hand; now that she is pregnant, Chipo is always playing with her stomach like maybe it's a toy. The stomach is the size of a football, not too big. We keep our eyes on the woman's mouth and wait to hear what she will say.

Oh, this? It's a camera, the woman says, which we all know; even a stone can tell that a camera is a camera. The woman wipes her hand on her skirt, pats the camera, then aims what is left of the thing at the bin by the door, misses, and laughs to herself like a madman. She looks at us like maybe she wants us to laugh with her, but we are busy looking at the thing that flew in the air before hitting the ground like a dead bird. We have never ever seen anyone throw food away, even if it's a thing. Chipo looks like she wants to run after it and pick it up. The woman's twisted mouth finishes chewing, and swallows. I swallow with her, my throat tingling.

How old are you? the woman asks Chipo, looking at her stomach like she has never seen anybody pregnant.

She is eleven, Godknows replies for Chipo. We are ten, me and her, like twinses, Godknows says, meaning him and me. And Bastard is eleven and Sbho is nine, and Stina we don't know because he has no birth certificate.

Wow, the woman says. I say wow too, wow wow wow, but I do it inside my head. It's my first time ever hearing this word. I try to think what it means but I get tired of grinding my brains so I just give up.

And how old are you? Godknows asks her. And where are you from? I'm thinking about how Godknows has a big mouth that will get him slapped one day.

Me? Well, I'm thirty-three, and I'm from London. This is my first time visiting my dad's country, she says, and twists the chain on her neck. The golden head on the chain is the map of Africa.

I know London. I ate some sweets from there once. They were sweet at first, and then they just changed to sour in my mouth. Uncle Vusa sent them when he first got there but that was a long time ago. Now he never sends anything, Godknows says. He looks up at the sky like maybe he wants a plane to appear with sweets from his uncle.

But you look only fifteen, like a child, Godknows says, looking at the woman now. I am expecting her to reach out and slap him on the mouth but she merely smiles like she has not just been insulted.

Thank you, I just came off the Jesus diet, she says, sounding very pleased. I look at her like *What is there to thank?* I'm also thinking, *What is a Jesus diet, and do you mean the real Jesus, like God's child?*

I know from everybody's faces and silence that they think the woman is strange. She runs a hand through her hair, which is matted and looks a mess; if I lived in Budapest I would wash my whole body every day and comb my hair nicely to show I was a real person living in a real place. With her hair all wild like that, and standing on the other side of the gate with its lock and bars, the woman looks like a caged animal. I begin thinking what I would do if she actually jumped out and came after us.

8

Do you guys mind if I take a picture? she says. We don't answer because we're not used to adults asking us anything; we just look at the woman, at her fierce hair, at her skirt that sweeps the ground when she walks, at her pretty peeking feet, at her golden Africa, at her large eyes, at her smooth skin that doesn't even have a scar to show she is a living person, at the earring in her nose, at her T-shirt that says Save Darfur.

Great, now, stand close together, the woman says.

You, the tall one, go to the back. And you, yes, you, and you, look this way, no, I mean you, with the missing teeth, look at me, like this, she says, her hands reaching out of the bars, almost touching us.

Good, good, now says *cheese*, say *cheese*, *cheese*, *cheeeeeeese* – the woman enthuses, and everyone says *cheese*. Myself, I don't really say, because I am busy trying to remember what *cheese* means exactly, and I cannot remember. Yesterday Mother of Bones told us the story of Dudu the bird who learned and sang a new song whose words she did not really know the meaning of and who was then caught, killed, and cooked for dinner because in the song she was actually begging people to kill and cook her.

The woman points at me, nods, and tells me to say *cheeeeeese* and I say it mostly because she is smiling like she knows me really well, like she even knows my mother. I say it slowly at first, and then I say, *Cheese* and *cheese*, and I'm saying *cheese cheeeeese* and everyone is saying *cheese cheese cheese* and we

9

are all singing the word and the camera is clicking and clicking and clicking. Then Stina, who is quiet most of the time, just starts to walk away. The woman stops taking pictures and says, Hey, where are you going? But he doesn't stop, doesn't even turn to look at her. Then Chipo walks away after Stina, then the rest of us follow them.

We leave the woman standing there, taking pictures as we go. Then Bastard stops at the corner of Victoria and starts shouting insults at the woman, and I remember the thing, and that she threw it away without even asking us if we wanted it, and I begin shouting also, and everyone else joins in. We shout and we shout and we shout; we want to eat the thing she was eating, we want to hear our voices soar, we want our hunger to go away. The woman just looks at us puzzled, like she has never heard anybody shout, and then quickly hurries back into the house but we shout after her, shout till we smell blood in our tickling throats.

Bastard says when we grow up we'll stop stealing guavas and move on to bigger things inside the houses. I'm not really worried about that because when that time comes, I'll not even be here; I'll be living in America with Aunt Fostalina, eating real food and doing better things than stealing. But for now, the guavas. We decide on Robert Street, on a huge white house that looms like a mountain. The house has big windows and sparkling things all over, and a red swimming pool at the front, empty chairs all around it. Everything looks really pretty, but I think it's the kind of pretty to look at and admire and say, Oh, that's pretty, not a pretty to live in.

The good thing is that the house is set far back in the yard, and our guavas are right at the front, as if they heard we were coming and ran out to meet us. It doesn't take long to climb over the Durawall, get into the tree, and fill our plastic bags. Today we are stealing bull guavas. These ones are big, like a man's angry fist, and do not really ripen to yellow like the regular guavas; they stay green on the outside, pink and fluffy on the inside, and taste so good I cannot even explain it.

Going back to Paradise, we do not run. We just walk nicely like Budapest is now our country too, like we built it even, eating guavas along the way and spitting the peels all over to make the place dirty. We stop at the corner of AU Street for Chipo to vomit; it happens most of the time she eats. Today her vomit looks like urine, only thicker. We leave it there, uncovered.

One day I will live here, in a house just like that, Sbho says, biting into a thick guava. She points to the big blue house with the long row of steps, flowers all around it. A really nice house, but not nicer than where we just got the guavas. Sbho's voice sounds like she is not playing, like she knows what she is talking about. I watch her chew, her cheeks bulging. She swallows, starts to peel what is left of the guava with her side teeth.

How are you going to do that? I ask. Sbho spits the peels and says, with her big eyes, I just know it.

She is going to do it in her dreams, Bastard says to the sun, and throws a guava at the Durawall of Sbho's house. The guava explodes and stains the wall. I bite into a sweet guava; I don't like grinding the bull guava seeds, because they are tough and it takes a long time to do, so I grind them just slightly, sometimes swallow them whole even though I know what will happen later when I'm squatting.

Why did you do that? Sbho looks at the stained Durawall of her house, and then at Bastard. Her face has turned ugly now, like a real woman's.

I said, why did you do that? Sbho's voice has hot coals in it, like maybe she will do something to Bastard, but really she won't because Bastard is bigger and stronger, plus he is a boy. He has beaten Sbho before, and myself, and Chipo and Godknows as well; he has beaten us all except Stina.

Because I can, kiss-knees. Besides, what does it matter? Bastard says.

Because you just heard me say I like the house, so you are not supposed to do anything to it. Why don't you pick another that I don't care about, they're many houses here! Sbho says.

Well, that doesn't make it your house, does it? Bastard wears black tracksuit bottoms and a faded orange T-shirt that says Cornell. Now he takes the top off, ties it over his head, and I don't know if it makes him look ugly or pretty, if he really looks like a man or a woman. He turns and starts walking backwards so he can face Sbho. He always likes whoever he is quarreling with to look right at him.

Budapest is not a kaka toilet for anybody to just walk in, it's not like Paradise. You'll never live here, he says.

I'm going to marry a man from Budapest. He'll take me away from Paradise, away from the shacks and Heavenway and Fambeki and everything else, Sbho says.

Ha-ha. You think a man will marry you with your missing teeth? I wouldn't even marry you myself, Godknows says, shouting over his skinny shoulder. He and Chipo and Stina walk ahead of us. I look at Godknows's shorts, torn at the back, at his buttocks peeping like strange eyes through the dirty white fabric.

I'm not talking to you, chapped buttocks! Sbho shouts at Godknows. Besides, my teeth will grow back. Mother says I'll even be more beautiful too!

Godknows flings his hand and makes a whatever sign because he has nothing to say to that. Even the stones know that Sbho is pretty, prettier than all of us here, prettier than all the children in Paradise. Sometimes we refuse to play with her if she won't stop talking like we don't already know it.

Well, I don't care, I'm blazing out of this kaka country myself. Then I'll make lots of money and

13

come back and get a house in this very Budapest. Or even better, many houses: one in Budapest, one in Los Angeles, one in Paris. Wherever I feel like, Bastard says.

When we were going to school my teacher Mr Gono said you need an education to make money, Stina says, stopping to face Bastard. And how will you do that now that we are not going to school anymore? he adds. Stina doesn't say much, so when he opens his mouth you know it's important talk.

I don't need any kaka school to make money, you goat-teeth, Bastard says.

He brings his face close to Stina's like he will bite his nose off. Stina can fight Bastard if he wants, but he only looks at him like he is bored and just eats the rest of his guava. Then he starts to walk, fast, away from us.

I'm going to America to live with my aunt Fostalina, it won't be long, you'll see, I say, raising my voice so they can all hear. I start on a brand-new guava; it's so sweet I finish it in just three bites. I don't even bother chewing the seeds.

America is too far, you midget, Bastard says. I don't want to go anywhere where I have to go by air. What if you get there and find it's a kaka place and get stuck and can't come back? Me, I'm going to Jo'burg, that way when things get bad, I can just get on the road and roll without talking to anybody; you have to be able to return from wherever you go.

14

I look at Bastard and think what to say to him. A guava seed is stuck between my gum and my last side tooth and I try to reach for it with my tongue. I finally use my finger; it tastes like earwax.

Yes, America is far, what if something happens to your plane when you are in it?

What about the Terrorists? Godknows says, agreeing with Bastard.

I really think flat-face, peeping-buttocks Godknows is only saying it to please ugly-face Bastard. I begin on a new guava and give Godknows a talking eye.

I don't care, I'm going, I say, and walk fast to catch up with Chipo and Stina because I know where the talk will end if Godknows and Bastard gang up on me.

Well, go, go to that America and work in nursing homes. That's what your aunt Fostalina is doing as we speak. Right now she is busy cleaning kaka off some wrinkled old man who can't do anything for himself, you think we've never heard the stories? Bastard screams to my back but I just keep walking.

I'm thinking how if I had proper strength I would turn right around and beat Bastard up for saying that about my aunt Fostalina and my America. I would slap him, butt him on his big forehead, and then slam my fist into his mouth and make him spit his teeth. I would pound his stomach until he vomited all the guavas he had eaten. I would pin him to the ground, jab my knee into his spine,

15

fold his hands behind him, and then pull his head back till he begged for his two-cents life. That is just what I would do, but I walk away instead. I know he is just saying this because he is jealous. Because he has nobody in America. Because Aunt Fostalina is not his aunt. Because he is Bastard and I am Darling.

By the time we get back to Paradise the guavas are finished and our stomachs are so full we are almost crawling. We stop to defecate in the bush because we have eaten too much. Plus it is best to do so before it gets too dark, otherwise no one will accompany you; it's scary to go out by yourself at night because you have to pass Heavenway, which is the cemetery, to get to the bush and you might meet a ghost. As we speak, those who know about things say Moses's father, who died last month, can be seen roaming Paradise some nights, wearing his yellow Barcelona football jersey.

We all find places, and me, I squat behind a rock. This is the worst part about guavas; because of all those seeds, you get constipated once you eat too much. Nobody says it, but I know we are constipated again, all of us, because nobody is trying to talk, or get up and leave. We just eat a lot of guavas because it's the only way to kill our hunger, and when it comes to defecating, we get in so much pain it becomes an almost impossible task, like you are trying to give birth to a country.

We are all squatting like that, in our different

places, and I'm beating my thighs with fists to make a cramp go away when somebody screams. It's not a scream that comes from when you push too hard and a guava seed cuts your anus; it's one that says *Come and see*, so I stop pushing, pull up my underwear, and abandon my rock. And there, squatting and screaming, is Chipo. She is also pointing ahead in the bush, and we see it, a tall thing dangling in a tree like a strange fruit. Then we see it's not a thing but a person. Then we see it's not just a person but a woman.

What's that? somebody whispers. Nobody answers because now we can all see what it is. The thin woman dangles from a green rope that's attached to a branch high up in the tree. The red sun squeezes through the leaves and gives everything a strange color; it's almost beautiful, it makes the woman's light skin glow. But still everything is just scary and I want to run but I don't want to run alone.

The woman's thin arms hang limp at the sides, and her hands and feet point to the ground. Everything straight, like somebody drew her there, a line hanging in the air. The eyes are the scariest part, they are almost too white, and they look like they want to pop out. The mouth is open wide in an O, as if the woman was maybe interrupted in the middle of saying something. She is wearing a yellow dress, and the grass licks the tip of her red shoes. We just stand there staring.

Let's run, Stina says, and I get ready to run.

Can't you see she's hanged herself and now she's dead? Bastard picks up a stone and throws; it hits the woman on the thigh. I think something will happen but then nothing happens; the woman does not move, just her dress. It swings ever so lightly in the breeze like maybe a baby angel is busy playing with it.

See, I told you she's dead, Bastard says, in that voice he uses when he is reminding us who is the boss.

God will punish you for that, Godknows says. Bastard throws another stone and hits the woman on the leg. The woman still does not move; she just dangles there, like a ragged doll. I'm terrified; it's like she's looking at me from the corner of her white, popped eye. Looking and waiting for me to do something, I don't know what.

God does not live here, fool, Bastard says. He throws another stone; it only grazes the woman's yellow dress and I am glad he missed.

I'll go and tell my mother, Sbho says, her voice sounding like she wants to cry. Stina starts to leave, and Chipo and Sbho and Godknows and myself follow him. Bastard stays behind for a little while, but when I look over my shoulder, I see him right there behind us. I know he can't stay in the bush by himself with a dead woman, even though he wants to make like he is fearless. We walk, but then Bastard jumps to the front, making us stop.

Wait, so who wants real bread? he says, tightening the Cornell T-shirt on his head and smiling.

18

I look at the wound on Bastard's chest, just below his left breast. It's almost pink, like the inside of a guava.

Where is it? I say.

Look, did you notice that woman's shoes were almost new? If we can get them then we can sell them and buy a loaf, or maybe even one and a half.

We all turn around and follow Bastard back into the bush, the dizzying smell of Lobels bread all around us now, and then we are rushing, then we are running, then we are running and laughing and laughing and laughing.

CHAPTER 2

DARLING ON THE MOUNTAIN

Jesus Christ died on this day, which is why I have to be out here washing with cold water like this. I don't like cold water and I don't even like washing my whole body unless I have somewhere meaningful to go. After I finish and dress, me and Mother of Bones will head off to her church. She says it's the least we can do because we are all dirty sinners and we are the ones for whom Jesus Christ gave his life, but what I know is that I myself wasn't there when it all happened, so how can I be a sinner?

I don't like going to church because I don't really see why I have to sit in the hot sun on that mountain and listen to boring songs and meaningless prayers and strange verses when I could be doing important things with my friends. Plus, last time I went, that crazy Prophet Revelations Bitchington Mborro shook me and shook me until I vomited pink things. I thought I was going to die a real death. Prophet Revelations Bitchington Mborro was trying to get the spirit inside me out; they say I'm possessed because they say my grandfather isn't properly buried because the white people killed him during the war for feeding and hiding the terrorists who were trying to get our country back because the white people had stolen it.

If you're stealing something it's better if it's small and hideable or something you can eat quickly and be done with, like guavas. That way, people can't see you with the thing to be reminded that you are a shameless thief and that you stole it from them, so I don't know what the white people were trying to do in the first place, stealing not just a tiny piece but a whole country. Who can ever forget you stole something like that? Nobody knows where my grandfather's body is, so now the church people say his spirit is inside me and won't leave until his body's buried right. The thing is I've never really seen or felt the spirit myself to say if it's true or people are just lying, which is what adults will do sometimes because they are adults.

Hey, cabbage ears, what are you bathing for? I hear somebody shout.

Who is it? I shout back, even though I don't like being called cabbage ears. I have soap all over my face so I can't really open my eyes.

We're going to play Andy-over, what are you bathing for?

I'm going to church with Mother of Bones, I say, tasting Sunlight soap in my mouth. I start to splash my face with water.

Don't you want to play with us? says a different voice, maybe Sbho's.

I have to go to church. Don't you know Jesus died today? I say.

My father says your church is just kaka, and that your Prophet Revelations Bitchington Mborro is an idio – I hear Bastard's voice start.

You you futsekani leave her alone you bloody mgodoyis get away boSatan beRoma! Mother of Bones spits from inside the shack. I hear giggling, then the stomp-stomp of running feet. I finish splashing my face, open my eyes, and they have disappeared; all I see is a brown dog lying behind MaDumane's shack, and Annamaria bathing her albino son, Whiteboy, in a dish. When I wave to him he starts to cry, and Annamaria looks at me with a peppered eye and says, Leave my son alone, ugly, can't you see you're scaring him?

Inside the shack, Mother of Bones has already laid out my good yellow dress, which I wouldn't dare wear if my mother were here; she went to the border to sell things so I have to stay with Mother of Bones until she returns. Sometimes Mother comes back after only a few days, sometimes after a week; sometimes she comes back when I don't even know when she is coming. Right now Mother of Bones is busy counting her money like she does every morning so I start to do my things quietly, the way I'm expected to. I reach under the bed for the Vaseline.

Yes be careful with that Vaseline I didn't say you should drink it khona and I told you not to play with those dirty imbeciles they are a bad influence,

Mother of Bones says, and I just pretend she hasn't spoken. After I finish Vaselining, I get dressed and sit on the edge of the bed and wait; I don't know why Mother of Bones has to go through her money every day like somebody told her it lays eggs overnight. To make the time go I start counting the faded suns on the bedspread; there's exactly twelve of them, like the disciples – Simon, Peter, Andrew, I don't know the rest, maybe if they had better names I'd remember them all.

After I finish with the suns I look at my father at the other end of the shack: he is dressed in a strange black dress, like a woman, and a silly square hat; there are ropes and things going around his neck and down his dress. He is carrying a paper in one hand, and a fat man in a suit is shaking the other. Mother of Bones says the picture was taken when Father was finishing university, just before I was born. She says that she was in the picture as well but we can't see her because that fat man got in front of her just when the camera was snapping, like it was maybe his own son who was finishing university. Now Father is in South Africa, working, but he never writes, never sends us money, never nothing. It makes me angry thinking about him so most of the time I just pretend he doesn't exist; it's better this way.

Then there is the long, yellow curtain with beautiful prints of proud peacocks, the feathers spread out like rays. It covers one side of the tin wall; I don't really see why Mother of Bones has the curtain in the first place since there are no real glass windows. After the curtain comes the calendar; it's old but Mother of Bones keeps it since it has Jesus Christ on it. He has women's hair and is smiling shyly, his head tilted a bit to the side; you can tell he really wanted to look nice in the picture. He used to have blue eyes but I painted them brown like mine and everybody's, to make him normal. Mother of Bones walloped me so much for it though, I couldn't sit for a whole two days.

Next to Jesus is my cousin Makhosi carrying me when we were little. Two years ago Makhosi went away to Madante mine to dig for diamonds, when they were first discovered and everybody was flocking there. When Makhosi came back, his hands were like decaying logs. He told us about Madante between bad bouts of raw, painful coughs, how when he was under the earth he forgot everything. He said all he knew inside that mine was the terrible pounding of the hammer around him, sometimes even inside him, like he had swallowed it. After a while, he too went to South Africa, like Father.

And hidden under the bed, inside the old, tattered Bible that Mother of Bones doesn't take to church, is a picture of my grandfather. He was killed before I was born, but I knew who he was the moment I laid my eyes on him for the first time; it felt as if I were looking at myself and Makhosi and Father and my uncle Muzi and my other relatives, like my grandfather's face was a folded fist and all our faces were collected like coins inside it.

In the hidden picture, Grandfather is speaking, his mouth pursed. There are frown lines on his forehead, and from the way his red eyes are looking deeply at the camera, you would think that he wants to eat it. He has a bone going through his nose and is wearing earrings. Behind him are fields of waist-high maize crops, just endless and endless green. Nobody likes to talk about him, it's as if he is something that never even happened, but there are times I have caught Mother of Bones muttering, and even though she doesn't say, I always have a feeling she is muttering to him. She doesn't know that I know about Grandfather's picture.

Why anyone would want me to throw away my suitcase of money is all I want to know and I mean money not bricks no but money, Mother of Bones says. She stays crouched on the floor like a praying mantis, her suitcase at her feet. Her brass bangles clink and clink as her hands go over the bricks of money.

You know what I don't understand? Mother of Bones asks. She raises her head and looks at me, but I don't say anything back because I know she is not even talking to me.

What I don't understand is how this very money that I have in lumps cannot buy even a grain of salt I mean that there is what I don't understand, she says, anger starting to churn in her voice.

Money is money no matter what this is still

25

money, she says. Now Mother of Bones is patting the money like it is a baby. Like she is trying to put the baby to sleep.

It's old money, Mother of Bones, it's useless now, don't you even get it? You just have to throw it away or use it to make fire like everybody else. Now they say we'll start using American money, I say, but to myself so Mother of Bones doesn't hear.

And the American money they are talking about just where do they think I'll get it do they think I can just dig it up huh do they think I will defecate it? Mother of Bones says. When she speaks, her words always come tumbling out, as if she is afraid that if she pauses, something will whisk them away. At first I want to jump up because I think she heard me even though I said it quietly, but she's not looking at me so I stay put. You can see the pain on her face now, like something inside her is breaking and bleeding.

Mother of Bones's face is the color of the shacks, a dirty brown, like it was made to match. There are deep lines on it; when I was little I thought somebody had taken a broken mirror and carved and carved and carved. A white scarf is tied around her head, and bright beads coil like snakes around her neck: purple beads, orange beads, pink beads, blue beads, their colors screaming against the quiet brown of the skin.

I make sure I walk behind Mother of Bones when we go to church; if I walk in front of her she'll just be telling me to walk like a woman, which I am not. On her small feet, Mother of Bones wears mismatched shoes, a flat green shoe and a red tennis shoe with a white lace, but that doesn't mean she's crazy.

We pass tiny shack after tiny shack crammed together like hot loaves of bread. I'm not wearing shoes because they are too small now, and the other made-in-China ones that Mother brought me from the border just fell apart, so I walk carefully and make sure to lift my feet to avoid things on the dusty red path: a broken bottle here, a pile of junk over there, a brownish puddle of something here, a disemboweled watermelon there. It's early in the morning but the sun is already frying the shacks; I feel it over my body, roasting me, like.

I keep my mouth shut like I'm supposed to while Mother of Bones shouts greetings to the people we see on the way; Bornfree's mother, MaDube, who is pounding nails on the roof of her shack with a rock; NaBetina holding her squatting grandson Nomoreproblems; Mai Tonde sitting on a stool and peering inside her screaming baby's ear; NaMgcobha dictating a letter to a tall boy I've never seen before.

We pass old Zuze looking at everything with his blind eyes, pass women sitting outside a shack and gossiping and doing one another's hair, and not too far off, the men huddled like sheep and playing draughts under the lone jacaranda. The blooming purple flowers almost make the men look beautiful

27

in the shade without their shirts on. They sit there, crouched forward like tigers, like the sun whipping their backs doesn't matter, like the bird droppings falling on their bare shoulders and splattering their skin don't matter. Mother of Bones shouts her greetings and waves but the men hardly take their eyes off the fading draughts board with its upturned and downturned bottle tops.

When we pass the people standing in line outside Vodloza's shack, Mother of Bones only waves; here she cannot shout because it's a healer's place. A few of the people wave back unsurely, like they don't even want to, looking worn out from sickness or troubles. They are waiting for Vodloza to divine with their ancestors because that's his job. A large white sign says in bold red English words: VODLOZA, BESTEST HEALER IN ALL OF THIS PARADISE AND BEEYOND WILL PROPER FIX ALL THESE PROBLEMSOME THINGS THAT YOU MAY ENCOUNTER IN YOUR LIFE: BEWITCHEDNESS, CURSES, BAD LUCK, WHORING SPOUSES, CHILDRENLESSNESS, POVERTY, JOBLESSNESS, AIDS, MADNESS, SMALL PENISES, EPILEPSY, BAD DREAMS, BAD MARRIAGE/ MARRIAGELESSNESS, COMPETITION AT WORK, DEAD PEOPLE TERRORIZING YOU, BAD LUCK WITH GETTING VISAS ESPECIALLY TO USA AND BRITAIN, NONSENSEFUL PEOPLE IN YOUR LIFE, THINGS DISAPPEARING IN YOUR HOUSE ETC. ETC. ETC. PLEASE PAYMENT IN FOREX ONLY.

When we pass the playground I walk a little

slower so I can see everything. They are playing Andy-over, and Bastard is jumping under a rope and the others are busy chanting – he went to America on a saucepan, and what-what. They pause to watch us, and when we get close, Godknows screams, Darling! Samu said she can beat you up, do you want to fight her when you get back? Did you hear NGO will be here next week! Are you coming to Budapest? as if he doesn't know he's not supposed to talk to me when I'm with Mother of Bones like this. I start to raise my hand to my lips to shut him up and Mother of Bones says, without even turning around, Leave those little heathens alone you hear me?

A little ways past the playground we meet Bornfree and Messenger carrying stacks of posters in their hands. They are trying to look like twins in the matching T-shirts with the little white hearts at the front and the word *Change* written in red just below the hearts. They stand aside to let us pass.

Good morning, Mother of Bones, they say together, like they rehearsed it.

Going to hunt for bones, Mother of Bones? Messenger says. He looks at Mother of Bones with a smile; if it were not for the one black tooth at the front, it would be a good smile. They don't say anything to me so I just look at my feet, covered now in red dust because that's just what happens when you use Vaseline and don't wear any shoes.

No my son today I'm going to the house of the

29

Lord don't you know what day it is? Mother of Bones says, walking on. She calls everybody my son or my daughter; I think that's because she cannot remember all the names.

Well, your God is listening because the change everybody's been crying for is finally here, Messenger says. He smiles again; Messenger likes to smile, like life is just too pretty, like everything is great.

Yes, it is, you watch, Bornfree adds. He waves his stack of papers and I see the words *Change, Real Change* at the front. His voice is bright and bold, like the red ink on his posters.

We're demonstrating tomorrow, on Main Street, come and walk for change! Be the future! Messenger shouts after us. We can hear them whistling and chanting about change, and in no time we hear the children's voices chanting as well. I turn to look and I see everybody has abandoned Andy-over and is now running after Bornfree and Messenger. Fists above their heads. Running and jumping and chanting, the word *change* in the air like it's something you can grab and put in your mouth and sink your teeth into.

Yes that Lot's wife turned to look back just like you're doing and turned to salt, Mother of Bones says, and I immediately stop even though I know that I, Darling, will not and cannot turn to salt.

Fools, Mother of Bones says. She picks up her pace a bit and I have to walk-run to catch up. What do they think they are doing yanking a lion's

30

tail don't they know that there will be bones if they dare? she continues. Now she turns back like she really is talking to me.

You will ask me tomorrow you will ask me what I'm saying now tomorrow when there are real bones, she says, and I just look away at the sky.

Further and further we go, and the sun keeps ironing us and ironing us and ironing us. When sweat trickles down my face I let it drip so I can try to reach it with my tongue; when I do, it is salty and stings. We stop underneath the mopane tree where we used to church until a little while ago so I can tie up Mother of Bones's one shoe-lace; I do this every time before we start on the trail up Fambeki. On the mopane is a big sign with an arrow that points upwards, towards our church. Beneath the arrow are the words HOLY CHARIOT CHURCH OF CHRIST – IT DOSNT GO BACKWARDS, IT DOESNT GO SIDEWAYS, IT DOESN'T GO FORWARDS. IT GOES UPWARDS, TO HEAVEN. AMEN! I think this is taken from the Bible, but I have forgotten the verse.

Mother of Bones is already singing her favorite church song, the one she always sings when she makes the climb. She sings it wrong because she doesn't know all the English words because she doesn't speak the right English because she didn't go to school, but I don't correct her since you can't tell an adult nothing. The truth of it is that the song says *My sins were higher than a mountain when the Lord*

31

sanctified me, not *sacrificed me*, like Mother of
Bones sings. I don't go to school anymore because
all the teachers left to teach over in South Africa
and Botswana and Namibia and them, where
there's better money, but I haven't forgotten the
things I learned.

By the time we finally get to the top of Fambeki
my thighs are like lead and I'm sick of the sun
and just want to sit down, but Mother of Bones
is singing away like she hasn't just climbed a
mountain. She has even raised her voice because
I know that she wants to show people that she is
a good Christian. There are only three other adults
there, Mr Hove and his pretty wife, Mai Shingi,
and a man in a green shirt I have never seen
before but maybe he is Mr Hove's relative because
they both have the large heads that look like
ZUPCO buses.

I sit on a rock with the Hove children like I'm
supposed to, but when the little boy smiles at me
and shows his toy soldier, I ignore him to let him
know he's just not my size. I also give the big-
nosed sister a good frown to show her that she,
too, doesn't count.

I see you're already here I see you beat me to it
today, Mother of Bones says to the adults. She
says it playing-like, laughing-like, but if you knew
her well, like I know her, then you would know
that she is in fact mad that they got here before
she did. Mother of Bones likes being the first in
everything.

In no time the rest of the church people begin to arrive, panting like dogs returning from a hunt. The only thing I like about getting here early is that I get to watch the fat adults toiling up the mountain, trying to look like angels in their flowing robes that have now lost their whiteness. They clap their hands and greet one another in the name of the Lord and what-what, and the women spread their ntsaroz and sit on one side, the men on the other, like they are two different rivers that are not supposed to meet. Chipo has come with her grandmother and grandfather, and I have already elbowed away one of the Hove kids so that Chipo can sit next to me. Then MaMoyo comes and puts her baby in my arms without even asking me if I want to hold him.

I hate babies, so I don't smile when MaMoyo's baby looks at me with his crazy bullfrog eyes. To make it worse, he is an ugly baby; his face looks shocked, like he has just seen the buttocks of a snake. I look at the pattern of ringworms on his bald head, at the mucus in his nose, and decide that no, I don't want to have anything to do with him. I ask Chipo in a whisper if she wants to hold him but she doesn't even look at me.

I make sure nobody is watching, and then I immediately start making faces to scare the baby. When he doesn't cry I pinch him on the arm. I watch the fat face scrunch up, reluctantly, as if he is deciding if he should cry at all, and when I think he is taking too long to make up his mind, I pinch harder. This time the baby explodes in a real cry like he's supposed to, and me and Chipo look at each other and smile. MaMoyo quickly comes to get him because no woman wants to be chided in front of the whole church.

The Evangelists and Prophet Revelations Bitchington Mborro arrive after everybody, like chief baboons. They look like something else with the colorful crosses emblazoned on their robes, their long sticks with the hooks at the ends, their bald heads glimmering in the sun, the long beards; you can just tell that they are trying to copy the style of those men in the Bible.

Today Prophet Revelations Bitchington Mborro is wearing a brand-new robe; it's milk white, with green and red stripes going down the sides. He is also carrying a new stick, and his doesn't look like the Evangelists' – it's way longer and fatter, like it can actually injure and do ugly things. At the end of the stick is a cross inside a circle. When the Evangelists and Prophet Revelations Bitchington Mborro come, you know that it has really begun, so a tall thin woman stands up and starts singing 'Mikoro' and I just want to die because the song bores me like I don't know what.

All of them are on their feet now, singing and shuffling and swaying, singing and shuffling and swaying, like maybe they have caught the spirit, but if they have, then it skipped me. The spirit always skips me. Chipo is swaying as well, her hands playing with her stomach, but she is not singing. I pretend to sing in case Mother of Bones looks to see, but I'm really just moving my lips because this 'Mikoro' song has no spark. All there is to it is the repeating of the words *Mikoro, Mikoro* while the woman who is leading the song does the singing, and she doesn't have the voice for it to begin with, even I myself can sing better, even a cat can do better. I look at MaMoyo and am not surprised the song is putting ugly baby to sleep.

To pass the time I let my eyes wander towards Paradise. When I'm on Fambeki like this I feel like I'm God, who sees everything. Paradise is all tin and stretches out in the sun like a wet sheepskin nailed on the ground to dry; the shacks are the muddy color of dirty puddles after the rains. The shacks themselves are terrible but from up here, they seem much better, almost beautiful even, it's like I'm looking at a painting.

Then I look up at the sky and see a plane far up in the clouds. First I'm thinking it's just a bird, but then I see that no, it's not. Maybe it's a British Airways plane like the one Aunt Fostalina went in to America.

It's what I will take myself when I follow Aunt Fostalina to America, I whisper in Chipo's ear. I look up so she can see what I'm talking about, and she follows my eyes.

But I don't know why I have to take a British Airways plane to go to America; why not an American Airways one? I say, but now I'm no longer talking to Chipo. Now I'm just talking to myself because I don't think she will understand. From here the sky appears very close, like somebody holy can reach a hand down and wipe the sweat off Prophet Revelations Bitchington Mborro's and the Evangelists' dripping heads. God told Prophet Revelations Bitchington Mborro in a dream that he needed to move the church to here; maybe God wanted us to be closer to him, just like in that verse, Simon on the mountain.

Prophet Revelations Bitchington Mborro brings me back with his roaring and I realize the singing has stopped. If Prophet Revelations Bitchington Mborro's voice were an animal it would be big and fierce and would knock things down. Once, when we still churched under the mopane, he told us how he used to have a small voice and that he rarely used it because he was a quiet, timid man, until the night an angel came to him and said, Speak, and he opened his mouth and thunder came out.

Now Prophet Revelations Bitchington Mborro is busy thundering about Judas and Golgotha and the cross and the two thieves next to Jesus and things, making like he was there and saw it all. When Prophet Revelations Bitchington Mborro is in form he doesn't stand in one place. He paces up and down like there are hot coals under his feet. He flails his arms, sometimes waving his stick at the sky, sometimes jumping around as if he is itching where nobody can see. Every once in a while a woman will scream Sweet

Jeeeeesus, or Hmmm-hmmm-hmmm, or Glory, glory, or something like that, which means that the spirit is touching her.

Prophet Revelations Bitchington Mborro is drenched in sweat now, and his robe clings to his chest; you can see his breasts and nipples. I look to the side and see Mother of Bones listening with all her might, eyes half closed, head tilted, and arms clutching at the stomach like she is feeling pain. All around, the adults are busy nodding their heads in agreement, or shaking them to show how terrible what Prophet Revelations Bitchington Mborro is saying is, or making guttural and moaning sounds. I look at Chipo and she is closing her eyes, taking a nap. My buttocks are so stiff they could be made of stone.

Now Prophet Revelations Bitchington Mborro reads from his English Bible even though he sounds like a grade-one reading. If he went to school, you can tell from the way he reads that he must have been just a dunderhead at it, even Godknows can read better. Prophet Revelations Bitchington doesn't spend much time on the Bible, maybe because he is afraid of running into a big word he won't know how to pronounce; he quickly moves on to preaching, which he is very good at. Then he starts to speak in a strange language that nobody understands. The people moan and clap and groan.

When the Mikoro woman interrupts Prophet Revelations Bitchington Mborro with another song, he just keeps thundering like he doesn't even hear her. For a moment their voices circle each other like crazy cocks, neither of them giving way; it becomes dizzying just listening until at last Prophet Revelations Bitchington Mborro says, I command the devil to shut up in the name of Jesus. When the Mikoro lady is silenced I bring my head to my armpit and giggle because she was making like God told her she is Celine Dion.

After the preaching somebody passes a big white bowl around for offerings, and Destiny's mother starts singing 'Blessed Are the Givers.' Her voice is quiet and beautiful and it makes me think about the Budapest lady; this is what her voice would sound like if she could sing; it would suit her better than it suits Destiny's mother, but she still needs to do something about that mess on her head. After a while the bowl comes back with strange monies I've never seen before, then Destiny's mother ends the song, then we move on to the confessing of sins, and those with sins stand up.

I think of what I would say if I were to stand up right now, among the confessors, but then I realize I have no sins. Prophet Revelations Bitchington Mborro goes around touching each of the sinners – there's seven of them, all women – on the forehead with his stick, and then sprinkles them with holy water before they confess.

We are listening to Simangele confessing about how last week she succumbed to the devil and went to seek Vodloza's help because she doesn't know what to do anymore about her jealous cousin. She says the cousin is also a witch who keeps sending her tokoloshes because she wants her dead so that she can then take over Simangele's husband, Lovemore. Somewhere near me, a voice says, Mnnnc, serves you right, you think your kaka doesn't stink. I turn to see who has spoken and Chipo's sister Constance gives me the look and so I quickly turn away.

We are waiting for Prophet Revelations Bitchington Mborro to pounce on Simangele for going to see a pagan, which is how he refers to Vodloza, when we hear a woman's scream coming from down the mountain. Some of the adults stand up to see but Prophet Revelations Bitchington Mborro sharply commands them to sit, and then he asks all the Evangelists to rise in the name of Jesus and get ready because God has told him the devil is coming.

The devil is a woman in a purple dress that's riding up her thighs and revealing smooth flawless skin like maybe she is an angel. A group of men are carrying her, struggling to get her to the top. I have never seen the woman before, or any of the men, but I think she is just so pretty even Sbho doesn't compare. She has long shiny hair that isn't really hers but it still looks good, nice skin, white teeth, and it seems like she eats well. Her breasts are the only thing that's wrong with her body – nobody needs breasts that are each the size of ugly baby's head.

You can see the woman's white knickers with the red kisses; they are really pretty knickers and they don't even have a single hole in them. The Evangelists and Prophet are already screaming prayers even before they've heard what is wrong. They pounce on the woman and pin her down. She is kicking and twitching like a fish in the sand; she obviously doesn't want them to hold her down like that and she's screaming for them to stop. I'm worried about her dress and knickers, about her skin getting scratched, about all that dirt they are getting on her. The men who brought the woman are standing to the side, watching.

Leave me alone, leave me alone, you sons of bitches! You don't know me! the woman screams at Prophet Revelations Bitchington Mborro and the Evangelists. Her voice is angry, like it can strike and kill things, but they don't even hear her; they are busy yelling prayers. I repeat her words – Leave her alone, leave her alone, you sons of bitches! You don't know her! – but I'm saying it quietly to myself.

When Prophet Revelations Bitchington Mborro tells them to, the women get up and stand behind him and the Evangelists like a wall, singing and dancing and waving Bibles in the air. Some of them pray. This is what they must do in order for the Holy Spirit to come properly, but they have to keep their voices kind of controlled so they don't sound like the pagans at Vodloza's. I have seen them calling the ancestors behind Vodloza's shack, the pagans – drums bark and men roar and women shriek, bodies leap in the air, bodies writhe, and sometimes clothes fall off.

The pretty woman keeps screaming for the sons of bitches to stop but the sons of bitches keep doing their thing. I try to catch her eye, to make her see that I'm not joining in the activities, that I'm with her, but she is too busy kicking and screaming to see me. The prayers grow louder and louder, some praying properly, some praying in strange languages, some chanting.

Then Prophet Revelations Bitchington Mborro raises both his hands for everyone to be quiet. He points his stick at the pretty woman and commands the demon inside her to get the hell out in the name of Jesus, his exact words, and in his most loudest voice. He says more things to the demon and insults it even. When nothing happens, he wipes his forehead with the back of his sleeve, throws the stick to the side, and leaps onto the woman like maybe he is Hulkogen, squashing her mountains beneath him.

Prophet Revelations Bitchington Mborro prays for the woman like that, pinning her down and calling to Jesus and screaming Bible verses. He places his hands on her stomach, on her thighs, then he puts his hands on her thing and starts rubbing and praying hard for it, like there's something wrong with it. His face is alight, glowing. The pretty woman just looks like a rag now, the prettiness gone, her strength gone. I'm careful not

41

to look at her face anymore because I don't want her to find me looking at her when she is like this. Chipo is just waking up and she is looking around like she was lost but has found herself.

He did that, that's what he did, Chipo says, shaking my arm like she wants to break it off. This is the first time in a long time that Chipo is talking, like maybe she has received the Holy Spirit or something. Her voice is shrill in my ear. Around us, the prayers grow louder; everybody is excited that Prophet Revelations Bitchington Mborro has stopped the woman. The men who brought her are happy, especially the tall one who makes like he is the husband, the church people are happy, Mother of Bones is happy, but I am sad the pretty woman is just lying there under Prophet Revelations Bitchington Mborro like Jesus after they clobbered him and nailed him on the cross.

He did that, my grandfather, I was coming from playing Find bin Laden and my grandmother was not there and my grandfather was there and he got on me and pinned me down like that and he clamped a hand over my mouth and was heavy like a mountain, Chipo says, words coming out all at once like she is Mother of Bones. I watch her and she has this look I have never seen before, this look of pain. I want to laugh that her voice is back, but her face confuses me and I can also see she wants me to say something, something maybe important, so I say, Do you want to go and steal guavas?

42

CHAPTER 3

COUNTRY-GAME

It's just madness inside Shanghai; machines hoist things in their terrible jaws, machines maul the earth, machines grind rocks, machines belch clouds of smoke, machines iron the ground. Everywhere machines. The Chinese men are all over the place in orange uniforms and yellow helmets; there's not that many of them but from the way they are running around, you'd think they are a field of corn. And then there are the black men, who are working in regular clothes – torn T-shirts, vests, shorts, trousers cut at the knees, overalls, flip-flops, tennis shoes.

We stand for a while at the entrance, underneath the huge red banner with the pretty, strange writing we can't read. We don't usually come to Shanghai because of how far it is but today MaS'banda, Sbho's grandmother, made us come and find this man Moshe, who works here, and tell him to come to Paradise because she wants to talk to him, about what, we don't know. To get here you have to pass Budapest and take Masiyephambili Road, head east all the way until you hit the fenced-off quarry, where not too long ago people were trying to dig for diamonds before the soldiers chased them away. Shanghai is on the other side of the quarry, separated by a bush.

They did all that already? Sbho says, her voice filled with awe. It's hard to believe just how much has been done. The last time we came they had only burned the grass and were bringing the machines and things in. Now there's this skeleton of a building that looks like it wants to belch in God's face.

Yes, didn't I tell you last time that China is a big dog? Was I lying? Isn't this major, all this? Bastard says, sounding pleased. He makes a sweep with his hand like he is the one who sent the Chinese to build, like they are his boys and are here just to follow his orders.

And when they get done, it's going to be something else up in here, just wait and see. Don't say I didn't tell you, Bastard says.

You talk like they are building your house, Stina says.

So what if they're not? Major. Major, major, major, Bastard says, chanting the word like it's a song. He is already starting towards the building and we follow him.

Around the construction site the men speak in shouts. It's like listening to nonsense, to people praying in tongues; it's Chinese, it's our languages, it's English mixed with things, it's the machine noise. Because the men don't really understand one another, hands and tools often rise in the air

44

to help the language. When we approach the black men shoveling earth into wheelbarrows, some of them pause to watch us. They look like they've been playing in dirt all their lives – it's all over their bodies, their clothes, their hair. They don't look the way adults always try to look, making like they are in charge, so we pity them a little bit.

We stand near the pipes and Bastard shouts that we want to see Moshe. Nobody answers us, but after a while the pitch-black one who is all muscles shouts for us to go away. Moshe went to South Africa a few days ago, he says, and he goes back to digging.

He did the right thing, Bastard says.

Who? Sbho says.

Moshe.

How?

By going to South Africa. That's what I would do, instead of working in this kaka place and getting all dirty. Do you see how they look like pigs? Bastard says, and laughs.

We stand around for a bit but since nobody else talks to us, we walk away from the men. When we get to the tent next to the large yellow Caterpillar we stop and peep to see what's inside. We are peeping like that and failing to see anything because it's dark in the tent when out walks this fat Chinese man fastening his belt, catching us. He must be the foreman because unlike the others, he is dressed in proper trousers, shirt, jacket, and tie.

It's surprise all over – he is obviously surprised to find us there peeping and we are surprised at being caught but we are more surprised at his fatness; the other Chinese workers here aren't even half his size, so what is wrong with this one? And then, to add to our surprise even more, the fat man starts ching-chonging to us like he thinks he is in his grandmother's backyard. He ching-chongs ching-chongs and then he stops, the kind of stop that tells you he is expecting an answer. Chipo giggles.

This one is crazy, Stina says.

Yes, somebody told Fat Mangena here that Chinese is our national language now.

Look at that drum of a stomach, it's like he has swallowed a country.

We are still standing there when out walk these two black girls in skinny jeans and weaves and heels. We forget about Fat Mangena and watch them twist past us, the large blue purse of the skinny one grazing my left side. Matching bling hangs around their necks like nooses. They twist past the Caterpillars, past the mountains of gravel, twist past the groups of men who stop working and stare at the girls until they eventually get out of Shanghai and disappear behind the bend near the main road.

So, you want something? this other regular-sized Chinese man who has come to join Fat Mangena says to us in slow English. This one is a worker; his face is dirty and he is dressed in the orange uniform and helmet, and he carries a rope in one hand, a cigarette in the other. We watch him take a drag, exhale, drag, exhale.

What are you building? A school? Flats? A clinic? Stina says.

We build you big big mall. All nice shops inside, Gucci, Louis Vuitton, Versace, and so on so on. Good mall, big, the Chinese man says, flicking ash off his cigarette and looking up at the building. We laugh and he laughs as well, and Fat Mangena laughs too.

Give us some zhing-zhongs. We got some before, Godknows says, getting straight to the point.

Last time, they gave us a black plastic bag full of things – watches, jewelry, flip-flops, batteries – but like those shoes that Mother bought me once, the items were cheap kaka and lasted us only a few days. But we also got these interesting brown, funny-shaped thingies wrapped in plastic. They were crunchy when we bit into them, and to our surprise we found little white pieces of paper tucked inside. Godknows's said *If you eat a box of fortune cookies, anything is possible.* Bastard's said *Your talents will be recognized and suitably rewarded.* Chipo's said *If I bring forth what is inside me, what I bring forth will save me.* Sbho's said *The nightlife is for you.* Stina's said *A new pair of shoes will do you a world of good; lucky numbers 7, 13, 2, 9, 4.* And mine said *Your future will be happy and productive.*

You get one time is enough. Now you want made in China, you work, nothing free, the Chinese man says.

47

Well, you are in our country, that counts for something, Stina says.

You want us to come at night and defecate all over? Or steal things? Godknows says, and the Chinese man laughs the kind of laugh that tells you he didn't understand a word. Then he and Fat Mangena start some really serious ching-chonging and we know they are now talking about other things. We wait until we grow tired of it, until Stina says, Let's just go, they are not giving us anything.

We are booing and yelling when we walk out of Shanghai. If it weren't for the noisy machines, the Chinese would hear us telling them to leave our country and go and build wherever they come from, that we don't need their kaka mall, that they are not even our friends. We are still yelling when we pass the black men but then the one with the muscles steps out to meet us like the Chinese made him a prefect and blocks our way with his giant body. He doesn't say a single word but we can tell from his face that this one can pinch a rock and make it wince so we shut up there and then and leave Shanghai in silence.

Okay, it's like this. China is a red devil looking for people to eat so it can grow fat and strong. Now we have to decide if it actually breaks into people's homes or just ambushes them in the forest, Godknows says.

That doesn't even make sense. Why does it need

48

to grow fat and strong if it's a devil? Isn't it all that already? I say.

We are back in Paradise and are now trying to come up with a new game; it's important to do this so we don't get tired of old ones and bore ourselves to death, but then it's also not easy because we have to argue and see if the whole thing can work. It's Bastard's turn to decide what the new game is about, and even after this morning, he still wants it to be about China, for what, I don't know.

I think China should be like a dragon, Bastard says. That way, it will be a real beast, always on top.

I think it must be an angel, Sbho says, with like some superpowers to do exciting things so that everybody will be going to it for help, like maybe pleading or dancing to impress it, singing *China China mujibha, China China wo!* Sbho says. She is dancing to her stupid song now, obviously pleased with herself. When she finishes she does two cart-wheels, and we see a flash of her red knickers.

What are you doing? Bastard says.

Yes, sit down, that's just kaka, who will play that nonsense? Me, I'm drawing country-game, Godknows says, and he picks up a fat stick.

Soon we are all busy drawing country-game on the ground, and it comes out great because today the earth is just the right kind of wet since it rained yesterday. To play country-game you need two rings: a big outer one, then inside it, a little one, where the caller stands. You divide the outer ring depending on how many people are playing and cut it up in nice pieces like this. Each person then picks a piece and writes the name of the country on there, which is why it's called country-game.

But first we have to fight over the names because everybody wants to be certain countries, like everybody wants to be the U.S.A. and Britain and Canada and Australia and Switzerland and France and Italy and Sweden and Germany and Russia and Greece and them. These are the country-countries. If you lose the fight, then you just have to settle for countries like Dubai and South Africa and Botswana and Tanzania and them. They are not country-countries, but at least life is better than here. Nobody wants to be rags of countries like Congo, like Somalia, like Iraq, like Sudan, like Haiti, like Sri Lanka, and not even this one we live in – who wants to be a terrible place of hunger and things falling apart?

If I'm lucky, like today, I get to be the U.S.A., which is a country-country; who doesn't know that the U.S.A. is the big baboon of the world? I feel like it's my country now because my aunt Fostalina lives there, in Destroyedmichygen. Once her things are in order she'll come and get me and I will go and live there also. After we have sorted the names we vote for the first caller. The caller is the person who stands in the little inner circle to get the game started. Everybody else

50

stands in the bigger circle, one foot in his country, the other foot outside.

The caller then calls on the country of his choice and the game begins. The caller doesn't just call on any country, though; he has to make sure it's a country that he can easily count out. It's like being in a war; in a war you don't just start to fight somebody stronger than you because you will get proper clobbered. Likewise in country-game, it's best to call somebody who is a weak runner so he can't beat you. Once the caller calls we scatter and run as if the police themselves are chasing us, except for the country that's been called; that one has to run right into the inner ring and shout, Stop-stop-stop!

Once everyone stops, the new country in the inner ring then decides who to count out. Counting out is done by taking at least three leaps to get to one of the countries outside. It's easier to just count out the country closest to the outer ring, meaning whoever did not run that far – you just do your leaps nice and steady; the other country is counted out and has to sit and watch the game. But if you are the new country in the inner ring and cannot count anybody out in three leaps because you were not fast enough to stop the other countries, you pick the next caller and leave the game. It continues like that until there is only one country left, and the last country standing wins.

We are in the middle of the game, and it's just getting hot; Sudan and Congo and Guatemala and

Iraq and Haiti and Afghanistan have all been counted out and are sitting at the borders watching the country-countries play. We are running away from North Korea when we see the big NGO lorry passing Fambeki, headed towards us. We immediately stop playing and start singing and dancing and jumping.

What we really want to do is take off and run to meet the lorry but we know we cannot. Last time we did, the NGO people were not happy about it, like we had committed a crime against humanity. So now we just sing and wait for the lorry to approach us instead. The waiting is painful; we watch the lorry getting closer and closer, but it seems far away at the same time, like it's not even here yet but stuck somewhere else, in another country. It's the gifts that we know are inside that make it hard to wait and watch the lorry crawl.

This time the NGO people are late; they were supposed to come on the fifteenth of last month and that month came and went and now we are on another month. We have already cleared the playground because it's where the lorry will stop. Finally, it arrives, churning dust, like an angry monster. Now we are singing and screaming like we are proper mad. We bare our teeth and thrust our arms upwards. We tear the ground with our feet. We squint in the dust and watch the doors of the lorry, waiting for the NGO people to come out, but we don't stop singing and dancing. We know that if we do it hard, they will be impressed, maybe they will give us more, give and give until we say, NGO, please do not kill us with your gifts!

The NGO people step out of the lorry, all five of them. There are three white people, two ladies and one man, whom you can just look at and know they're not from here, and Sis Betty, who is from here. Sis Betty speaks our languages, and I think her job is to explain us to the white people, and them to us. Then there is the driver, who I think is also from here. Besides the fact that he drives, he doesn't look important. Except for the driver, all of them wear sunglasses. Eyes look at us that we cannot really see because they are hidden behind a wall of black glass.

One of the ladies tries to greet us in our language and stammers badly so we laugh and laugh until she just says it in English. Sis Betty explains the greeting to us even though we understood it, even a tree knows that *Hello, children* means 'Hello, children.' Now we are so excited we start clapping, but the other small pretty lady motions for us to sit down, the shiny things on her rings glinting in the sun.

After we sit, the man starts taking pictures with his big camera. They just like taking pictures, these NGO people, like maybe we are their real friends and relatives and they will look at the pictures later and point us out by name to other friends and relatives once they get back to their homes. They don't care that we are embarrassed by our dirt and torn clothing, that we would prefer they didn't do it; they just take the pictures anyway, take and take. We don't complain because we know that after the picture-taking comes the giving of gifts.

Then the cameraman tells us to stand up and it continues. He doesn't tell us to say *cheese* so we don't. When he sees Chipo, with her stomach, he stands there so surprised I think he is going to drop the camera. Then he remembers what he came here to do and starts taking away again, this time taking lots of pictures of Chipo. It's like she has become Paris Hilton, it's all just click-flash-flash-click. When he doesn't stop she turns around and stands at the edge of the group, frowning. Even a brick knows that Paris doesn't like the paparazzi.

Now the cameraman pounces on Godknows's black buttocks. Bastard points and laughs, and Godknows turns around and covers the holes of his shorts with his hands like he is that naked man in the Bible, but he cannot completely hide his nakedness. We are all laughing at Godknows. When the cameraman gets to Bastard, Bastard takes off his hat and smiles like he is something handsome. Then he makes all sorts of poses: flexes his muscles, puts his hands on the waist, does the V sign, kneels with one knee on the ground.

You are not supposed to laugh or smile. Or any of that silly stuff you are doing, Godknows says.

You are just jealous because all they took of you

are your buttocks. Your dirty, chapped, kaka buttocks, Bastard says.

No, I'm not. What's to be jealous about, you ugly face? Godknows says, even though he can be beaten up for those words.

I can do what I want, black buttocks. Besides, when they look at my picture over there, I want them to see me. Not my buttocks, not my dirty clothes, but me.

Who will look at your picture? I ask. Who will see our pictures? But nobody answers me.

After the pictures, the gifts. At first we try and line up nicely, as if we are ants going to a wedding, but when they open the back of the lorry, we turn into dizzied dung flies. We push and we shove and we yell and we scream. We lurch forward with hands outstretched. We want to grab and seize and hoard. The NGO people just stand there gaping. Then the tall lady in the blue hat shouts, Excuse me! Order! Order, please! but we just laugh and dive and heave and shove and shout like we cannot even understand spoken language. We are careful not to touch the NGO people, though, because we can see that even though they are giving us things, they do not want to touch us or for us to touch them.

The adults have come from the shacks and are standing slightly to the side like they have been counted out of country-game. They don't order us to stop pushing. They don't look at us with talking eyes. But we know that if the NGO people were not here, they would seize switches or pounce

55

on us with their bare hands, that if the NGO people were not here, we would not even dare act like we are doing in the first place. But then the NGO people are here and while they are, our parents do not count. It's Sis Betty who finally gets us to stop by screaming at us, but she does it in our language, maybe so that the NGO people do not understand.

What are you doing, masascum evanhu imi? Liyahlanya, you think these expensive white people came all the way from overseas ipapa to see you act like baboons? Do you want to embarrass me, heh? Futsekani, don't be buffoons zinja, behave at once or else we'll get in the lorry and drive off right this minute with all this shit! she says. Then Sis Betty turns to the NGO people and smiles her gap-toothed smile. They smile back, pleased. Maybe they think she just told us good things about them.

We stop pushing, stop fighting, stop screaming. We stand in a neat line again and wait patiently. The line moves so slowly I could scream, but in the end we all get our gifts and we are happy. Each one of us gets a toy gun, some sweets, and something to wear; I get a T-shirt with the word *Google* at the front, plus a red dress that is tight at the armpits.

Thank you much, I say to the pretty lady who hands me my things, to show her that I know English. She doesn't say anything back, like maybe I just barked.

56

After we get our things, it's the adults' turn. They stand in their own line, trying to look like they don't really care, like they have better things to do than be here. The truth is that we hear them all the time complain about how the NGO people have forgotten them, how they should visit more often, how NGO this and NGO that, like maybe the NGO are their parents. Soon the adults get small packets of beans and sugar and mealie-meal but you can see from their faces that they are not satisfied. They look at the tiny packages like they don't want them, like they are embarrassed and disappointed by them, but in the end they turn and head back to the shacks with the things.

It's MotherLove alone who does not join the line for food. She stands there like a baobab tree, looking at everything from the side, in her bright gown with the many stars. There is a sadness on her face. One of the NGO ladies takes her sunglasses off and waves to MotherLove, but MotherLove just stands there, not waving back, not smiling, not anything. Sis Betty holds out some packages.

Hawu, MotherLove! Sis Betty shouts in a silly voice like she is coaxing a stupid child. Please come, bantu, can't you see we've brought you gifts? she says. The NGO people hold out more little packages to MotherLove, and the two white women even bare their teeth like grinning dogs. Everybody is waiting to see what MotherLove will do. She turns and strides away, head held high, the bangles on her arms jingling, the stars on her dress shining, her scent of lemon staying in the air even after she is gone.

When the NGO lorry finally leaves, we take off and run after it; we have got what we wanted and don't care how they want us to do. We wave our toy guns and gifts in the air and shout what we want them to bring us next time: shoes, All Stars, balls, cell phones, cake, underwear, drinks, biscuits, U.S. dollars. The groaning sound of the lorry drowns our voices but we continue to run and shout regardless. When we get to Mzilikazi, we stop because we know we cannot get on the road. Sbho screams, *Take me with you!* and we're all screaming the words, screaming and screaming, like somebody said the lorry would turn around and take whoever screamed the loudest.

We watch the lorry get smaller and smaller until it's just a dot, and when it finally disappears we turn around and walk back towards the shanty. Now that the lorry is gone-gone, we do not scream anymore. We are as quiet as graves, sad like the adults coming back from burying the dead. Then Bastard says, Let's go and play war, and then we take off and run to kill each other with our brand-new guns from America.

CHAPTER 4

REAL CHANGE

The adults are preparing to vote and so for now everything is not the same in Paradise. When we wake up, the men are already parked under the jacaranda, but this time they are not crouching over draughts, no. They sit up straight, chests jutting out, and hold their heads high. They have their shirts on and have combed their hair and just look like real people again.

When we pass, they smile and wave like they can actually see us, like maybe they like us now, like we are their new friends. We are surprised that they still remember how to smile, but we don't smile back. We just stand together and carefully look at them, at the hairs peeping through the tops of their shirts, at the foreheads that we know can turn to ridges anytime, at the eyes that we have seen become lightning whenever they're angry, at the bricks in the arms that have clobbered us before, and we know that this smiling at us means nothing.

Now when the men talk, their voices burn in the air, making smoke all over the place. We hear about change, about new country, about democracy, about elections and what-what.

They talk and talk, the men, lick their lips and look at the dead watches on their wrists and shake their hands and slap each other and laugh like they have swallowed thunder. We listen, and then we grow tired of listening but we know, from the men's faces, from their voices, that what they are talking about is supposed to be a good thing.

The women, when the women hear the men, they giggle. Now there is something almost lovely in the women's eyes, and from the way they are looking, you can tell that they are trying to be beautiful. Painted lips. Made-up hair. A pink ribbon pinned to the dress, just above the left breast. A thick figure belt. A bangle made from rusty, twisted wire. A fur coat, most of the fur fallen off. A flower tucked behind an ear. Hair straightened by a red-hot rock. Earrings made from colorful seeds. Bright patches of cloth sewn onto a skirt. We haven't seen the women look like this in a while and their beauty makes us want to love them.

What happens when the adults go and vote? Godknows asks. We are busy putting up the Change, Real Change posters like Bornfree and Messenger told us to. We are supposed to put one on the door of each shack, to remind people they need to go and vote on the twenty-eighth.

Weren't you even listening to the adults? Sbho says. There'll be change.

Yes, but what exactly is it, this change? Godknows says. He has just finished putting up a poster and is now looking into it like it has eyes, like it is a person. Sbho starts to speak, but then bends down to pick up a broken mirror and smiles into it, admiring herself.

We continue putting up the posters; the thing is, we don't even care about any change, we're doing this only because Bornfree says he has some Chinese yams for us when we finish the job. Maybe we'll go to Green Zonke and buy something with the yams. I've never seen Chinese money before, but what I know is that their shoes are plain kaka; I wore them just four times and they turned to rubbish.

You know, one day I'll become president, Bastard says. We have put up most of the posters and we're now doing the last of the shacks, towards Heavenway Cemetery.

President of what? I say.

President of a country, this country, Bastard says. What do you think I'm talking about, you dumb donkey?

But you have to be an old, old man to become president, Stina says.

Who told you that? How do you know? Bastard says, slapping a poster onto a door. He does it so hard that the tin trembles, and a voice inside says, You, you damage my door and I'll make you wipe your asses with razor blades, fools! and we look at each other and giggle, hands covering our mouths. In reply, Bastard raises his fist and makes like he will pound the shack. His poster is tilted, but he doesn't try to fix it. He turns to look at Stina over his shoulder.

I said, how do you know? Bastard says again.

I know, Stina says. I saw a picture of the president in a magazine. He was also with the president of Zambia and Malawi and South Africa and other presidents. They were all old; you have to be like a grandfather first.

Bastard's poster falls, and he picks it up and tears it into two. He stretches out his leg and rolls one piece on his thigh to make like it's a cigarette. He puts the rolled-up paper in his mouth, reaches into his tracksuit, and takes out a box of matches. We all watch him light up his cigarette and smoke it.

What are you doing? I say.

Can't you see he's practicing? Godknows says.

It doesn't matter, Bastard says. It doesn't matter that I'll be old and white-haired, as long as I'll have money. Presidents are very rich, he says. He laughs like the men, takes a drag on the cigarette, and the smoke chokes him he coughs and coughs and spits. Nobody asks him for a smoke.

When we're finished, there's a poster on every shack, except Mother of Bones's because she told us she would kill us if we ever put our nonsense on her door. Now, with all the posters, Paradise looks like a colorful thing. We are proud of ourselves; we clap and we dance and we laugh.

Let's sing a Lady Gaga, Sbho says.

No, let's sing the national anthem like we used to do at school assembly, I say.

Yes, let's sing, and me, I'll stand in front because I'll be president, Bastard says. We line up nicely by Merjury's shack and sing at the top of our voices, sing until the little kids come and gather around us, but they know they must not join.

Wayyyt, wayyyt, wih neeeeed tuh tayke a pictchur, whereh ease mah cemera? Godknows cries, making like he is the NGO man, and we laugh and we laugh and we laugh. Godknows runs and picks up one of those bricks with holes in them and holds it like it's a camera and takes and takes and takes pictures. We smile and we strike poses and we look pretty and we shout, Change! Cheese! Change!

I am not sleeping. It's just that Mother expects me to be sleeping, that's why my eyes are closed like this. Mother of Bones tells me that because he is always hunted, the hare sleeps with his eyes wide open. This is to fool everybody; when his eyes are shut, he is actually awake. Right now I am the hare but I have to be careful not to be found because Mother is busy parading all over the place. She paces a lot, as if we live in a Budapest house.

We didn't always live in this tin, though. Before, we had a home and everything and we were happy. It was a real house made of bricks, with a kitchen, sitting room, and two bedrooms. Real walls, real windows, real floors, and real doors and a real shower and real taps and real running water and a real toilet you could sit on and do whatever you wanted to do. We had real sofas and real beds and real tables and a real TV and real clothes. Everything real.

Now all we have is this small bed that sits on some bricks and poles. Mother made the bed herself, with the help of Mother of Bones. The inside of the mattress is made of plastic and chicken's and duck's feathers and old pieces of cloth and all sorts of things. That's our parents' bed, but Father is not home to sleep on it because he is in South Africa. He does not return to see us or bring us things, which is why Mother is sometimes worried and sometimes mad and sometimes disappointed in him. Because Father does not do anything for us, Mother complains. About our tinned house, Paradise, the food that is not there, the clothes she wants, and everything else.

Mother is sitting on the bed now, I can tell by the noise of the mattress. It makes different noises, depending on how a body is positioned on the bed. Mother is silent; I wonder what she is thinking. Sometimes she is just silent like that, with her head held like a heavy melon in both hands, like somebody told her, Be careful or your head will fall on the ground and smash into red, impossible pieces.

Now there is a very soft tap on the door. It's that

man again. I don't know his name but I know it's him and nobody else because he always knocks five times, not four, not six, just five, and so softly too, like he fears he will make dents in the tin. Mother pulls the blankets over my head and then blows out the candle before opening the door. But what she doesn't know is that I am always awake most of the time this happens, because I am the hare.

I hear the door creaking open, and Mother whispers something to the man and he whispers back. I cannot hear the words properly; they are speaking like they are stealing.

Now Mother is laughing. I like it when she laughs like this. It's like how she used to laugh when we lived in a house. I don't know what he said, this man, to make Mother laugh like this. I also don't know what he looks like because I can never see his face in the dark. I don't even know his name, but I know that I don't like him. He never asks after me, like I'm just a country that is far away. He also never brings us anything. All he does is just come in the dark like a ghost and leap onto the bed with Mother.

Now Mother is moaning; the man, he is panting. The bed is shuffling like a train taking them somewhere important that needs to be reached fast. Now the train stops and spits them on the bed of plastic, and the man lets out a terrific groan. Then Mother and the man are still; I hear nothing more, only some heavy breathing. Maybe they are sleeping, but in the morning the man will be gone;

he gets up and sneaks away during the night and when day comes he is gone, like something too terrible to be seen in the light.

Now I am counting inside my head; this way I will not sleep. Nobody knows that sometimes I do not sleep. I am the hare. Even if I want to sleep I cannot because if I sleep, the dream will come, and I don't want it to come. I am afraid of the bulldozers and those men and the police, afraid that if I let the dream come, they will get out of it and become real. I dream about what happened back at our house before we came to Paradise. I try to push it away and push it away but the dream keeps coming and coming like bees, like rain, like the graves at Heavenway.

In my dream, which is not a dream-dream because it is also the truth that happened, the bulldozers appear boiling. But first, before we see them, we hear them. Me and Thamu and Josephat and Ncane and Mudiwa and Verona are outside playing with More's new soccer ball, and then we hear thunder. Then Ncane says, What is that? Then Josephat says, It's the rain. I say, No, it's the planes. Then Maneru's grandfather comes sprinting down Freedom Street without his walking stick, shouting, They are coming, Jesus Christ, they are coming! Everybody is standing on the street, neck craned, waiting to see. Then Mother shouts, Darling-comeintothehousenow! but then the bulldozers are already near, big and yellow and terrible and metal teeth and spinning dust.

The men driving the bulldozers are laughing. I hear the adults saying, Why why why, what have we done, what have we done, what have we done? Then the lorries come carrying the police with those guns and baton sticks and we run and hide inside the houses, but it's no use hiding because the bulldozers start bulldozing and bulldozing and we are screaming and screaming. The fathers are throwing hands in the air like women and saying angry things and kicking stones. The women are screaming the names of the children to see where we are and they are grabbing things from the houses: plates, clothes, a Bible, food, just grabbing whatever they can grab. And there is dust all over from the crumbling walls; it gets into our hair and mouths and noses and makes us cough and cough.

The men knock down our house and Ncane's house and Josephat's house and Bongi's house and Sibo's house and many houses. Knockiyani knockiyani knockiyani: men driving metal, metal slamming brick, brick crumbling. When they get to Mai Tari's house she throws herself in front of a bulldozer and says, Kwete! You'll have to bulldoze me first before I see my house go down, you dog shit. One ugly policeman points a gun to her head to make her move and she says, Kill me, kill me now, for you have no shame, you could even kill your own mother and eat her up, imbwa! The policeman does not kill Mai Tari, he only hits her with a gun on the head, because all eyes are on him and maybe he has to do something important. Blood gushes from Mai Tari's head and turns the policeman's boots red-red.

When the bulldozers finally leave, everything is broken, everything is smashed, everything is wrecked. It is sad faces everywhere, choking dust everywhere, broken walls and bricks everywhere, tears on people's faces everywhere. Gayigusu kicks broken bricks with his bare feet and rips his shirt off and jabs at the terrible scar running across his back and bellows, I got this from the liberation war, salilwelilizwe leli, we fought for this facking lizwe mani, we put them in power, and today they turn on us like a snake, mpthu, and he spits. Musa's father stands with his hands in his pockets and does not say anything but the front of his trousers is wet. Little Tendai points at him and laughs.

Then Nomviyo comes running from the bus stop in her red high-heeled shoes, because she is just returning from town. She sees all the broken houses and she throws all her groceries and bags down, screaming, My son, my son! What happened? I left my Freedom sleeping in there! Then they are helping her dig through the broken slabs and then Makubongwe appears carrying Freedom, and his small body is so limp and covered in dust you think it's just a thing and not a baby. Nomviyo looks at the thing that is also her son and throws herself on the ground and rolls and rolls, tearing at her clothes until the only things she has on are her black bra and knickers. The mothers scream

68

to put our hands over our eyes and we put them there but me, I spread my fingers so I can still see; Nomviyo weeps, beats the earth with her head and hands until somebody wraps her in a gray blanket and carries her away.

Then later the people with cameras and T-shirts that say BBC and CNN come to shake their heads and look and take our pictures like we are pretty, and one of them says, It's like a tsunami tore through this place, Jesus, it's like a fucking tsunami tore this up. I say to Verona, What is a fucking tsunami? and she says, A fucking tsunami walks on water, like Jesus, only it's a devil, didn't you see that time on TV, how it came out of the water and left all those people dead in that other country?

It is a bad dream, and I don't want it to come, which is why I am being the hare. Now Mother's man is snoring; I hate people who snore because it's an ugly sound, how are we even supposed to sleep? Now MotherLove is singing out there. Nobody ever sings like that in Paradise, voice swinging like ripe fruit you can pick and put in your mouth and taste its sweetness. When you hear MotherLove, you know that her shebeen is now open for people to go and drink.

The day the adults go to vote we stand at the edge of Paradise, near the graveyard, and watch them leave. They are silent when they go, none of that talk-talk of the days before. We are quiet because we've never seen them silent, not like this. We

69

want them to open their mouths and speak. To talk about elections and democracy and new country like they have been doing all along. We want them to look over their shoulders and tell us they will know what we are doing while they are gone. We want them to say something but they are just silent like they are suddenly unsure, like something crept upon them while they slept and cut out their tongues.

When they eventually disappear down Mzilikazi, we don't go running to Budapest even though we're free to do as we please. We don't go to Heavenway to read the names of the dead, don't start to light a fire or get inside the shacks to try on the adults' clothes or mess with their things. We don't play Find bin Laden or country-game or Andy-over or anything. We just go to sit quietly under the jacaranda all morning and all afternoon.

Maybe they're just not coming back, Godknows says. Nobody answers him, which means we don't want to think about the adults not coming back.

Maybe there's a party and right now they are busy feasting and dancing without us, Godknows says. We keep looking far out towards the playground, where the adults are supposed to appear. There is nothing but trees and dry grass and brown earth and Fambeki and emptiness.

Or maybe they are still voting. Maybe all the adults in this country went to vote for change and there are so many of them there they have to stand in an endless line. Maybe the line is not moving, like when you are waiting for a doctor. Maybe the line will never finish, Godknows says.

Somebody's stomach makes a loud long sound and I remember I am hungry. We are all hungry but right now we do not care. All we want is to see the adults come back, we so badly want to see the adults come back, it's like we will eat them when they do.

They will come. Maybe they are just on the other side of Fambeki and they are appearing any minute, Godknows says. He has stood up now and has both his hands on his egg-shaped head. Then it starts raining, like maybe Godknows has made it rain by all his talking. It's light rain, the kind that just licks you. We sit in it and smell the delicious earth around us.

Me, I want my mother, Godknows says after a long while. His voice is choking in the rain and I look at his face and it's wet and I don't know which is the rain, which are the tears. I am thinking I want my mother too, we all want our mothers, even though when they are here we don't really care about them. Then, after just a little while, even before we are proper wet, the rain stops and the sun comes out and pierces, like it wants to show the rain who is who. We sit there and get cooked in it.

By the time the adults return we are dizzy from waiting. We see the first ones appear from behind Fambeki and we stand up. They are walking like floating and speaking with their hands, and we can tell, even though they are so far, that they are happy. We forget they are not really our friends and take off to meet them. We collide with their bodies and they catch us with those hands with black ink on them, because that is how they have voted, with their fingerprints, they tell us. They catch us and toss us in the air, toss us so far up we see the blue so close we could stick our tongues out and taste it.

That night, nobody sleeps. We all go to MotherLove's shack, which is the biggest shack in Paradise; the adults don't even have to bend inside. What MotherLove does is cook brew in huge metal madramuz by day, and by night people go to her shack to drink. The shack is painted a fun color and when dark comes the paint glows like a living thing. We always wait for it to light up in the night, and when it does we blaze towards the light, holding our breath like we are under-water. We get to the shack, touch it with just our fingertips, and run back the way we came, screaming, Fire! Fire!

We crowd in MotherLove's shack like sand, and it is stuffy and hot inside and smells like adult sweat and armpits and brew. The adults are passing the brew around, even to us, because they tell us change is coming. We don't drink it because it sears our lips and stings our noses, so we just stand there and fold our arms and watch the adults drink and burn their throats and laugh and talk and what-what.

Then MotherLove stands beside this giant poster of Jesus and starts singing. At first there is this hush, as if people don't know what music is for, but then they start swaying. Soon they are gyrating and twisting and writhing and shuffling and rocking. MotherLove's head is tilted up like she's drinking the stuffy air, her eyes closed. Her mouth is open just a little, you'd think she didn't even want to sing, but her voice is boiling out of her and steaming up the place. Then we are caught in the arms of the adults and twirled in the air, their skin sweaty and warm against ours.

Get ready, get ready for a new country, no more of this Paradise anymore, they say when they steady us on our feet. They say *Paradise* like they will never say it again: the *Pa* part sounding like it is something popping; letting their tongues roll a while longer when they say the *ra* part; letting their jaws separate as far as possible when they say the *di* part; and finally hissing like a bus's wheels letting out air when they say the *se* part. And once they say it like that, *Pa-ra-di-se*, we know that it is a place we will soon be leaving, like in the Bible, when those people left that terrible place and that old man with a long beard like Father Christmas hit the road with a stick and then there was a river behind them.

CHAPTER 5

HOW THEY APPEARED

They did not come to Paradise. Coming would mean that they were choosers. That they first looked at the sun, sat down with crossed legs, picked their teeth, and pondered the decision. That they had the time to gaze at their reflections in long mirrors, perhaps pat their hair, tighten their belts, check the watches on their wrists before looking at the red road and finally announcing: Now we are ready for this. They did not come, no. They just appeared.

They appeared one by one, two by two, three by three. They appeared single file, like ants. In swarms, like flies. In angry waves, like a wretched sea. They appeared in the early morning, in the afternoon, in the dead of night. They appeared with the dust from their crushed houses clinging to their hair and skin and clothes, making them appear like things from another life. Swollen ankles and blisters under their feet, they appeared fatigued by the long walk. They appeared carrying sticks with which they marked the ground for where a shack would begin and end, and these, they carefully passed around, partitioning the new land with hands shaking like they were killing something. Squatting to mark the ground like that, they appeared broken – shards of glass people.

They appeared with tin, with cardboard, with plastic, with nails and other things with which to build, and they tried to appear calm as they put up their shacks, nailing tin on tin, piece by piece, bravely looking up at the sky and trying to tell themselves and one another that even here, in this strange new place, the sky was still the same familiar blue, a sign things would work out. But far too many appeared without the things they should have appeared with.

Woman, where is my grandfathers' black stool? I don't see it here.

What, are you crazy, old man? I don't even have enough of the children's clothes and you're here talking about your dead grandfathers' stool!

You know it was meant to stay in the family – my greatest grandfather Sindimba passed it on to his son Salile, who passed it on to his son Ngalo, who passed it on to his son Mabhada, who passed it on to me, Mzilawulandelwa, to pass on to my son Vulindlela. And now it's gone! Now what to do?

I am not the one who killed Jesus Christ and Mbuya Nehanda; why don't you go to those who are responsible?

All I'm saying is that stool was my whole history—
And like that, they mourned perished pasts.
There were some who appeared speechless,

without words, and for a long while they walked around in silence, like the returning dead. But then with time, they remembered to open their mouths. Their voices came back like tiptoeing thieves in the dark, and this is what they said:

They shouldn't have done this to us, no, they shouldn't have. Salilwelilizwe leli, we fought to liberate this country.

Wasn't it like this before independence? Do you remember how the whites drove us from our land and put us in those wretched reserves? I was there, you were there, wasn't it just like this?

No, those were evil white people who came to steal our land and make us paupers in our own country.

What, but aren't you a pauper now? Aren't these black people evil for bulldozing your home and leaving you with nothing now?

You are all wrong. Better a white thief do that to you than your own black brother. Better a wretched white thief.

It's the same thing and it isn't. But what's the use, we are here now. Here in Paradise with nothing. And they had nothing, except of course memories, their own, and those passed down by their mothers and mothers' mothers. A nation's memory.

Some appeared with children in their arms. There were many who appeared with children held by the hands. The children themselves appeared baffled; they did not understand what was happening to them. And the parents held their children close to their chests and caressed their dusty, unkempt heads with hardened palms, appearing to console them, but really, they did not quite know what to say. Gradually, the children gave up and ceased asking questions and just appeared empty, almost, like their childhood had fled and left only the bones of its shadow behind.

MotherLove appeared with enormous barrels in which to brew a potent liquor that would make people forget. She also appeared with songs in her throat and the most colorful dresses in her sacks. Despite the circumstances, she refused to appear like something coming undone.

Generally the men always tried to appear strong; they walked tall, heads upright, arms steady at the sides, and feet firmly planted like trees. Solid, Jericho walls of men. But when they went out in the bush to relieve themselves and nobody was looking, they fell apart like crumbling towers and wept with the wretched grief of forgotten concubines.

And when they returned to the presence of their women and children and everybody else, they stuck hands deep inside torn pockets until they felt their dry thighs, kicked little stones out of the way, and erected themselves like walls again, but then the women, who knew all the ways of weeping and all there was to know about falling apart, would not be deceived; they gently rose from the hearths, beat dust off their skirts, and planted themselves like rocks in front of their men and children and shacks, and only then did all appear almost tolerable.

CHAPTER 6

WE NEED NEW NAMES

Today we're getting rid of Chipo's stomach once and for all. One, it makes it hard for us to play, and two, if we let her have the baby, she will just die. We heard the women talking yesterday about Nosizi, that short, light-skinned girl who took over MaDumane's husband when MaDumane went to Namibia to be a housemaid. Nosizi is dead now, from giving birth. It kills like that.

We get out of the shanty really careful because the adults must not know. We are also leaving the boys, Bastard and Godknows and Stina, out of this one because it's really a woman thing, so it's just me and Sbho and Forgiveness. Forgiveness is not a friend-friend because her family only just recently appeared in Paradise – this makes her a stranger. On top of that, she is not even like us; if you look at her really closely you'll see her skin is too light, and her hair almost wants to be curly. Maybe she was born just different, maybe God couldn't decide to make her black or white or even albino. We are still reading Forgiveness for now, but we let her come today because Sbho and I

78

need an extra person since Chipo herself cannot help.

We are doing it in the mphafa behind Heavenway; the tree has a nice big shade. Sbho starts by spreading her mother's ntsaro on the ground. She doesn't say how she got the ntsaro but I know she stole it because no mother in Paradise will give her things to anybody to spread on the dirt. Chipo does not waste time, maybe because she's afraid of dying; she quickly gets on the ntsaro and lies flat on her back, her eyes squinted against the sun.

I begin gathering small stones, and after I pick maybe seven I change my mind. I throw them away and start gathering medium-sized rocks. I haven't decided what exactly we'll do with the rocks, but since nobody asks or stops me, I just gather and gather. Gather. Maybe we'll use them to smash the stomach, I don't know. Soon enough, I have a nice little pile collected beside Chipo, near her shoulder. I pat the pile to make sure it's steady.

Forgiveness has found a rusted clothes hanger and she is busy with it. We don't ask her what it's for, but I lean against the tree and watch her undo it. She is biting her lower lip and untwisting the wire, which is struggling in her hands. Sbho emerges from behind a bush carrying a twisted metal cup, half of a man's brown leather belt, and a purple round thingy I don't know what it is. She lines the items up beside my rocks, and put together like that, everything starts to look like an important collection. Chipo is smiling up at us, and we know she's happy about not dying, and we know we are not going to let her die.

Do you want to pee? Sbho says, looking at me.

No. I don't know, why? I say.

Because we need pee, she says.

We need pee?

Well, I can pee, Forgiveness says, but Sbho doesn't even look at her.

I just peed before I came here, so I have no pee in me, Sbho says.

I said, I can pee, Forgiveness says again, her voice raised this time. She is almost done pulling the hanger apart.

I heard you; you think I'm deaf? It has to be my pee or Darling's pee, remember, we don't know you yet, Sbho says, and I smile because I am pleased with Sbho for telling Forgiveness.

Well, I will pee, I say, feeling important now. I want to pee.

Pee in this, Sbho says, and hands me the twisted cup. There is a spider and a web inside so I get a stick to squash the spider, but then I just decide to flip the cup and bang it against a rock instead. The spider crawls away and I clean the web off with a stick. I set the cup on the ground and squat over it, my back turned so I do not have to look anyone in the eye when I pee.

At first it comes in small drops; that's how pee does, if somebody is watching, then it just won't come. I get more tiny drops, like I'm squeezing a lemon, so I close my eyes tight and concentrate.

Why are you taking so long? Forgiveness says, irritated-like, like she is somebody.

Leave her alone, is she peeing with your thing? Sbho says. Then when I'm beginning to think the pee is really not coming, it comes, so I turn around and give Forgiveness a talking eye that says Say something, uh-uh, uh-uh. Afterwards I pick up the cup carefully, it is warm now, and the foam reaches about halfway. I hand the cup to Sbho, who sprinkles earth into it and stirs with a stick and then hands the cup to Chipo, who sits up and takes the cup and drinks the urine without asking questions.

Sbho tells Chipo to lie back down, and then she kneels and lifts Chipo's dress, pushes it up all the way to her chest, exposing her growing stomach. Underneath, Chipo is wearing a boy's khaki shorts. There is a long scar on her thigh from when she was pierced by a broken branch when we were stealing guavas and the owners appeared out of nowhere and chased us out of the tree and down the road. Sbho and I start poking Chipo's stomach with our fingers. It feels hard at the front, like she has swallowed stones, soft at the sides.

It tickles, Chipo says, now that she is back to speaking again. She covers her face with her hands and giggles so hard, I stop pressing her stomach and go for the armpits, where I know it tickles for real. Chipo giggles and giggles until tears start coming in her eyes, until Forgiveness says, Shhhhh, if you make too much noise they will find us. I stop tickling Chipo and stab Forgiveness with my eyes; I mean, who does she think she is?

Sbho has moved on to massaging and so I start massaging as well. We knead the flesh and knead the flesh until Chipo closes her eyes. There is drool coming from the corner of her mouth and I tell her to wipe it off because it's disgusting.

This is what they do in ER, Sbho says. I think, *What is ER?* I cannot remember, so I just keep quiet. Forgiveness doesn't say anything either, and I know she too doesn't know.

I saw it on TV in Harare when I visited Sekuru Godi. ER is what they do in a hospital in America. In order to do this right, we need new names. I am Dr Bullet, she is beautiful, and you are Dr Roz, he is tall, Sbho says, nodding at me.

You said *he*, I don't want to be a man, I say.

Well, that's who I remember, either you are that or you are nothing, Sbho says, making a cutting motion across Chipo's stomach.

And you, you are Dr Cutter, Sbho says to Forgiveness, and Forgiveness spits and ignores Sbho.

Who am I? Chipo says.

You, you are a patient. Patients are just called patients, Sbho says.

Dr Cutter has finished undoing the clothes hanger; now she is trying to straighten it. I think about how Dr Bullet and I collected the rocks, the metal cup, and the belt between us and are now rubbing the patient's stomach without

Dr Cutter, then I realize that maybe she is running away from helping.

How come you are not even doing anything? I ask Dr Cutter.

What? Can't you see I'm busy with this? she says, pointing the hanger straight to my head like she wants to plunge it in my eye. I suck my teeth, swat it away.

So? That's not even doing anything, I say. Look at what Dr Bullet and I have done all by ourselves, look at what we are doing now.

Well, you need a clothes hanger to get rid of a stomach.

Who told you that? Dr Bullet says.

No, you don't, she's lying, I say.

It's true too. You can't do without a clothes hanger, everybody knows that. Even those rocks over there know that. It's like common sense, Dr Cutter says.

The patient props herself up and rests on her elbows. She squints at Dr Cutter but she does not say anything. Then she lies back down and looks up, maybe at the branches, maybe at the sky. Dr Cutter picks up a stone, goes to a flattened rock, and starts bashing the clothes hanger with the rock to make it straighter. Small sparks of fire fly.

What exactly will you do with the clothes hanger? I say.

Remove the stomach, Dr Cutter says.

Yes, we know, but how? Dr Bullet says.

You'll see, Dr Cutter says.

My arms feel tired from massaging the patient's stomach so I stop and just sit on my haunches. Dr Bullet doesn't stop; she keeps massaging and massaging. When she puts an ear to the stomach I don't ask her what she is doing, listening to a stomach like that.

I wish I had a stethoscope, Dr Bullet says, which I don't know what it is.

I want a doll, the patient says. A proper doll with a battery that you can turn off when you want it to stop crying.

When I go to live with Aunt Fostalina in America I'll send you the doll. There are lots of nice things over there, I say. The patient just looks at me like I haven't even said anything.

Dr Cutter finishes with the clothes hanger and lays it besides the patient. It looks straight, like it was never bent to begin with. Then she kneels and pulls at the patient's boy's shorts.

Wait, what are you doing? the patient asks, giggling, but Dr Cutter keeps tugging at the shorts. The patient sits and snatches them back up.

I said, what are you doing? the patient asks again. Now she has a look on her face.

Taking off your shorts. You have to be naked, Dr Cutter says, all serious.

No, I don't. If I take off my shorts then you'll see my thing, the patient says and crosses her legs. She looks at Dr Bullet and me, to see if we think she needs to take off her shorts. I frown and shake my head no, and she pulls her dress back down her thighs.

Why do you want to see her thing? Don't you have yours to look at if you really want to see one? Dr Bullet says.

Because it's what you have to do. The clothes hanger goes through the thing. You push it in until all of it disappears inside; it reaches deep into the stomach, where the baby is, hooks it, and then you can pull it out. I know because I overheard my sister and her friend talking about how it's done, Dr Cutter says. She is holding the hanger in the air and pushing and twisting it this way and that to show how the whole thing is going to go. We are silent for a while, just watching the wire dance and letting it all sink in. I cannot read anything on Dr Bullet's face to see if we are going to go through with it or what. She is looking up into the tree, lips pressed tight, maybe thinking.

Well, is it painful or not? Dr Bullet says at last.

How do I know? It's not like I've done it. But we are not cutting anybody so how can it be painful? Dr Cutter says.

You are lying, the patient says. Her thighs are pressed together, her face contorted as if the hanger is inside her already. I notice her eyes are wide now, fearful. They remind me of the eyes of the woman dangling in the tree, the one whose shoes we took.

Okay. Do you want to die or not? Dr Cutter asks in this stop-nonsense voice.

Don't you know that if you use a clothes hanger, there will be blood? We can't have blood, people will know, Dr Bullet says.

Well, what, then? Dr Cutter asks. She picks up the clothes hanger and jabs the earth. Dirt flies from the hole, onto my dress. I brush it off. Dr Cutter gets up and walks away. We watch her stop before a bush and spread her legs. She hikes up her dress and starts to pee.

I don't see MotherLove coming but I suddenly smell lemon and look up and she is towering over us, her long shadow falling over everything. She frowns and looks around, her nose crinkled. She has yellow butterflies flying on her green gown. We start to get up but she tells us not to move.

Jesus, what is going on here? MotherLove asks. I see Forgiveness finish peeing and start to run off but MotherLove calls her right back and points her to the ground, next to Sbho. Forgiveness sits like a dog told to sit. I am just wringing my hands and thinking what will happen if MotherLove marches us all to the shanty and tells our mothers. I would rather she wallop me herself, here and now; I would rather anybody, even Satan himself, wallop me instead of my mother. Mother wallops like she wants to draw blood and break bone, like she wants to kill and bury you at Heavenway.

Anybody want to tell me what in the Lord's name is going on? MotherLove asks. She looks from one face to another. I turn away, look at the church people going up Fambeki for the afternoon

86

prayers, and I almost want them to pray for me so I can escape this.

Look at me when I talk to you, child, MotherLove says. She brings her face close to mine like she wants to kiss me. Her eyes are large, the white part like it's been dipped in milk. She is beautiful, but now the way she is looking makes her ugly.

So. What is this? she says with a frown. And don't lie to me because I have better things to do than be lied to.

We didn't even do anything, Forgiveness says. Sbho is drawing patterns on the earth with her toe. Chipo starts to cry.

MotherLove bends down to pick up the hanger. Her gown sweeps the earth and leaves lines.

What is this? she says, looking at Chipo, who just keeps crying. MotherLove turns to Sbho.

What is this? she asks again.

It's a clothes hanger, Sbho says. But I'm not the one who made it like that. Sbho and I look at Forgiveness to say, without saying it, that she did it.

I was just – we were trying to remove Chipo's stomach, Forgiveness says, looking down at the ntsaro. Then she bursts into tears. Chipo raises her voice and starts to wail.

MotherLove shakes her head, and then her body heaves downward, like she is a sack falling. But she is not angry. She doesn't yell. She doesn't slap or grab anybody by the ears. She doesn't say she will kill us or tell the mothers. I look at her face and see the terrible face of someone I have never seen before, and on the stranger's face is this look of pain, this look that adults have when somebody dies. There are tears in the eyes and she is clutching her chest like there's a fire inside it.

Then MotherLove reaches out and holds Chipo. We are all watching and not knowing what to do because when grown-ups cry, it's not like you can ask them what's wrong, or tell them to shut up; there are just no words for a grownup's tears. Then Chipo stops crying and wraps her arms around MotherLove, even though they don't really reach around. A purple lucky butterfly sits at the top of Chipo's head and when it flies away, Forgiveness chases it. Then Sbho and I take off after Forgiveness, and we are all chasing the butterfly and screaming out for luck.

CHAPTER 7

SHHHH

Father comes home after many years of forgetting us, of not sending us money, of not loving us, not visiting us, not anything us, and parks in the shack, unable to move, unable to talk properly, unable to anything, vomiting and vomiting, Jesus, just vomiting and defecating on himself, and it smelling like something dead in there, dead and rotting, his body a black, terrible stick; I come in from playing Find bin Laden and he is there.

Just there. Parked. In the corner. On Mother's bed. So thin, like he eats pins and wire, so thin at first I don't even see him under the blankets. I am getting on the bed to get the skipping rope for playing Andy-over when F – when he lifts his head and I see him for the first time. He is just length and bones. He is rough skin. He is croco- dile teeth and egg-white eyes, lying there, drowning on the bed.

I don't even know it's Father at the time so I run outside, screaming and screaming. Mother meets me with a slap and says, Shhhh, and points me back to the shack. I go, one hand covering my pain, the other folded in a fist in my mouth. By the time we are at the door I know without Mother saying anything. I know it's Father. Back. Back after all those years of forgetting us.

His voice sounds like something burned and seared his throat. My son. My boy, he says. Listening to him is painful; I want to put my hands on my ears. He is like a monster up close and I think of running again but Mother is standing there in a red dress looking dangerous. My boy, he keeps saying, but I don't tell him that I'm a girl, I don't tell him to leave me alone.

Then he lifts his bones and pushes a claw towards me and I don't want to touch it but Mother is there looking. Looking like Jesus looks at you from Mother of Bones's calendar so you don't sin. I remain standing until Mother pushes me by the back of my neck, then I stagger forward and almost fall onto the terrible bones. The claw is hard and sweaty in my hand and I withdraw it fast. Like I've touched fire. Later, I don't want to touch myself with that hand, I don't want to eat with it or do nothing with it, I even wish I could throw the hand away and get another.

My boy, he says again. I do not turn to look at him because I don't even want to look at him. He keeps saying, My boy, my boy, until I finally say, *I'm not a boy, are you crazy? Go back, get away from our bed and go back to where you come from with your ugly bones, go back and leave us alone,* but I'm saying it all inside my head. Before I have finished saying all I'm trying to say he has shat himself and it feels like we're inside a toilet.

Mother had not wanted Father to leave for South Africa to begin with, but it was at that time when everybody was going to South Africa and other countries, some near, some far, some very, very far. They were leaving, just leaving in droves, and Father wanted to leave with everybody and he was going to leave and nothing would stop him.

Look at how things are falling apart, Felistus, he said one day, untying his shoes. We were sitting outside the shack and Mother was cooking. Father was coming from somewhere I don't know where, and he was angry. He was always angry those days; it was like the kind and funny man with the unending laugh and the many stories, the man who had been my father all those years, had gone and left an angry stranger behind. And little by little I was getting afraid of him, the angry stranger who was supposed to be my father.

Mother kept on stirring the pot on the fire, choosing to ignore him. Those days, you knew when and when not to talk to Father from the tone in his voice, that tone that could switch on and off like the lights. The tone he was using at that moment was switched to on.

We should have left. We should have left this wretched country when all this started, when Mgcini offered to take us across.

Things will get better, Mother said, finally. There

is no night so long that doesn't end with dawn. It won't stay like this, will it? And besides, we can't all abandon our country now.

Yes the wife is right it will get better my son and the Lord God is here he will not forsake us he will not for he is a loving God, Mother of Bones said, rubbing her hands together like she was washing them, like she was apologizing for something, like it was cold outside. Mother of Bones said *God* like she knew God personally, like God was not even something bigger than the sky but a small, beautiful boy with spaced hair you could count and missing buttons on his Harvard shirt, who spoke with a stammer and played Find bin Laden with us. That's how it felt, the way Mother of Bones said *God*.

Then Father laughed, but it wasn't a laughing-laughing laugh.

You all don't get it, do you? Is this what I went to university for? Is this what we got independence for? Does it make sense that we are living like this? Tell me! Father said.

All I know is that I'm certainly not clamoring to go across the borders to live where I'm called a kwerekwere. Wasn't Nqobile here from that Hillbrow just two days ago telling us the truth of how it is over there? Mother said. She stirred more mealie-meal into the pot.

And besides, all my family is here. What about my aging parents? What about your mother? And you, get away, imbecile, go and play with your friends before I chop off those big ears, what are you listening for? she said to me, like she always did every time there was adult talk or they argued, and they argued a lot those days.

Father left not too long after that. And later, when the pictures and letters and money and clothes and things he had promised didn't come, I tried not to forget him by looking for him in the faces of the Paradise men, in the faces of my friends' fathers. I would watch the men closely, wondering which of their gestures my father would be likely to make, which voice he would use, which laugh. How much hair would cover his arms and face.

Shhhh – you must not tell anyone, and I mean *an-y-one*, you hear me? Mother says, looking at me like she is going to eat me. That your father is back and that he is sick. When Mother says this I just look at her. I don't say yes or nod, I don't anything. Because I have to watch Father now, like he is a baby and I am his mother, it means that when Mother and Mother of Bones are not there, I cannot play with my friends, so I have to lie to them about why.

In the beginning, when they come over to our shack to get me, I stand outside the door and yawn as wide as I can and tell them I am tired. Then I tell them I am having the headaches that won't go away. Then I tell them I am having the flu. Then diarrhea. It's not the lying itself that

93

makes me feel bad but the fact that I'm here lying to my friends. I don't like not playing with them and I don't like lying to them because they are the most important thing to me and when I'm not with them I feel like I'm not even me.

One day I'm standing at the door with just my head out and I'm telling them I have measles. I don't know why I think it, but the word is suddenly there, on my tongue, speaking itself. *Measles.*

Is it painful? Sbho says. She is looking at me with her head tilted-like, the way a mother is supposed to do when you tell her about anything serious.

Yes, it is, I say. And then I add, It itches. Soon, it will become wounds and then I won't be able to come out to play for a while, I say. I cannot read the look on Stina's face but Godknows is looking at me with his mouth open. Bastard is just narrowing his eyes, watching me like I'm stealing something, and Sbho's face is twisted, as if she's sick with measles herself. Chipo is sitting down, drawing patterns with a stick on the ground.

What about the World Cup? Godknows says. You are not playing in the World Cup? We even found a real leather ball in Budapest because somebody forgot it outside.

Maybe my measles will be gone by the time it's World Cup, then I can come and be Drogba, I say, scratching my neck to make like it's itching.

True? Godknows says.

Yes, cross my heart and hope to die, I say.

94

Good, but you can't be Drogba, can't you see I'm already Drogba? Godknows says.

Liar, you're lying, Bastard says. You don't have measles and you're not sick and you haven't been sick. He is standing on one leg like a cock and chewing a blade of grass. He looks me in the eye and I know he wants me to say something back so he can say something worse. We are all standing there, everybody waiting for me to say something to Bastard, but I know I'm not opening my mouth.

We remain like that, and the silence is big and fat between us like it's something you can touch when the coughing starts. It is loud and raw and terrible and at first it takes me by surprise. I start, but then I quickly remember that he is in the shack. By now it's too late for me to do anything to hide it, and everybody is looking me in the eye, looking and waiting for me to say something, to explain.

I can't think what to say so I just stand there, sweating and listening to the cough pounding the walls, pounding and pounding and pounding, and I'm saying in my head, *Stop, please stop, stop stop stop stop please*, but he keeps pounding and pounding and pounding until I just turn around and slam the door shut, behind me a voice saying, Wait!

What you got in there? What you got?

I hear Bastard's voice close to the door, like he is going to maybe turn the handle and come in. I pull the latch and listen to him saying things and telling me to open and making jokes. When, finally, he goes quiet I sink down to the floor and just sit there, feeling tired. I look to the corner and he is looking at me with those eyes, wild, like he is some kind of animal caught in the glare of light on Mzilikazi Road, looking at me with his shrunken head, with his pinking lips, with his stench of sickness.

He coughs some more and I listen to the awful sound tearing the air. His body folds and rocks with each cough but I don't even feel for him because I'm thinking, *I hate you for this, I hate you for going to that South Africa and coming back sick and all bones, I hate you for making me stop playing with my friends*. When the coughing finally ceases he is sweating and breathing like somebody chased him all the way from Budapest and up and down Fambeki, and when he says, Water, in that tattered voice, I make like I don't even hear him because I'm hating him for making me stop my life like this. In my head I'm thinking, *Die. Die now so I can go play with my friends, die now because this is not fair. Die die die. Die.*

Father cannot climb Fambeki since he is sick, so Mother of Bones asks Prophet Revelations Bitchington Mborro to come and pray for him in the shack. We sit in a corner, me and Mother and Mother of Bones, watching. Prophet Revelations Bitchington Mborro sprinkles Father with holy water and then lights four candles: one red, maybe for the Father; one white, maybe for the Son; one yellow, maybe for the Holy Spirit; and one black, I don't know for what, maybe for the black majority, which is what the black of our flag stands for. Prophet Revelations Bitchington Mborro is crouching and humming to himself as he does all this, and finally, when he is done, he spreads a white cloth on the floor, kneels on it with a Bible at his side, and thunders.

At first my eyes are closed just like they are supposed to be when somebody is praying but then I get tired of closing them because Prophet Revelations Bitchington Mborro just keeps thundering and thundering. To make the time go I count to one hundred and when I finish he is still going on and on. On and on and on and on and on and on and on and on and on on on on on on on on on on on on on: I warn you in the name of Jesus, demon – cleanse him, Father – you mighty lion and healer of the sick – I lay myself before you Jehovah Jaira, what-what. I just sit there, biting the insides of my mouth till I taste blood.

Father's eyes are open and the look inside them is that of waiting, like waiting for a miracle. I look to the side and Mother of Bones has her eyes closed and is praying fervently, a vein popped on her forehead. Mother's eyes are open. She doesn't give me a look that says she will kill me for keeping my eyes open during prayer, so I just stay like that, watching.

Mother's eyes are tired and her face is tired; ever since Father came she has been busy doing things for him – watching him and cooking for him and feeding him and changing him and worrying over him. I think of praying for her so that her tiredness goes away but then I remind myself I have decided that praying to God is a waste of time. You pray and pray and pray and nothing changes, like for example I prayed for a real house and good clothes and a bicycle and things for a long, long, time, and none of it has happened, not even one little thing, which is how I know that all this praying for Father is just people playing.

I've thought about it properly, this whole praying thing, I mean really thought about it, and what I think is that maybe people are doing it wrong; that instead of asking God nicely, people should be demanding and questioning and threatening to stop worshipping him. Maybe that way, he would think differently and try to make things right, like he is supposed to; even that verse in the Bible says ask for anything and you shall receive and, I mean, whose words are those?

After the longest time, Prophet Revelations Bitchington Mborro finally says Amen, and opens his eyes. He wipes his dripping face and head with the back of his sleeve as he tells Mother of Bones that God showed him that my grandfather's spirit, which has been in me all along, has left. When I hear this I smile; even though I never felt like there was something in me, it had still bothered

98

me to hear Prophet Revelations Bitchington Mborro say there was to begin with.

He goes on to tell Mother of Bones that it doesn't mean the spirit is gone because it has now got into Father and is devouring his blood and body, making him all bony and sick and taking his strength away. In order to avenge the spirit and heal Father, Prophet Revelations Bitchington Mborro says, we need to find two fat white virgin goats to be brought up the mountain for sacrifice, and that Father has to be bathed in the goats' blood. In addition, Prophet Revelations Bitchington Mborro says he will need five hundred U.S. dollars as payment, and if there are no U.S. dollars, euros will do. When he says this, Mother gets up angry-like and boils out of the shack, slamming the door behind her.

God also told me that the wife is possessed too, by three demons. One causes her to be unhappy all the time, one is the spirit of the dog, and the last one gives her a bad temper, rendering her a dangerous woman. But for now we have to deal with the husband, seeing how he is the most urgent case, Prophet Revelations Bitchington Mborro says, pointing his stick at Father.

They are huddling outside the shack when I open the door. Mother has gone to the border to sell and Mother of Bones is on Fambeki praying because she is fasting for Father's health. She cannot afford the two virgin goats and the five hundred U.S. dollars that Prophet Revelations Bitchington Mborro said to get and there are no doctors or nurses at the hospital because they are always on strike, so that's what Mother of Bones must do for now, fast and get on Fambeki and pray and pray and pray even though God will just ignore her.

It's your father in there. He has the Sickness, we know, Godknows says.

It's no use hiding AIDS, Stina says. When he mentions the Sickness by name, I feel a shortness of breath. I look around to see if there are other people within earshot.

It's like hiding a thing with horns in a sack. One day the horns will start boring through the sack and come out in the open for everybody to see, Stina says.

Where did he get it, South Africa? He wasn't sick when he left, was he? Godknows says.

Who told you all this? I say, looking from face to face. In my head I'm thinking just how much I hate him again, but now it's for a different reason. It's for putting me in this position where I have to explain to my friends and I don't know how anymore because I'm tired of all the lying.

Everybody knows, you ugly, Bastard says. We want to come in and see for ourselves.

There is nothing to see, I say. There is nobody in here. I realize that I am whispering, like I'm just talking to myself.

We saw your mother leave and we know your

100

grandmother is on that kaka mountain wasting her time, so why don't you let us come in and see, Bastard says. He is already opening the door and letting himself in like he lives here. They all pile in, and I follow them like it's their shack and I'm just visiting.

We kneel around the bed, around Father, who is perched there like a disappearing king. This is the first time I am coming this close to him without Mother making me. I keep expecting for somebody to laugh at Father's bones but nobody makes a sound; it is all quiet like we are maybe at church and Jesus just entered and coughed twice. I am careful not to look anyone in the face because I don't want them to see the shame in my eyes, and I also don't want to see the laughter in theirs.

We don't speak. We just peer in the tired light at the long bundle of bones, at the shrunken head, at the wavy hair, most of it fallen off, at the face that is all points and edges from bones jutting out, the pinkish-reddish lips, the ugly sores, the skin sticking to the bone like somebody ironed it on, the hands and feet like claws. I know then that what really makes a person's face is the meat; once that melts away, you are left with something nobody can even recognize.

Bastard picks up the stick-like hand lying there beside Father as if somebody left it behind on the way to play. He cradles it in his like it's an egg and says, How are you, Mr Darling's father? I have never heard Bastard sound like this, all

101

careful and gentle like his words are made of feathers. We all lean forward and watch the thin lips move, the mouth struggling to mumble something and giving up because the words are stunning themselves on the carpet of sores around the inner lips, the tongue so swollen it fills the mouth. We watch him stop struggling to speak and I think about how it would feel to not be able to do a simple thing like open my mouth and speak, the voice drowning inside me. It's a terrifying feeling.

Where do you think he is going to go? Sbho says.

Can't you see he is stuck here and he is never getting out? Chipo says.

I mean when he dies, Sbho says.

I turn to look at her and she shrugs. I know Father is sick but the thought of him dead and gone-gone scares me. It's not like he'll be in South Africa, for example, where it is possible to tell yourself and other people that since that's where he went then maybe one day he will return. Death is not like that, it is final, like that girl hanging in a tree because as we later found out from the letter in her pockets, she had the Sickness and thought it was better to just get it over with and kill herself. Now she is dead and gone, and Mavava, her mother, will never ever see her again.

To heaven. My father is going to heaven, I say, even if I don't really think there is a heaven; I just don't like the thought of him not going anywhere. I hear myself saying *my* like he is maybe my favorite thing, like he is mine, like I own him. He is looking like a child, just lying there, unable to do anything, and then I'm wishing I were big and strong so I could scoop him up and rock him in my arms.

Is that why Mother of Bones is always on that mountain praying? Is she praying for God to let him into heaven? Sbho says.

I don't know, maybe, I say.

Heaven is boring. Didn't you see, in that picture book back when we used to go to school? It's just plain and white and there is not even any color and it's too orderly. Like there will be crazy prefects telling you all the time: Do this, don't do that, where are your shoes, tuck in your shirt, shhh, God doesn't like it and will punish you, keep your voice low you'll wake the angels, go and wash, you are dirty, Bastard says.

Me, when I die I want to go where there's lots of food and music and a party that never ends and we're singing that Jobho song, Godknows says.

When Godknows starts singing Jobho, Sbho joins in and we listen to them sing it for a while and then we're all scratching our bodies and singing it because Jobho is a song that leaves you with no choice but to scratch your body the way that sick man Job did in the Bible, lying there scratching his itching wounds when God was busy torturing him just to play with him to see if he had faith. Jobho makes you call out to heaven even though you know God is occupied with better

103

things and will not even look your way. Jobho makes you point your forefinger to the sky and sing at the top of your voice. We itch and we scratch and we point and we itch again and we fill the shack with song.

Then Stina reaches and takes Father's hand and starts moving it to the song, and Bastard moves the other hand. I reach out and touch him too because I have never really touched him ever since he came and this is what I must do now because how will it look when everybody is touching him and I'm not? We all look at one another and smile-sing because we are touching him, just touching him all over like he is a beautiful plaything we have just rescued from a rubbish bin in Budapest. He feels like dry wood in my hands, but there is a strange light in his sunken eyes, like he has swallowed the sun.

CHAPTER 8

BLAK POWER

The guava season is getting ready to end so now we prowl Budapest like we're hunting animals. We carefully comb and comb the streets, eyes trained on the trees so hard our necks could strain. We don't really talk about it but I know all of us are thinking of the end of the season, when Budapest will have nothing for us anymore, of the long, boring months before the next season starts.

Maybe we should start hitting inside, Bastard says, speaking really slow and thoughtful-like.

No. We're not thugs, Godknows says, and I almost clap for him for talking sense for a change.

Yes, we're not those kind of people, Sbho says.

I tell you, we're really missing out, Bastard says, his face all screwed up with seriousness.

We are strolling down Queens and underneath our feet, the road is burning from the sun. It's when we turn the corner of Mandela that we see the man. We can tell from his uniform that he is a guard. We haven't seen any guards in Budapest before so at first we are not so sure what to do with him. He beckons us with his black baton stick, and because we are too close to turn around and run we just walk towards him.

Yes, so what prompts your presence in this territory? the guard says. We're right there with him but he is busy shouting like we are on Mount Everest. He looks us over with his dirty eyes, and we look him back, not answering, just watching him to see what he is all about.

I can't figure out if he is frowning or it's his general ugliness. He is tall and his navy uniform looks like it's just been slapped on him. On his left arm is a discolored white patch with a picture of a gun and the word *Security* embossed in red letters, and on his breast is a ZCC church badge. The trousers barely reach the ankles, and his boots are unpolished. He is wearing a black woolen hat and matching gloves, never mind the heat. Everything about him looks like a joke and we know he is a waste of time – if we weren't this close we'd probably call him names and laugh and throw stones.

I command you to immediately turn around and retrace your steps. Extricate yourselves from these premises and retreat to whatever hole you crawled out of. Under no circumstances should I ever lay my eyes on you again, you follow? the guard says, pointing us to the road. He speaks with this tone like he owns things, but we know that even the baton stick in his hands is not his, that if he weren't on this street he'd be nothing.

Why are you talking like that, did you go to university? My cousin Freddy went too and can speak high-sounding English as well, Godknows says, but the guard doesn't even look at him.

Are your ears malfunctioning? the guard says with a raised voice. Then he bends a bit so his face is level with ours. Be on your way right at this juncture, he says, but we just stand there, unmoving.

We don't know you, Bastard says, and spits. That does it, the guard gets all animal-like as if he were a dog and somebody yanked his tail.

Who accorded you the permission to perform filthy functions on this street? Who? the guard says. He is rapidly jabbing a crooked finger at Bastard now, and then the spit, and then back at Bastard.

What, you are complaining about just spit? Our friend has vomited on these streets before, Godknows says, pride in his voice. And why didn't they give you a gun, or a guard dog? What if we were armed and dangerous? Godknows adds.

I demand that you wipe it off right now, the guard says to Bastard, his face all dead serious.

Do you even have handcuffs? Godknows says.

Wipe what? Bastard says.

Your filth; do you think you can just come here and desecrate the place as you see fit? Do you know I can perform a citizen's arrest on you right now and ferry your despicable personage to jail? You really wish to see the inside of a cell, don't you, big head? You are begging for it, huh? You want me to take you there? the guard says. He is walking towards Bastard, motioning with his baton

107

stick all menacing-like as if he is going to use it.

But how will you take him to jail? Where is your car? Do you have a driver's license? Godknows says.

You, you seal your trap, cantankerous idiot, don't play with me. I can arrest you too, the guard says, half turning to Godknows and making like he will poke him with the stick. He thinks Godknows is making fun of him but Godknows is real.

So where are the handcuffs and squad car, or are you going to call the police for that part? Where is your roger-over, can I see it? Is it true that they can kill you there, in jail? Godknows says.

Ah, last week, when Sekuru Tendai was coming to see us, the police stopped him at a roadblock near town, Sbho says.

Did they put handcuffs on him? Is he in jail now? Did they beat him up? Godknows says.

No, they begged him for a bribe and then they just let him go, Sbho says.

You, cease all conversation, right now, both of you, you hear me? Refrain from utilizing your vocal organs unless and until you are addressed, the guard says to Godknows and Sbho. I giggle quietly. Then the guard turns back to Bastard.

You believe this to be your father's street, boy? You see the sign says Mandela and you think he is your father, is that it?

But the spit has dried up, see, Stina says, pointing to where Bastard's spit was, and we yell and clap and laugh.

So you fancy I'm a piece of entertainment, huh? You think I wake up in the morning and don this uniform specifically for your pleasure? You think I have no pressing matters to attend to but your nonsense, huh? the guard says, waving his long arms and baton for emphasis.

Since when did you even start guarding this place? We've never seen you before, Bastard says, looking at his fingernails. These days he is growing them, for what, I don't know.

Since your uncultured fathers started terrorizing this neighborhood. It's your fathers who've been coming here, preying on the sweat of decent citizens, isn't it? Isn't it? And now you are surveying this place on their behalf, aren't you? Well, tell you what, let them come and I will reduce them to size. Go and get them right now, you hear me? Go and get them, not tomorrow, not in three hours, but right now, I want them, the guard says. He is sweating on the nose and foaming at the mouth, looking at us from one face to the next like he really believes we have time for him. I am starting to get bored and just want us to get on with guava hunting.

But really, how much are they paying you? Bastard says. He walks to the gate like it's his and leans against it.

Stop that, just stop, you dirty pest, hear me? Don't you ever – remove yourself, get away, right now! the guard hisses.

We watch him do a brief trot over to the gate,

baton stick raised above his head, all ready to strike. Immediately we start shouting and booing. He unleashes the stick on Bastard, who ducks, runs, and stands at a safe distance. The guard starts to pursue Bastard; he slips and staggers briefly like he is going to fall, but he manages to steady himself. He stands there looking at Bastard, who is just having fun because he loves this kind of thing. You can tell from the guard's face that he is getting frustrated, that if he could land his hands, his stick, on Bastard right now, he would do him bad.

I will catch you and you will wish you were never born, you pathetic, fatally miscalculated biological blunder, he says, his mouth all quivering. Then he turns to us like he has just remembered we are there.

Go, get away from here at once. Is this what they teach you at school, huh? To behave like animals? Move, depart! he says.

Ah, we don't go to school anymore. The teachers left, don't you even know what is happening? Godknows says. The guard starts saying something but then just stands there like all his big words are gone. You can tell he doesn't really know what to do with us.

When the small red car comes gliding from down the street the guard takes off towards the other gate. We clap and cheer for him, then we watch the car like maybe it's a bride. Unlike Stina, I don't know much about cars, like I can't look at

110

one and tell you what kind it is, but even I can see that this is an interesting car. It's low like a child can drive it, with this strange design, all points and edges and creases. Up close, the sound of it is like there's something humming inside the metal. Stina nods his head, whistles, and laughs. If he could run and hug the car and talk to it, he would.

The guard is already at the gate of the cream house with the big satellite dish and massive grounds. We watch him hold the gate open for the car, standing all tall and puffed up now like he has grown some height and muscle in the last few minutes, like he is actually the owner of the car and whoever had borrowed it is bringing it back to him. When the car passes we see a hand flash a wave. The guard waves back and smiles. He is still waving and smiling long after the buttocks of the car have disappeared into the large yard. He doesn't look our way and we know he is avoiding us.

Okay. There's nothing else to do, let's go, Sbho says.

Yes, let's get away from this place, he'll arrest us, Godknows says, and we laugh.

That, right there, was a Lamborghini Reventón, Stina says.

When I go to live with Aunt Fostalina, that's the kind of car I'll drive, see how it's even small like it was made for me? I say. I just know, because of this feeling in my bones, that the car is waiting for me in America, so I yell, My Lamborghini, Lamborghini, Lamborghini Reventon! My voice rings in the empty street and I laugh and do a hop-step-and-jump.

Ah, shut up, you, Bastard says.

Let's just look for guavas and leave this clown alone, Godknows says.

On Julius Street, we finally find a tree with guavas, not a whole lot but just enough, and we're in the middle of harvesting when we hear this crazy noise. We look and they are pouring down Julius like angry black water and we know immediately that it was a mistake for us to come to Budapest today. They are just everywhere, walking, rushing, running, toyi-toying, fists and machetes and knives and sticks and all sorts of weapons and the flags of the country in the air, Budapest quivering with the sound of their blazing voices:

Kill the Boer, the farmer, the khiwa!

Strike fear in the heart of the white man!

White man, you have no place here, go back, go home!

Africa for Africans, Africa for Africans!

Kill the Boer, the farmer, the khiwa!

They are going to kill us, Sbho says. I can't see her face because she is on a branch right behind me, but I know, just from the tremor in her voice, how tears are already streaming down her cheeks and that they will eventually get into her mouth.

I don't want to die. I want my mother, she says.

Now she starts to proper wail like she is a radio and somebody just turned up the volume.

Shut up, what are you doing, you want us to get killed? Godknows says.

Shhhh. Sbho, listen, keep quiet. If we don't make noise, if we just stay here and be quiet, they won't see us. They'll just pass, then we'll go, Stina says in a whisper, sounding like he is somebody's sweet mother. Sbho stops the crying but you can still hear her sniffling.

Ah, what, they won't do anything to us. Me, I'm not even afraid, Bastard says, and we all look down at him. He is sitting on a fat branch, one arm wrapped around the tree, his cracked feet dangling in the air. It's like he is just striking a pose and is maybe waiting for someone with a camera.

Can't you hear that they are looking for white people? I'm telling you, they won't touch us, we're not white, he says. We watch him spit, reach out for a guava, wipe it on the picture of the rainbow at the front of his T-shirt, and start attacking it in quick bites.

What if they don't find any white people? Godknows says. Then they'll come for us.

Stupid nonsense, they always find white people, Bastard says.

The gang has spread out in packs now, and they go about kicking down gates or jumping over Durawalls to get into yards, where they pound on doors, shouting for the people to come out. They are wild, chanting and screaming and yelling and

113

baring teeth and waving weapons in the air, and I'm reminded of the gang that came for Bornfree; that is how they did. One group charges in our direction. They kick down the gate, pass right beneath us. That's when we notice the guard from before; they have taken his baton stick and bound his wrists behind him. He is walking barefoot now and is looking like the nothing that he really is. If we weren't up here like this we'd laugh at him.

Then one of them stops, puts his weapons down, and just as we are wondering what will happen, he unzips his trousers, takes his big thing out, and starts urinating against our tree. Now I'm just perched there trembling. Even though I know it won't do anything, I've prayed twice already, to God and then to Jesus's mother as a just-in-case. There is guava in my mouth, sitting there like a bitter stone; I can't swallow it and I can't spit it out. I have all sorts of thoughts in my head, like *What are we going to do? What if he looks up? What will they do to us if they find us?*

When the man finishes urinating he zips his trousers, gathers his weapons, and rejoins the gang. I have to hold tight because I think I'm just going to faint.

Ah! Did you see how big his thing is? Godknows whispers. We don't answer.

When I am big my thing will be like that too, he says.

Open up! If you don't open now, we smash this door. Open now, now now now, open! they yell

114

down below. Then the tall one in the red overalls, the one who's brandishing an ax, goes to the big window. We hear the sound of shattering glass.

They have broken the window! Godknows says.

Shhhh, shut up, somebody whispers.

Then one of them pounces on the door with a machete and starts hitting it and hitting it, and the others join in with their weapons. The guard is standing to the side as if to say he doesn't want to be caught doing anything bad. I wonder what his face looks like right now, I wonder what big words he would use for this. They continue with the slashing pounding clobbering, but before they can really break the door down it swings open, and they cheer. Then two white people, a man and a woman, come out of the house looking like rats pulled from a hole.

The man is tall and fat and is wearing khaki shorts and a khaki shirt and a khaki hat, like he is maybe a schoolboy. He is barefoot, which is the first time I'm seeing a white person going barefoot like he is trying to say he can't afford shoes. His legs are so hairy you could comb them. The woman, who follows behind, is thin like maybe the man eats all her food, like she has the Sickness. She is wearing a black dress and white shoes. We didn't really know, coming here, that it was a white people's house.

Then there is this sound, and a small white thing that looks like a toy comes out of the house after the couple.

What is that? Godknows says. At first nobody answers because we are all looking at the thing, trying to see what it is.

It has four legs, it has a tail, it barks, even if it's a strange bark, Stina says.

It's a dog! Sbho says. I know, it's a dog!

Then slowly I realize that indeed it must be a dog, and that the sound is really supposed to be a bark. It's just a weird bark, like the dog is playing, or is not even used to barking. It's the littlest dog I have ever seen. I start to laugh but then I remember where I am and what is happening. The dog rushes towards the gang as if it will gobble somebody up, then it stops suddenly and just stands there barking its crazy little bark. Now the gang is busy killing itself with laughter. Listening to them, you would think that it is what they woke up and told themselves they needed to do for the day: just throw their heads back and laugh long and loud. You would not tell, from the sound of it, that they are also brandishing things that can cut a person and make it rain blood.

But it doesn't look like a dog, it looks like a plaything and it can't even bark. How will it bite and kill anybody? How will it hunt? Godknows says.

It's a white people's dog, it's supposed to be strange, Bastard says.

Me, I wouldn't even be afraid of it, Godknows says.

Then the white woman bends down and scoops the dog into her arms. She cradles it against her chest like she is cradling a baby. The gang explodes with laughter again; I keep thinking they will throw their weapons down and slap each other and clutch their stomachs or something. Then a man in a pink shirt snatches the dog and throws it to somebody, who catches it and throws it to the next person. They are making like they are playing netball now, and they cheer as the dog is passed from one person to another.

The woman throws her hands in the air, exasperated-like. She looks as if she is saying something. We can't hear her above the noise but you can tell she is begging them to let the dog go. Finally, one of them catches the dog and takes a few steps away from the group, towards our tree.

He's coming, he'll see us, somebody whispers, but just as we are wondering what will happen, the man stops. He throws his machete onto the ground, holds the dog in front of him by one paw, so it is dangling in the air like a rag. Then we watch him take a few steps back and shake his leg. Then he extends the leg back and up, and we know he is aiming to kick.

He is going to – somebody starts, but before he even finishes, the man's leg shoots out and connects. There is a *bhu* sound and the dog sails in the air like it has borrowed wings. It keeps rising and rising and then finally disappears on the other side of the Durawall with a thud and a sharp yelp.

The men in the gang jump up and down and whistle and cheer and scream, *Goal!*

What do you want? The white man is shouting now, and you can tell that if his voice had teeth, it would devour. Then we see one of them, the only one who is not carrying any weapons, step forward and hand the white man a piece of paper. He does it like a bride, slow and respectful-like, the proper way you are supposed to do with white people. We watch the white man snatch the paper, open it, and look at it for a while, and then his face turns a deeper color, like somebody is cooking it.

What is this? What is this? the white man says, jabbing at the paper with a finger. The anger in his voice is as if there's a lion inside him. He towers above everyone, head leaning forward as if he is about to do something. The woman is there beside him, wringing her hands.

Can't you read? You brung English to this country and now you want it explained to you, your own language, have you no shame? one of them says. The guard shifts on his feet like maybe he wants to be asked to read the piece of paper; I think it's something he would just love doing.

Bloody nonsense! This is illegal, I own this fucking property, I have the papers to prove it, the white man says. The lion inside him is raising its hairs now.

We know, sir. I'm sorry, but it's just the times, you know. They are changing, you know. Maybe

118

you'll understand one day this has to be done, you know, says a new voice. It is soothing, like a woman's, and I'm craning my neck to see what kind of man speaks with a voice like that.

You, stop reasoning with these people, I always tell you that! And stop your bullshit colonial mentality, what are you calling him sir for, is he your father? Are you gonna act like that sellout over there, says the one with the red overalls, who also looks like he is the boss. He points to the guard to indicate sellout, and the guard shrinks away.

And you, stupid white man, we don't care, you hear me? If you didn't bring this land with you on a ship or plane from wherever you came from, then we don't bloody fucking care, says the boss. He is waving his ax in the white man's face now.

Listen—

What, do you hear him, Sons of the soil, do you even hear him? the boss says, tilting his head towards the gang.

Just like a white man! He has the testicles to tell a black man to listen in his own country. Somebody please tell this white man here that this is not fucking Rhodesia! the boss says. He has turned back to the gang now and is addressing them with his ax in hand. His face is tilted up like he is speaking to us as well. The boss has an ordinary face; his skin is the color of the earth. He turns back to the white man and starts waving the ax again.

Know this, you bloody colonist, from now on

the black man is done listening, you hear? This is black-man country and the black man is in charge now. Africa for Africans, the boss says to thunderous applause.

Who are you? the white man says, looking the boss up and down. You can tell from his voice that he despises him, despises them all, and that if he could see us up here, he would despise us as well.

Don't you know him? This is Assistant Police Commissioner Obey Marima, and watch that tone, white man, because you don't talk to him like that, talking like you're shitting, a raspy voice says.

No, you listen, the white man says, like he didn't just hear the boss warn him about telling black men to listen.

I am an African, he says. This is my fucking country too, my father was born here, I was born here, just like you! His voice is so full of pain it's as if there is something that is searing him deep in his blood. The lion has bared its fangs now. The veins at the sides of the white man's neck are like cords, his face dark with anger. But nobody minds him. They are leaving and storming into the house, their chants about Africa for Africans filling the air. The white man and woman remain standing there near the guard like sad plants, just standing and looking after the gang; maybe they are afraid of the weapons and that's why they don't try to stop them or follow them inside.

What exactly is an African? Godknows asks.

Shhh, look, Bastard says.

The white man starts tearing the paper in his hands; he rips it and rips it and rips it, throws the pieces onto the ground. Then he starts trampling them with his feet, his enormous legs moving swiftly. A small cloud of dust lifts. He moves like dancing, stomp-stomp-stomp, as if he is hearing a drum somewhere in his head. The woman watches but doesn't do anything.

Then, as if that is not enough, the white man gets on the ground and starts pummeling it with his fists, just pummeling and pummeling, and I think of Prophet Revelations Bitchington Mborro when he fights with a demon. I picture the white man's knuckles cut and bleeding, the brown earth drinking the blood. When he finally, finally stops, maybe because he has worn himself out, and just stays there on all fours, dangling his golden head like he will never look up again, the woman kneels there besides him and lays her hand on his broad back as if she is about to pray for him. Then her shoulders start heaving and heaving and heaving like she is crying for the world. The guard just stands there looking. Then Sbho starts sniffling again.

What, are you crying for the white people? Are they your relatives? Bastard says.

They are people, you asshole! Sbho says in this hard, hot voice we have never heard before, and I almost fall out of the tree because nobody has ever called Bastard that. Never ever. I wait to see

121

what he will do but he is looking at Sbho with confusion on his face.

What are they going to do? Godknows says, and just as the question leaves his lips we hear the sounds of smashing. The white man and woman keep kneeling as if they don't even hear the noise but the guard is pacing around nervously. I don't know why he doesn't run away, it's not like his legs are tied, like his hands.

Maybe they are killing things, Godknows says, answering himself. We sit there and listen to the sound of things breaking and crashing and falling and damaging.

I want to be in there, in there smashing things, Bastard says, and he laughs. He has taken out his pocketknife and is stabbing at the tree, tattooing it.

Me, I'm going home; I should have stayed behind with Chipo, I'm going home right now, Godknows says, his voice sounding like somebody who is fed up with playing.

Wait. Wait until they leave, Stina says. Plus, look at the white people still down there, they'll see us.

I don't care, I'm going. I'm not even hitting Budapest anymore, Godknows says. He starts to move, but Stina slides down his branch like a snake, reaches, and grabs Godknows by his Don't Be Mean, Go Green T-shirt. There is a sound of cloth ripping. We sit in silence and wait, Stina holding Godknows by the shirt as if he's a mad dog that shouldn't be let loose. Bastard has finished tattooing the tree. It reads *Bastad*; he has left out the *r* but I doubt he even knows this.

After a long while, after we are tired from sitting in the tree, the smashing stops and they come out of the house. The boss walks in front, ax dangling at his side. They are no longer making that much noise and they look a little tired even. Like they have been exorcising demons and devils in there. They do not talk to the white people, they just grab them and lead them away, together with the guard, herding them like cattle. When the group passes under our tree, the woman looks up like God whispered to her to look up, like something told her we were up here. I see a black shadow flash over her kind of beautiful face; it's like she's a chameleon trying to change color and take ours.

I cannot look away from the woman's eyes, but I'm ashamed that she is seeing us up in her tree, ashamed for her that we are seeing them being taken away like that. The black shadow remains on her face, and she keeps looking, like maybe she wants to pluck us out of the tree with her eyes, and I begin to think we will fall out from being looked at like that. We know from the look, because eyes can talk, that she hates us, not just a little bit but a whole lot. She doesn't say anything; they move her past, and we exhale.

Where are they taking them? Godknows says, sounding like himself now.

Maybe they are going to kill them, he answers himself. Maybe they'll take them to the forest so their screams for help are not heard, and kill them there.

When we are sure they are gone-gone we quickly climb down the tree and head straight for the house. It's the first time we are entering a white people's house so we pause by the door, like we don't know how to walk through a door. Godknows, who is at the front, wipes his feet on the mat that says Wipe Your Paws but then just keeps standing. Bastard comes from behind, pushes Godknows aside, and steps in like he is the real owner of the house and he has the keys. We all pour in after him.

Inside, the cold air hits us and we put our hands on our bare arms and feel goose bumps. We look around, surprised.

How is it cold in here when it is so hot outside? Sbho says in a whisper, but nobody answers her, which means we don't know. Around us everything is strewn about and broken. Chairs, the TV, the large radio, the beautiful things we don't know. We stand in the wreckage; nobody says it but we are disappointed by the senseless damage, as if it's our own things that they have destroyed.

In the sitting room, we stand before the large mask on the wall and stare at the black face, the eyes gouged out. It is a long, thin face, white lining the eyebrows and the lips. The forehead is high and protrudes a little, and yellow dots divide it in half. The nose is long, and the round mouth is open, like it's letting out a howl. And finally a horn grows at the top of the head.

Bastard picks his way through the strewn furniture and unhooks the mask from the wall. He covers his face with it and starts barking like the white people's dog.

That's what pagans do, they wear things like that, Prophet Revelations Bitchington Mborro said so at church, I tell Bastard, but he keeps the mask on and continues barking and barking and barking. It's not funny so nobody laughs. We leave the sitting room and go to the next large room with the long table that's now broken and the many chairs that are lying all over the place. Dangling from the center of the ceiling is a large light, part of it smashed.

Why do they have two sitting rooms? Godknows says.

This is not a sitting room, it's a dining room, Bastard says. And get out of my way and stop asking kaka questions. We poke our way through the room, then we stop by one end of the wall to look at the pictures that have been left untouched.

Why do white people like to take pictures? Godknows says.

It's because they are beautiful, Sbho says.

The pictures?

No, the white people.

In the pictures we see women in long dresses and funny hats. A boy rides a black horse; he looks happy, the horse doesn't. A man stands next to a long rock, pointing a gun. He bites his lower lip in concentration, like maybe he is constipated and

125

he is trying to push it out. Another man is dressed in a soldier's uniform and carries a red beret. His left breast is flashy with metal thingies. He looks at the camera like he doesn't know where to look. A man dressed in khaki stands in front of a field of maize. A man and woman are getting married, surrounded by happy people carrying drinks in their hands.

It's like a museum, Sbho said. This is what they do in a museum, look at pictures and things.

It's called a gallery, Stina says.

In a very large picture that takes up a big part of the wall, a tall, thin man with graying hair parted at the side is dressed in a suit that matches his kind of blue eyes. He holds a cup and saucer in one hand. His free hand is raised slightly, like he is speaking with it. At the bottom of the picture are the words *The Hon. Ian Douglas Smith; Rhodesians never die*. In the next picture, a little toddler stands holding hands with a monkey. They are dressed in identical blue thingies that are half shirts, half vests, like they are twins.

And in another photo, next to the twins, a nice-looking woman with a round face smiles. She is all bling: a sparkling crown sits on her head, with a necklace and earrings to match. The picture is not even interesting, and she is not even crazy beautiful, but we all stand there and lift our eyes to her like maybe we are looking at a flag.

Why does she look like that? Bastard says.

Like what? Sbho says.

126

Like that thing is heavy, Bastard says.

It's called a crown, I say. And she is called a queen. I know her.

How do you know her? Bastard says.

She was at our house. A long time ago.

You're lying. What would a white person even be doing at your kaka house? Bastard says.

Yes, she was. Under the bed. Under Mother of Bones's bed.

The queen was under your grandmother's bed? Godknows says.

Mnncccc. Sbho sucks her teeth and rolls her eyes.

Her face was on this British money that Mother of Bones kept in her Bible under the bed. That's how I know her, I say.

That crown on her head is very heavy, that's why she is smiling like that, smiling like she just ate a whole bunch of unripe guavas. It's heavy because it's made of gold, Godknows says.

I thought crowns were made of thorns. I saw a picture of it in the Bible, there when they were killing Jesus, Sbho says.

Maybe you saw another Bible. In the one I saw myself, Jesus had a real crown made of gold too. I mean, his father owns the whole world, Godknows says.

You are both lying, gold is not heavy, and you wouldn't carry it on your head, Bastard says.

How do you know? Godknows says.

My uncle Jabu told me. He worked in the mine, remember? He said it was yellow and sparkling,

127

but he never mentioned any heavy. He was going to bring it for us to see but then those kaka soldiers shot him down there, Bastard says, his voice starting to rise with show-off-ness.

We know the story. You've already told us, Sbho says.

Yes, but I didn't tell you about how they tried to hide his body. It was in all the newspapers, Bastard says, but we are already moving to another room. I am thinking of my cousin Makhosi's hands of rubble, when he too worked the mine. When I look behind me, Bastard is busy patting his Afro like there's a crown there he wants to fix in place.

In the bedroom everything is smashed as well but we still get on the bed and jump on it, except Sbho, who stands in front of a broken mirror and paints her lips red, then sprays herself with this blue bottle of perfume. We jump and we jump and we jump, the springs lifting us so high we raise our hands and almost slap the white ceiling each time we go up. Then after we get tired of jumping we get under the sheets and close our eyes and make snoring sounds. The bed is soft and smells so nice I don't even want to get up from it.

We are like Goldidogs, I say from under my sheets. The three bears are coming, I say, but nobody says anything and I know it's because they never read the story back in school.

Let's do the adult thing, Sbho says, and we giggle. Now her lips look like she's been drinking blood, and she smells expensive. We look at each other shy-like, like we are seeing one another for the first time. Then Bastard gets on top of Sbho. Then Godknows moves over but I push him away because I want Stina, not chapped-buttocks Godknows, to get on top of me. Stina climbs on me and lies still and we all giggle and giggle. I feel him crushing my stomach under his heavy body and I'm thinking what I'd do if it burst open and things splattered all over.

We are lying like that, giggling and doing the adult thing on the white people's soft bed, when we hear the ringing. We jump up and look around, unsure what to do.

What is that? Godknows says.

It's a phone, Stina says.

It's a phone! It's a phone! It's a phone! we yell, running out of the bedroom towards the sound. We hunt for the phone in the living room and quickly find it under a towel. Stina flips the phone open and says, Hallo. Then he laughs and gives it to Sbho, who laughs and gives it to Bastard, who laughs and gives it to me. I am the one who speaks better English, so I say, Hallo, how are you, how can I help you this afternoon?

Who is this? a voice says on the other end. It is surprised, the way you sound when you find something you were not expecting.

It's me, I say.

What? Who are you?

Darling.

Darling?

Yes, Darling.

Okay, is this a joke? How did you get the phone?

No, it's not a joke, and I got the phone from Bastard, I say.

Bastard? Okay, wait, can you just give the phone to the owner?

The owner is not here.

Where is she? Where are they?

We don't know. They took them away.

What? Who is we? Who took them away? I can hear from her voice that she is maybe frowning. I also remember that I haven't been using the word *ma'am* like we were taught to at school and I almost want to start the conversation over just so I can do it right.

The gang, ma'am, I say, doing it the right way now.

What gang?

The one with the weapons and flags, ma'am.

Where did they take them?

I don't know, ma'am.

Jesus, Dan, can you find out what's going on here? I just called Mum and Dad and some weird African kid has Mum's phone, the woman says to somebody called Dan.

By now everybody is looking at me like I'm something and as for me I'm just proud that I'm finally talking to a white person, which I haven't ever done in my life. Not like this. Then a new voice, a man's voice, comes on. When he starts speaking

130

to me in my language I laugh; I have never heard a white person speak my language before. It sounds funny, but I'm a little disappointed because I want to keep speaking in English.

The white man asks me what has happened and I tell him everything, but I don't tell him the part about us stealing the guavas. In the end he tells me that I should put the phone back and that we should get out of the house because it's not our house and we have no right to be there. I close the phone and put it back under the towel, where we found it, but I don't tell the others what the man said about getting out of the house. I am already thinking of how many people from Paradise can live here in this big house. Maybe five families, maybe eight.

In the kitchen, water gushes from opened taps and we stop them. The table and chairs have been overturned, and plates and cups and pots and gadgets litter the floor. When we open the fridge we find it untouched, which surprises us. We gorge ourselves on the bread, bananas, yogurt, drinks, chicken, mangoes, rice, apples, carrots, milk, and whatever food we find. We eat things we have never seen before, things whose names we don't even know.

Wee fawgoat the fowks, wee fawgoat the fowks, Godknows says, sounding like a white man, and we giggle. He starts towards the cupboards and rummages and rummages and rummages, and then he is back with the glinting forks and

131

knives and we eat like proper white people. When we miss our mouths we laugh, fling the things away, and go back to using our hands. We stuff ourselves and we stuff ourselves, stuff ourselves until we almost cannot breathe.

I want to defecate, Godknows says, and we all leave the kitchen to hunt for the toilet. Our stomachs are so full they could explode. We walk like elephants because we are heavy, and the food has made us tired. We find the toilet at the end of the long passage. There is a big white round thing where they bathe, then there is the glass shower, the soaps, the gadgets and things. There is also a terrible reeking smell, and we look at the other end, and there, near the toilet, we see the words *Blak Power* written in brown feces on the large bathroom mirror.

CHAPTER 9

FOR REAL

The singing is so distant it's like the voices have been buried under the earth and they are now trying to get out. We've been waiting for it all afternoon, so when we hear it we stop all play and make a dash for the big tree right in the middle of Heavenway. We climb the tree double-fast, and within a few minutes we are high up. Me, I prop myself nicely, find a good strong branch for support, and make sure I am well covered by the leaves.

Look over there, now they are coming, Godknows says, and we see the mourners bursting from behind the big anthill and coming towards Heavenway. They are here to bury Bornfree even though they were told what would happen if they were found doing it. We are watching it this way because we can't go to the funeral since children are not allowed inside Heavenway. But what the adults don't know is that we sneak in whenever we want to watch funerals like this, or just to roam around or even play.

Heavenway is mounds and mounds of red earth everywhere, like people are being harvested, like

133

death is maybe waiting behind a rock with a big bag of free food and people are rushing, tripping over each other to get to the front before the handouts run out. That is how it is, the way the dead keep coming and coming.

And on the red mounds, the artifacts memorializing the dead: Smashed plates. Broken cups. Knobkerries. Heaps of stones. Branches of the *mphafa* tree. Everything looking sad and clumsy and ugly. I don't know why people don't try to make the place look pretty – for example, by painting the crosses and weeding the khaki grass and planting nice flowers – since the dead cannot do it themselves. That is what I would want if I were dead. For my grave to look nice, not this kaka.

I used to be very afraid of graveyards and death and such things, but not anymore. There is just no sense being afraid when you live so near the graves; it would be like the tongue fearing the teeth. My favorite part about Heavenway are the crosses bearing the names of the dead. If we are not watching funerals we sometimes walk around reading the names on the graves. I always try to imagine I knew the people and make up stories about them in my head, or I tell them things that have been happening while they have been under the earth.

When you look at the names together with the dates you see that they are really now names of the dead. And when you know maths like me then you can figure out the ages of the buried and see that they died young, their lives short like those of house mice. A person is supposed to live a full life, live long and grow old, like Mother of Bones, for example. It's that Sickness that is killing them. Nobody can cure it so it just does as it pleases – killing killing killing, like a madman hacking unripe sugarcane with a machete.

The coffin men appear first, marching ahead of the rest of the mourners. They pass right under our tree, shouldering the coffin, their long shoes, brick-colored from the earth, punching the ground and lifting at exactly the same time – up-down, left-right, up-down, left-right – like the feet are playing marimbas tucked just beneath the red, callused skin of the earth.

That is how they move, the six men with faces of rock and lightning in their eyes and zero nonsense in their march – up-down, left-right, up-down, left-right. It's nice, the way they are marching, and so we all look at one another and smile. Bornfree's coffin is draped by a flag with black, red, yellow, and green stripes, with a white heart on the front. We have seen quite a few coffins like that lately; it's the Change people, like Bornfree, in the coffins.

And next comes the throng of mourners. This is the first time we are seeing this many people at Heavenway; it's just bodies all over, clogging the narrow paths. Many of them are wearing the black

T-shirt with the white heart at the front or with the word *Change*. But these ones are not like the mourners we have seen before. These ones do not cry; they do not wail. They do not lower their eyes to the ground; they do not cross their hands behind their backs. They do not measure their footsteps. These ones rush after the coffin. They whistle; they raise their fists. They chant Bornfree's name like they want him to appear from wherever he is. These mourners are angry.

In the sea of bodies are some of the adults from Paradise. There is Mother, there is MaMoyo, and Mother of Bones even. MotherLove. Dignity. Chenzira. Soneni. The men. The Holy Chariot Church people. Almost all the adults are here, but now they don't look the same, they look like bones after you have chewed away the meat.

In the days right after the voting, after the party at MotherLove's shack, Paradise didn't sleep. The adults stayed up for many nights, dizzy and restless with expectation, not knowing how to sit still, not knowing how to bend low inside the shacks, not knowing how to sleep, not knowing how to do anything anymore except stand around fires and talk about how they would live the new lives that were waiting for them.

The first thing I'll do is get a house where I'll stand up to my full height. Ya, a real house fit for a big man like me.

I'm going back to finish my final year at university. I'll go and get my children from those ugly streets, you know, call back those who have gone abroad, tell them to come back home. Have my family again, you know, like a human being, you know?

We'll start living. It won't be the same again. Come, change, come now.

They talked like that, stayed up night after night and waited for the change that was near. Waited and waited and waited. But then the waiting did not end and the change did not happen. And then those men came for Bornfree. That did it, that made the adults stop talking about change. It was like the voting and the partying and everything that had happened had not even happened. And the adults just returned quietly to the shacks to see if they could still bend low. They found they could bend; bend better than a branch burdened with rotting guavas. Now everything is the same again, but the adults are not. When you look into their faces it's like something that was in there got up and gathered its things and walked away.

Messenger is there too, among the mourners, and there is so much anger and pain on his face you almost cannot tell it's Messenger, you almost cannot tell it's even a face you are looking at. If Messenger were to open his mouth right now, his voice would be a terrible wound; it's all there, on his face, the pain. I don't know what he will do now without his Bornfree because they went everywhere and did everything together, like maybe they were a pair of ears.

After everybody comes the two men with the BBC caps. One is looking at everything through a thing, and the other is busy taking pictures. Bornfree's mother, MaDube, is wearing a dress the color of blood even though when people die, you are supposed to wear black, not red, not any other color. Black is for the dead, red is for danger. She is writhing and roaring like an injured lion. She is in pain; you can see and hear for yourself that this is proper pain. Pain-pain. Other women are holding on to MaDube like they heard the lion will leap skyward and rip the sun into bloody chunks.

The mourners stop and form a circle. The coffin has been set just by the grave. It's hard to see with all the bodies so I climb to the topmost branches. When I step on a branch and it crackles, Stina looks at me and frowns, a finger on his lips. I frown back to tell him to leave me alone, nobody will see us with all these leaves, or hear us with all the noise.

A tall man with big hair stands at the head of the grave and begins to speak. The mourners hush, but still you can hear that there is something underneath the silence. Like anger. The man shouts, and his voice rises like smoke, past us, towards God. The man speaks about country and runoff and heroes and democracy and murder and freedom and human rights and what-what. The sound of it maddens the mourners; it's as if they've just been insulted. The BBC man clicks away at his camera like he is possessed.

Now the mourners are restless and cannot hold themselves. They murmur and nod their heads. They shout, they stomp the ground. They toyi-toyi. They dance, feet beating hard on the earth like they want to tear it up. Then Prophet Revelations Bitchington Mborro raises his Bible and starts saying holy things. The mourners quiet. Prophet Revelations Bitchington Mborro reads a verse and says a prayer and he calls Bornfree Moses who was trying to lead his people to Canaan. He says more holy things and keeps going and going until I begin to wonder if he doesn't get tired of talking to a god who doesn't even do anything to show that he is a god.

In the days immediately following the voting, Prophet Revelations Bitchington Mborro and the Holy Chariot people kept vigil on Fambeki, praying for change and encouraging everyone to come up the mountain and pray for the country. They were awesome to see, and when they were in full form, their noise lit Fambeki like a burning bush, songs and chants and sermons and prayers rising to the heavens before tumbling down the mountain like rocks and mauling whoever happened to pass by. And when afterwards no change came, the voices of the worshippers folded like a butterfly's wings, and the worshippers trickled down Fambeki like broken bones and dragged themselves away, but now they are back like God didn't even ignore them that time.

Now the mourners are restless, and they begin to shuffle and mumble, so Prophet Revelations Bitchington Mborro finishes his talk, maybe because he is afraid of the people's anger. Then the burial begins. By the time the men carefully lower Bornfree's coffin into the grave, the lion that is MaDube has become a raging bull. Blinded by the maddening red of its dress, the bull bellows, They murdered my son! They murdered my only son! Bornfree, my son! Who will bury me now that you are gone! The bull bellows and bellows, struggling against its captors and trying to charge after the coffin. I look at Bastard and see he has tears in his eyes, which surprises me. When he sees I'm looking at him he frowns and turns his face away.

The mourners throw their handfuls of soil, and shovels hurriedly scoop earth into the grave. This part is done quickly, maybe so the raging bull does not escape and get in there and turn into a worm burrowing deep and refusing to come out; I have seen some people want to jump inside a grave or do plain strange things. Once the earth is formed into a neat mound, and after they put a sign with Bornfree's name to mark the grave, MaDube sinks to the ground on her knees as if in prayer. Now that she has calmed down, they let go of her. She sits on her haunches and begins to pat the grave with her bare hands, like she is a little girl making mud cakes. Then the mourners start singing a funeral song:

Tshiya lumhlaba, lentozawo,
thabath' isphambano ulandele,
ngcono ngiz' hambele mina ngalindlela,
tshiya lumhlaba, lentozawo—

Right at the point the song says lentozawo, the bull leaps into the air and bolts right across the graveyard. MaDube runs, all the while screaming for her son. Sbho starts to laugh and Bastard says, Shut your kaka mouth, can't you see this is a funeral? People start shouting for MaDube to stop and come back. They yell her name, but she just keeps running, heels almost licking the back of her head. MaDube runs.

After all the people leave, some going after MaDube and some just leaving because there is nothing else to do, we get down from our tree. We can see the prints of MaDube's hands on Bornfree's grave, from where she was patting the earth – a dozen furrowed palms neatly lined together to make a nice pattern. The sign on Bornfree's grave says BORNFREE LIZWE TAPERA, 1983–2008, RIP OUR HERO. DIED FOR CHANGE.

What happens when somebody dies? Godknows says.

We don't know, we've never died. Who are you asking? Sbho says.

Yes. Go and ask your mother, Bastard says.

When people die because they are killed they become ghosts and roam the earth because they are not resting in peace, Stina says. We turn to

141

look at him; he is standing there and not taking his eyes off the grave, like it's his.

Well, maybe if Bornfree is a ghost then he will find all those people who killed him and burn them. I hear ghosts can drop red-hot coal and burn things, Godknows says.

My grandfather was killed before we were born. Maybe he is a ghost – I start, but big-head Bastard interrupts me and says, I am Bornfree. Kill me!

At first we just stand there, looking at the grave like we want it to give us the how to instructions for a game about the dead since we've never played one before. Then Godknows starts making hooting and groaning sounds and we know he is becoming the lorry that brought the armed men who came for Bornfree. He gets louder and louder, and we move. We quickly pick up our knobkerries and machetes and knives and axes and get in the lorry. Stina takes off his What Would Jesus Do? T-shirt and waves it because it's now the flag of the country, and we point to it with our weapons and sing the president's name.

Godknows is a terrific car; he groans and hoots and churns dust until he parks for us to get out, then he changes and becomes one of us. He takes off his Arsenal T-shirt and waves the flag of the country in the air. By now we are laughing and chanting and singing war songs and waving our weapons. We are proper drunk with verve; we are animals wanting blood.

But first, we dance. We lift our weapons above

our heads and sing and chant and whistle. We jump high, stomp the ground, and raise dust. We swing our bodies like they are things, maul the air with our weapons. Our faces are contorted now; we look at each other and we have become fierce and really ugly men. Stina's mouth is open so wide I can see the pink of his throat. He waves his ax and makes chomping motions with his dog teeth and I laugh.

After the dancing we pounce on Bastard, who is now Bornfree. We scream into his face while we clobber him.

Who are you working for?

Sellout!

Who is paying you? America and Britain?

Why don't you scream for America and Britain to help you now?

Friend of the colonists!

Selling the country to whites!

You think you can just vote for whoever you want?

Vote right now, we want to see, sellout!

You want Change, today we'll show you Change!

Here's your democracy, your human rights, eat it, eat eat eat!

Then Godknows swings a hammer, making a straight line in the air. It hits Bornfree at the back of the head and I hear the sound of something breaking. Sbho swings an ax and hooks him at the side, above the ear. Next, a machete catches Bornfree in the face, splits him from the eye to the chin. Then we are just all on him. Thrashing beating pounding clobbering. Axes to the head, kicks to the ribs, legs, knobkerries whacking all over. With all our weapons clamoring for one person like that, it looks like we are hitting a grain of sand; there are just so many weapons they crash into one another. But we only laugh and keep hitting. Hitting hitting hitting. In all this, Bornfree doesn't even make a sound.

There is blood everywhere, so much blood, just blood. Then we stop the beating and some-body says, Get up and go. Get up. But Bornfree cannot stand. He crawls on the ground, slowly, slooooooowly, like a fat, poisoned cockroach.

How do you like the taste of change now?

Come on, get up. You need to get up and vote!

How will you see change when you're just lying there not doing anything?

We jeer and laugh and go back to clobbering.

Chipo, who couldn't climb up the tree with us, has become Bornfree's mother, MaDube. She is off to the side, rolling on the earth. Sbho runs to hold her but MaDube thrashes about like a fish out of water, like a possessed snake, screaming and screaming. Screaming screaming screaming.

Let me go! Let me go and rescue my son! Why isn't anybody rescuing my son! Why are you all standing there watching! You assholes, why are you just standing there and letting this happen! MaDube screams at the graves, which are also the people of Paradise who are standing there doing nothing.

144

Please, MaDube, please don't do this, do you want them to kill you? Sbho has become a kind woman with a soothing-like voice.

Let me go! Let me go! Better they kill me than kill my son. Better they—

And then, right there, a fountain of blood shoots in the air like an arrow and sprays all over. MaDube's hands fly to her chest and she faints.

But the pounding doesn't stop. We chant and sing louder and loudest. We stomp the ground and raise more dust. Bornfree is half naked now and looking like a ragged, bloodied thing and not a person. He still doesn't make a sound, like he is trying to be Jesus, but I don't think Jesus himself would do it like this because there is even that verse in the Bible that says 'Jesus wept.'

The people of Paradise too don't make any sounds. There is this big black silence, like they are watching something holy. But we can see, in the eyes of the adults, the rage. It is quiet but it is there. Still, what is rage when it is kept in like a heart, like blood, when you do not do anything with it, when you do not use it to hit, or even yell? Such rage is nothing, it does not count. It is just a big, terrible dog with no teeth.

And then finally, finally, we just stop. We are tired. Our voices are hoarse. Our faces are drained. Our weapons dangle at our sides, all bloodied. Our clothes are bloodied. The flag of our country is bloodied.

They killed him, somebody whispers. Jesus, he has died death.

We pack ourselves in the lorry, and Godknows drives off, hooting and groaning.

What kind of game is that? we hear somebody say behind us. We turn around to see the two BBC men have returned. They are watching us with their things, standing there among the graves. The camera clicks a few times, taking our pictures. Then the tall one with hair all over and a jungle on his face asks again, What kind of game were you just playing? and Bastard puts his shirt on and says, Can't you see this is for real?

CHAPTER 10

HOW THEY LEFT

Look at them leaving in droves, the children of the land, just look at them leaving in droves. Those with nothing are crossing borders. Those with strength are crossing borders. Those with ambitions are crossing borders. Those with hopes are crossing borders. Those with loss are crossing borders. Those in pain are crossing borders. Moving, running, emigrating, going, deserting, walking, quitting, flying, fleeing – to all over, to countries near and far, to countries unheard of, to countries whose names they cannot pronounce. They are leaving in droves.

When things fall apart, the children of the land scurry and scatter like birds escaping a burning sky. They flee their own wretched land so their hunger may be pacified in foreign lands, their tears wiped away in strange lands, the wounds of their despair bandaged in faraway lands, their blistered prayers muttered in the darkness of queer lands.

Look at the children of the land leaving in droves, leaving their own land with bleeding wounds on their bodies and shock on their faces and blood in their hearts and hunger in their stomachs and grief in their footsteps. Leaving their mothers and fathers and children behind, leaving their umbilical cords underneath the soil, leaving the bones of their ancestors in the earth, leaving everything that makes them who and what they are, leaving because it is no longer possible to stay. They will never be the same again because you just cannot be the same once you leave behind who and what you are, you just cannot be the same.

Look at them leaving in droves despite knowing they will be welcomed with restraint in those strange lands because they do not belong, knowing they will have to sit on one buttock because they must not sit comfortably lest they be asked to rise and leave, knowing they will speak in dampened whispers because they must not let their voices drown those of the owners of the land, knowing they will have to walk on their toes because they must not leave footprints on the new earth lest they be mistaken for those who want to claim the land as theirs. Look at them leaving in droves, arm in arm with loss and lost, look at them leaving in droves.

CHAPTER 11

DESTROYEDMICHYGEN

If you come here where I am standing and look outside the window, you will not see any men seated under a blooming jacaranda playing draughts. Bastard and Stina and Godknows and Chipo and Sbho will not be calling me off to Budapest. You will not even hear a vendor singing her wares, and you will not see anyone playing country-game or chasing after flying ants. Some things happen only in my country, and this here is not my country; I don't know whose it is. That fat boy, TK, who is also supposed to be my cousin even though I have never seen him before, says, This is America, you, you won't see none of that African shit up in this motherfucker.

What you will see if you come here where I am standing is the snow. Snow on the leafless trees, snow on the cars, snow on the roads, snow on the yards, snow on the roofs – snow, just snow covering everything like sand. It is as white as clean teeth and is also very, very cold. It is a greedy monster too, the snow, because just look how it has swallowed everything; where is the ground now? Where are the flowers? The grass? The stones? The leaves?

The ants? The litter? Where are they? As for the coldness, I have never seen it like this. I mean, coldness that makes like it wants to kill you, like it's telling you, with its snow, that you should go back to where you came from.

In the sitting room, Aunt Fostalina is busy walking and walking and walking. It is very strange how she just walks in one place. Maybe if it were not for all this snow lying all over, she would be walking outside, like how a person is supposed to do. MaDube used to walk like this too, just walk and walk and walk, not really going anywhere in particular. That was because MaDube suffered from madness after they killed her son, Bornfree, but I don't really know about Aunt Fostalina here, like what her issue is.

When she walks, she whips her arms front to back like a mjingo and counts at the same time. Three-four-five-six, and walk, and walk. Uncle Kojo, TK's father, who is like Aunt Fostalina's husband but not really her husband because I don't think they are married-married, comes in from work and says, Fostalina, the Lions and the Giants still actually on, no? Uncle Kojo's voice sounds like something in his mouth is running after the words and making them scatter with fright. But Aunt Fostalina does not reply; she has to keep up with the women on TV – four-five-six, and walk, and walk.

This is me in the picture, wearing the pink shirt; I was still living in my country then. Aunt Fostalina took the picture when she came for me. For memories, one day all you'll have are these pictures, that's what she said. This is Bastard and this is Godknows and this is Chipo and this is Stina and this passing by is Godknows's sister S'bahle. I don't know where Sbho was when we took the picture. This is Aunt Fostalina and Mother in this picture, they are twins. Aunt Fostalina is pretty but I think Mother is a lot prettier; if she had been born here she would have maybe become a model or something. What I've seen, though, is that some of the models aren't really beautiful so I don't even know what they are doing on TV; I look at them walking on the runway and think, *If you were born in my country you'd just be ordinary, your runway would be the border, where you'd just be selling things like my mother.*

When I was leaving, Mother wouldn't let go of my hand I thought she was going to rip it off. Mother of Bones looked at me with kindness, which was the first time she ever looked at me like that, and said, I don't know I really don't know child this could be the last time I see you I don't know I'll still be here when you return but what kind of life is this when you are all born to scatter to foreign lands in droves what will the country become a ruin? she said. I didn't say anything because even though it was a question, Mother of Bones was talking to herself as usual.

A few days before I left, Mother took me to Vodloza, who made me smoke from a gourd, and I sneezed and sneezed and he smiled and said,

The ancestors are your angels, they will bear you to America. Then he spilled tobacco on the earth and said to someone I could not see: Open the way for your wandering calf, you, Vusamazulu, pave the skies, summon your fathers, Mpabanga and Nqabayezwe and Mahlathini, and draw your mighty spears to clear the paths and protect the child from dark spirits on her journey. Deliver her well to that strange land where you and those before you never dreamed of setting foot.

Finally he tied a bone attached to a rainbow-colored string around my waist and said, This is your weapon, it will fight off all evil in that America, never ever take it off, you hear? But then when I got to America the airport dog barked and barked and sniffed me, and the woman in the uniform took me aside and waved the stick around me and the stick made a *nting-nting* sound and the woman said, Are you carrying any weapons? and I nodded and showed my weapon from Vodloza, and Aunt Fostalina said, What is this crap? and she took it off and threw it in a bin. Now I have no weapon to fight evil with in America.

With all this snow, with the sun not there, with the cold and dreariness, this place doesn't look like my America, doesn't even look real. It's like we are in a terrible story, like we're in the crazy parts of the Bible, there where God is busy punishing people for their sins and is making them miserable with all the weather. The sky, for example, has stayed white all this time I have been here, which tells you that something is not right. Even the stones know that a sky is supposed to be blue, like our sky back home, which is blue, so blue you can spray Clorox on it and wipe it with a paper towel and it wouldn't even come off.

And another thing: you won't see them from where I am standing but there are tokoloshes too in that snow. At night I dream they come out of it and they say, Hey, do you want to make a snowman? How are you doing? Where are you from? Then they say, Do you like *High School Musical* or *That's So Raven*? They say, Do you want McDonald's or Burger King? They say, Do you like Justin Bieber? I shout at the tokoloshes to go away.

Uncle Kojo looks at Aunt Fostalina walking in one place and folds his arms across his chest and says, You know, me, I actually don't understand why you are doing all this. What are you doing to yourself, Fostalina, really-exactly-what? Kick. And punch. And kick. And punch. Look at you, bones bones bones. All bones. And for what? They are not even African, those women you are doing like, shouldn't that actually tell you something? Three-four-five-six, and kick. And punch. That there is actually nothing African about a woman with no thighs, no hips, no belly, no behind. Squat. Bend your knees. Squat. Bend your knees. Squat.

He says, Uncle Kojo, he says, And last time I sent family pictures to my mother, she actually cried, Ah ah ah, my son, oh, please please please feed your wife and don't nah bring her here looking like this, you will embarrass us. That's what she said, my mother. Squat, bend your knees. Squat. Bend your knees. Squat. Bend your knees. Move to the left now, two jabs. And uppercut. One more time.

When Uncle Kojo comes from work all he does is sit in front of the TV. Aunt Fostalina says, When are you going to do something with the kids, Kojo? You are never home, and when you are, you just park in front of that damn TV and watch that damn football. Can't you take them to the movies or the mall or something? But I think she is only saying it just so she can have the TV to herself so she can watch her walking women. Uncle Kojo doesn't seem to bother about listening to her; he only says, Touchdown! And then speaks in his language that nobody understands. He is not from our country, that's why we don't under-stand his language or he ours; he is from Ghana. TK doesn't understand his father's language either because he is not from Ghana, his mother is American and he was born here.

Uncle Kojo says to TK, You, just how many times do I actually need to tell you to pull up your trousers, eh? If you will let them drop like that, why not just get rid of them? Why not just go around in your underwear? Why not actually just lose all your clothes and run about naked, eh? Now you want to be like these raggedy boys standing around corners and smoking things and talking profanity because they are too stupid to realize how easy they have it? That's who you want to be, eh? TK mutters and pulls his trousers up and then goes to his room, where he spends hours and hours.

Once I went up there to see what he was doing and I found him just sitting on his bed with that thing on his lap and *tobedzing* and *tobedzing* and *tobedzing*, bullets and bombs raining on the screen. I said, What are you doing, and he said, Can't you see I'm playing a game? and I said, What kind of game do you play by yourself? and he said, Get the fuck out. I will not be friends with TK; he shuts himself up there like he lives in his own country by himself. He also doesn't even speak my language and says I talk funny.

If I were at home I know I would not be standing around because something called snow was preventing me from going outside to live life. Maybe me and Sbho and Bastard and Chipo and Godknows and Stina would be out in Budapest, stealing guavas. Or we would be playing Find bin Laden or country-game or Andy-over. But then we wouldn't be having enough food, which is why I will stand being in America dealing with the snow; there is food to eat here, all types and types of food. There are times, though, that no matter how much food I eat, I find the food does nothing for me, like I am hungry for my country and nothing is going to fix that.

★　　★　　★

155

I have been watching that black car across the road trying to move but it cannot; the snow sneaked down last night and has bewitched the car's poor wheels. The car manages to move only a little, just a little bit and then stalls, like a dung beetle struggling uphill with a big ball of cow dung. Now whoever is inside that car is stuck in the cold snow.

When the snow falls it doesn't even make a sound. That's why I am watching it – because it is just so sneaky. You can wake up to find even more heaps and heaps of it without you ever hearing it. How does something so big it shrouds everything come down just like that and you don't even hear it coming? No sound – a crash, slam, bam, clatter, something, anything, so that this snow can carry a proper story. Right now I know what it is trying to do: it is waiting for me to come out so it can cover me too, but I will not be going out of that door. Aunt Fostalina says we are snowed in and will not be going out of the house anytime soon. I say I am staying in this house because I know what this snow is trying to do.

If it wasn't for that the houses here have heat in them, I think we'd all be killed by now. Killed by this snow and the cold it comes with; it's not the normal cold that you could just complain about and then move on to other things. No. This cold is not like that. It's the cold to stop life, to cut you open and blaze your bones. Nobody told me of this cold when I was coming here. Had it been that somebody had taken me aside and explained the

156

cold and its story properly, I just don't know what I would have done, if I would really have gotten in that plane to come.

Aunt Fostalina's cousin Prince arrived yesterday from our country but he will be moving on to live with his brother in this place called Texas in two weeks. Right now he is sleeping because he is tired from sitting in the plane too long. Prince has burn scars on his arms and back where they burned him. He is young but now he looks aged, older than Uncle Kojo, looks maybe like Mdawini back home, who has six children. His face is hard and terrible and the light in his eyes is gone, like the snow maybe sneaked in there and put it out.

When Aunt Fostalina finishes walking she asks, You think I'm losing weight? Who is fatter, me or Aunt Da? Who is fatter, me or your mother? Then she sits on that big ball and then she sleeps on it. Then she lifts those metals and says, I will be going on a fruit diet. Then she gets up and starts walking again, her arms swinging front to back, front to back. Aunt Fostalina is thin and very soon she will begin to look like Father's bones, drowning there on the bed and just waiting to die.

Uncle Kojo comes home from work and says to Aunt Fostalina, You know, me, I actually don't understand why there is never any hot food in this house, Fostalina. Aunt Fostalina looks up from squeezing an orange and says, No food in this house, Kojo, really? But I just did groceries yesterday, what do you think that fridge over there

157

is full of, huh, bricks? And he says, Fostalina, ever since you started this weight thing you never cook. When was the last time we actually had a real dinner in this house, heh? You know in my country, wives actually cook hot meals every day for their husbands and children. And not only that, they actually also do laundry and iron and keep the house clean and everything.

Fat boy TK pulls up his trousers and mutters, Patriarchal motherfucker, and Aunt Fostalina throws the rest of the orange in the bin and says, Yes, in your country maybe, but this is America, and nxa ubon' engan' ulebhoyi lapha manj' uzatshetshela ngereza fanami! and Uncle Kojo shakes his head and walks away since he doesn't understand a word of it. But I think it is better that Uncle Kojo did not understand what Aunt Fostalina just said to him, otherwise he would actually be very, very angry.

On TV that pretty man Obama who has been saying, Yes We Can, America, Yes We Can, is becoming president. He does not look old like our own president; he looks maybe like our president's child. There are crowds and crowds of white people and black people and brown people, just people, and they are happy and cheering and clapping. Prince looks at it all with tears in his eyes and shakes my hand until I think he wants to break it and says, See? That is democracy, we can't even say that word back home, and then he shakes his head and laughs and laughs and laughs

158

until fat boy TK says, Crazy-ass motherfucker. Prince talks to himself like there are a lot of people inside his head that he needs to tell things.

When the microwave says *nting*, fat boy TK takes out a pizza and eats it. When the microwave says *nting* again, he takes out the chicken wings. And then it's the burritos and hot dogs. Eat eat eat. All that food TK eats in one day, me and Mother and Mother of Bones would eat in maybe two or three days back home.

They are out there digging the snow, because so much of it has fallen. I think it is a very good thing that they are digging it; that is just too much whiteness, as if somebody told the snow the other colors don't even count. I think if it were a pretty color, like maybe purple or pink, or even rainbow-like, then it would at least be interesting to look at. They dig and fling the snow to the sides, where it piles into dirty heaps.

There are also little children playing in the snow. They touch it, kick it, throw it at each other, just play with it like it is meant to be played with. Now they have even gone on to make a thing that almost looks like a round person, and they have put a hat on it and a red rag around its neck and a carrot on its face. Maybe that is an American tokoloshe, maybe when night comes it will start walking and do evil. I do not know what I would do because I cannot even fight evil now because they made me throw away my weapon at that airport.

In the living room Prince is polishing his wooden

animals; he brought them with him from home and plays with them as if he is a young child. The animals are all lined up there on the table: the lion, the elephant, the rhino, the giraffe. Prince talks to his animals like they will hear and talk back to him. He says to the lion, Silwane, bhubesi, nkunzi! Then he picks it up and holds it against his cheek and roars for it, and the dead light in his eyes almost comes back.

Then he picks up the elephant and says, Ndlovu, ntaba, umkhulu! Then he holds it against his other cheek and trumpets for it. I say to him, It's a good thing they are made of wood because they do not have to go outside and die in that snow, but Prince does not look like he hears me. He just butts the heads of the elephant and lion against each other and bares his teeth like a dog and growls and asks them, Who will rule this jungle, who will rule it? Uncle Kojo says to him, Shouldn't you actually be looking at colleges, Prince? You are in America now and you can actually be anything you want to be, look at Obama. Aunt Fostalina looks at Uncle Kojo like she wants to cut him with her eyes and says, Wena silima, can't you see he is coping with everything that happened there?

The snow has not fallen in a while, and on the ground, it looks like it is starting to melt. It is much thinner and you can see puddles of water in some places. It is also falling off the branches, and you

160

can see the roofs and the road. Maybe the snow has decided to go away, to go back where it came from because it knows I am watching it. I do not want to go outside yet, and I shake my head no when Aunt Fostalina asks if I want to go places with her. She leaves me alone and does not force or beat me up like perhaps Mother or Mother of Bones would if I was not doing what they wanted me to. She always asks me if I want to do things – Do you feel like eating mac and cheese? Do you want to go to bed? Do you prefer this or that? Are you sure? – as if I have become a real person.

Prince is talking to himself more and more, like maybe the people in his head have really come out and he can see them. Sometimes he yells and screams and kicks like somebody is trying to do things to him. Aunt Fostalina shakes Prince to make him stop but she is not strong enough. He is flailing his burned arms and screaming for help now. When he stops, Aunt Fostalina wraps him in her thin arms like he is a baby. He quietens down and she rocks him and rocks him and rocks him. When he starts talking again she sings him a lullaby, and he sings along with her, though he sings a different song, his fists hammering his head like he wants to make himself bleed:

Sobashiy' abafowethu
Savuka sawela kwamany' amazwe
Laph' okungazi khon' ubaba lomama
S'landel' inkululeko—

161

Once the snow is gone it will be possible to go outside and see what this Detroit is all about, to see the grass, the flowers, the leaves, the birds, and the litter. Maybe I will finally see things that I know, and maybe this place will look ordinary at last. I will go out there and smell the air, maybe catch some grasshoppers and find out what kind of strange fruits grow on all these big trees. I will draw country-game on the ground, or even arra, which Bornfree taught us to play. He said they played it when they were boys, when the country was still a country.

Stina said a country is a Coca-Cola bottle that can smash on the floor and disappoint you. When a bottle smashes, you cannot put it back together. One day when we were squatting in the bush after eating guavas, Mukoma Charlie found us and said, You are the most unfortunate children this broken bottle has ever seen. When it was still a country you would all be at school doing some serious learning so you would grow up and be somebodies, but here you are, squatting in the bush, guavas ripping your anuses.

Stina also said leaving your country is like dying, and when you come back you are like a lost ghost returning to earth, roaming around with a missing gaze in your eyes. I don't want to be that when I go back to my country, but then I don't really know because will Paradise be there when I return? Will Mother of Bones be there when I return? Will Bastard and Godknows and Sbho and Stina and

162

Chipo and all my friends be there when I return? Will the guava trees be there when I return? Will Paradise, will everything, be the same when I return?

The onliest time that it's almost interesting here is when Uncle Themba and Uncle Charley and Aunt Welcome and Aunt Chenai and others all come to visit Aunt Fostalina. I call them uncles and aunts but we are not related by blood, like me and Aunt Fostalina are; I never knew them back home, and Uncle Charley is white, for instance. I think the reason they are my relatives now is they are from my country too – it's like the country has become a real family since we are in America, which is not our country.

Whenever they come, Uncle Kojo leaves the house for most of the time because everybody will be speaking our real language, laughing and talking loudly about back home, how it was like when they were growing up before things turned bad, then ugly. They always forget Uncle Kojo cannot understand them and he sits there looking lost, like he just illegally entered a strange country in his own house.

The uncles and aunts bring goat insides and cook ezangaphakathi and sadza and mbhida and occasionally they will bring amacimbi, which is my number one favorite relish, umfushwa, and other foods from home, and people descend on the food like they haven't eaten all their lives. They tear off the sthwala with their bare hands, hastily roll and dip it in relish and pause briefly to look at one another before shoving it in their mouths. Then they carefully chew, tilting their heads to the side as if the food speaks and they are listening to the taste, and then their faces light up. When they cook home food, even Aunt Fostalina will forget she is on a fruit diet.

After the food comes the music. They play Majaivana, play Solomon Skuza, play Ndux Malax, Miriam Makeba, Lucky Dube, Brenda Fassie, Paul Matavire, Hugh Masekela, Thomas Mapfumo, Oliver Mtukudzi – old songs I remember from when I was little, from Mother and Father and the adults singing them. Some of the songs I don't know because Uncle Charley says I wasn't even born then. When they dance, I always stand by the door and watch because it is something to see.

They dance strange. Limbs jerk and bodies contort. They lean forward like they are planting grain, sink to the floor, rise as whips and lash the air. They huddle like cattle in a kraal, then scatter like broken bones. They gather themselves, look up, and shield their faces from the sun and beckon the rain with their hands. When it doesn't come they shake their heads in disappointment and then get down, sinking-sinking-sinking like ships drowning. Then they get up, clutch their stomachs and hearts like women in pain, raise their arms in prayer, crouch low as if they are burying themselves. They rise again, abruptly, stand on their toes and stretch their hands like planes headed for faraway lands.

CHAPTER 12

WEDDING

Things begin to go wrong when we miss our turn and get lost on the way to Dumi's wedding in South Bend, Indiana. But it's not like we know we're lost; Aunt Fostalina is taking a nap in the front seat because she worked overnight, and TK, sitting beside me, is busy as usual, iPod on his lap, loud headphones in his ears. I am behind Uncle Kojo, who's driving, nodding to that weird Ghanaian music that sometimes makes him forget himself, like maybe there's something inside his head that's calling him away to somewhere far.

We've long left the houses and stores behind, now we're just driving between stretches and stretches of maize fields, which make me keep expecting to see hoers bent double, tilling; boys walking in front of ox-drawn plows, leading the oxen, the sounds of their whistles and cracking whips in the air, hoes hitting the earth, voices of women urging one another with song. There are always moments like this, where it almost looks like the familiar things from back home will just come out of nowhere, like ghosts.

No matter how green the maize looks in America, it is not real. They call it corn here, and it comes out all wrong, like small, sweet, too soft. I don't even bother with it anymore because eating it is really a disappointing thing, it feels like I'm just insulting my teeth. I watch the fields stretch endlessly and it starts to make me nervous because I can't imagine what could be coming next. Maybe thick forests with lions and tigers and monkeys swinging from branches and stuff because you just never know.

Uhmmn, maybe we need to use the navigator, Uncle Kojo, I say, leaning forward and speaking into his ear. I know he doesn't like being told what to do, but still. I am not surprised when he just keeps nodding to his music like I haven't spoken. A long while ago, after we got off the highway, Uncle Kojo started cussing the navigator in his language because it kept saying, Recalculating, turn right, turn right, recalculating, even though we were on a long stretch and there was no way to turn right. In the end Uncle Kojo just yanked the navigator off its thing, handed it to me over his shoulder, raised the volume on the radio, and started listening to his music.

When I get tired of looking at the endless fields and the back of Uncle Kojo's head I fish my Hello Kitty case from my purse and take out my mirror and lip gloss. I kind of like my face today, even though it looks strange, because Aunt Fostalina did it with makeup for the wedding since she says

I'm now a teen. If I were standing outside of myself and saw this face I would maybe say, Who is that? because I wouldn't recognize it at first, but at the same time it also looks interesting and I'm happy with it. My only regret is that it's summer and schools are closed so I really can't show it off, but I've decided that come fall, this is the face I'm taking to Washington Academy.

When I first arrived at Washington I just wanted to die. The other kids teased me about my name, my accent, my hair, the way I talked or said things, the way I dressed, the way I laughed. When you are being teased about something, at first you try to fix it so the teasing can stop but then those crazy kids teased me about everything, even the things I couldn't change, and it kept going and going so that in the end I just felt wrong in my skin, in my body, in my clothes, in my language, in my head, everything. When I talked to Aunt Fostalina about it she told me how when she was going to boarding school at home, the bullies would eat the other students' food and generally made them maids – had them washing their clothes and cleaning after them and stuff. She has this weird thing of constantly referring to back home when she doesn't want to deal with anything – When I was growing up back home we only got new clothes on Christmas and we turned out just fine; back home you wouldn't ever dream of talking to your elders in that tone; back home this, back home that.

The teasing stopped only when Tom joined our class; I don't know where he came from but he came with these crooked teeth and long, greasy hair and these large glasses and this sad stutter. Somehow he made them forget about me and I almost felt like thanking him for it. I remember they teased him harder, maybe because he was a boy. I remember they always wanted him to fight and called him freak, which I had to Google since I had never heard the word before; there were a lot of American words and things I was still learning.

I remember it was the way they said *freak* that made me want to look it up; said it like they wanted to puncture their bottom lips with their teeth when they said the *f* part and then making the rest of the word explode from their mouths. I remember I waited until I was alone in my room to Google it. I searched for the word, then hit Images, and when all these crazy pics popped up I just stared at the screen and wondered how it felt for Tom, but I knew, we all knew just a week later, when they found him hanging near the lockers at school, the word *freak!* scrawled in a red marker on a locker behind him.

You need to watch out for the hall, it must actually be here somewhere, Uncle Kojo says.

Here? In the fields? I say, and I'm immediately sorry because it comes out like Uncle Kojo just said something lame and I cannot believe my ears.

He doesn't respond, so I finish putting on my lip gloss, smack my lips together like I've seen Aunt Fostalina do. I put the lip gloss and mirror away, push my purse under Uncle Kojo's seat, next to the navigator. My shoes are starting to pinch my feet so I kick them off.

You see, at your age, the best thing to do is forget makeup and actually think about school. What you want to be when you grow up, that kind of thing, Uncle Kojo says. When he turns down the volume I roll my eyes because I know what's coming.

You know how many young women actually want to come into this country to study? How many of them are just – just dying to be where you are?

Uncle Kojo sounds all upset now, and this annoys me very much because it's not like I've done anything wrong. And besides, I've been getting all As in everything, even maths and science, the subjects I hate, because school is so easy in America even a donkey would pass, so I don't know what Uncle Kojo wants, what else I'm supposed to do. He looks at me from the rearview mirror and his eyes have this disappointment in them that I know I don't deserve, so I borrow TK's word and say inside my head, *Leave me alone, motherfucker.*

I think it's at that moment when Uncle Kojo is giving me the look that the deer runs in front of the car. Next thing I know there's the sound of smashing and the car lurches to the side and we're being jolted all over. There's a blaring horn from a second car coming straight at us, and Uncle Kojo is shouting in his language and Aunt Fostalina has woken up and is shouting in our language and TK is saying, What the fuck? and I'm screaming. By the time Uncle Kojo gets the car back on our lane and slams the brakes, the deer is already limp-hopping away into the bushes, a large blood-stain on its side. I'm worried about the deer but I'm also thankful because now Uncle Kojo has finally left me alone.

What in the world are you doing, Jameson, you want to kill us? Aunt Fostalina says. Her voice is sleep and shock and panic. Uncle Kojo ignores her and gets out of the car, muttering. For a while he just stands there shaking his head, hands in his pockets. Then he bends down to take a closer look at the right side.

Jesus, it's 3:35, we're missing the wedding! How did this happen? Aunt Fostalina says, a new panic in her voice, like this is more serious than the accident that almost happened.

Where are we? she asks, turning back to TK and myself, and we answer her with silence.

We were supposed to be at the wedding an hour and a half ago, an hour and a half! Where is my navigator? What did he do with it? she says, and I quickly retrieve the navigator from under Uncle Kojo's seat and hand it over. Aunt Fostalina snatches it; she is all mad now, making phone calls and asking for directions. Uncle Kojo gets back into the car and says, That deer actually broke my light. Now I have to replace it. I just fixed the exhaust only last week!

After Uncle Kojo has turned the car around and we're on the way back toward 94, TK says, Oh shit, the police are right behind us, maybe somebody saw.

The police? Is it actually the police? Uncle Kojo says, his voice so high and panicky you wouldn't think it was Uncle Kojo speaking but a terrified young boy. The way he says the word *police*, as if they were witches, monsters.

Just don't turn around, you know how they don't really like that, TK says. The car starts to slow down toward the right, getting off the road and preparing to stop. Uncle Kojo is muttering; it sounds like prayer. I look over my shoulder, and when I don't see any police I put a fist in my mouth and giggle. Beside me, TK is busy dying. When Uncle Kojo hears us he looks over his shoulder and screams at TK in his language, his voice now loud and angry and sounding like his again. He doesn't think it's funny.

By the time we finally get to the wedding, we figure the most important parts must be over, which doesn't bother me a bit because I don't really know Dumi, the guy who's getting married. But Aunt Fostalina does, and I know she is mad because for the past few weeks she's been talking

171

about the wedding like it was her own. She gets out of the car, slams the door, and storms off like she doesn't even know us.

About three weeks ago, I went with Aunt Fostalina to JCPenney to buy her dress for the wedding. We spent hours and hours trying this and that dress, until finally, when I wanted to just run out of JCPenney, she found the one she really wanted, a long, strapless cream dress that clung to her body. The zipper wouldn't close, but she bought it all the same, which meant she would have to lose some pounds for it. This morning, when she came to my room and asked me to zip the dress up for her, it zipped without a problem, like she had poured herself inside.

You look good, Aunt Fostalina, I said, because she really looked beautiful, and also because she likes hearing that.

Really, you think so? she said, turning around, and finally standing still in front of the mirror. Her face appeared a little tired in the reflection.

Don't tell anyone: me and the groom used to date, but that was way back at home when we were in college. It ended when he moved to the States a while ago, but it's all in the past now. I'm just going to see who he's marrying, that's all, Aunt Fostalina said with a mischievous grin I had never seen before, and I didn't even know if she was speaking to me or herself or her reflection.

The first thing I notice when we get inside the hall are the white people. I know that of all the Americans, it's really the white people who love Africans the most, but still, looking at how many of them are at the wedding, I can't help but think, *This can't be just love*. It's only when I see the bride that I understand why there's this many white people: she is white. Besides that, she is just rolls and rolls of flesh; I cannot help staring, cannot help thinking, *But this is not just fatness.*

In America, the fatness is not the fatness I was used to at home. Over there, the fatness was of bigness, just ordinary fatness you could understand because it meant the person ate well, fatness you could even envy. It was fatness that did not interfere with the body; a neck was still a neck, a stomach a stomach, an arm an arm, a buttock a buttock. But this American fatness takes it to a whole 'nother level: the body is turned into something else – the neck becomes a thigh, the stomach becomes an anthill, an arm a thing, a buttock a I don't even know what.

The tall husband, Dumi, is sitting there beside the bride in his white suit. He has this smile that never goes away; his tinted dreadlocks reach his shoulders, and his body looks like a stick in comparison to his wife's. I look at his carved smile and ask myself what he's smiling for because I don't see why anyone would be smiling with a bride like that because it's not like you're saying, Look at my beautiful wife; it's not like other women are busy envying her and wanting to kill her for her beauty or hating her for it. I look at

Aunt Fostalina and she is all smiles looking at the couple, and I know the reason she is so happy is that Dumi's bride is fat and ugly.

We sit through the reading of messages from home. The MC explains that Dumi's parents and family couldn't make it to the wedding because they couldn't get visas so they wrote down their messages, which were later sent by e-mail. Dumi's friend, who introduces himself as Mtha, reads the messages, and another, Siza, translates for the white people.

The first message is from Dumi's grandmother, who starts by addressing Dumi with his totems, the way old people like to do. They sound like a tumbling poem, the totems, and it's just beautiful to hear them read in our language. The grandmother congratulates her first grandson, and she says she hopes he has chosen a healthy, pretty, respectful, and grounded wife who will bear strong sons and teach them our beautiful culture and come home and revive the ancestral homestead as expected of the first daughter-in-law. A wife who knows her place and who will listen to and obey her husband and make him a man among men. A wife who is quick on her feet and talented with her hands and hardworking and pure and faithful.

The bride keeps nodding and smiling like she can understand the language, but now I know that smiling at nothing is really a white-people thing so I'm not surprised. I notice, though, that when the translator translates, he leaves out things like reviving the ancestral home and teaching the grandsons our beautiful culture and being quick on her feet and hardworking and obeying the husband. When the messages start to go on and on like Bible verses, I get up to find the restroom.

I am in the middle of peeing when I hear two voices talking in our language. They talk in tones that are lowered and guarded, just like you are supposed to do when you gossip, but I can still hear. I hold my pee and listen.

The nerve! I think she's the sister. Talking about African men and their love for big women! I seriously wanted to laugh.

Well, that's you, 'coz I so wanted to slap that dumb whore. Like, bitch, what the fuck do you know about Africa? And since when did big become fat?

Girl, that's not even fat.

Damn right. *Obese* is the word. Like, she is a freaking mountain!

Here, the voices explode in laughter. I giggle inside until two drops of pee come out, so I stop giggling and concentrate so I can hold the rest.

All I'll say is that he is a brave man. I mean, if it's not bravery, then I don't know what it is. Stupidity?

Ah, what a waste, and such a fine-ass brother too.

But the things people will do for these *papers*, my sister, I tell you.

I am surprised by the sudden change in the

second voice now, by the pity, and I can almost picture the speaker: not a girl, like the voice suggests, but an old, old woman with a kind face, maybe shaking her white head in sorrow. Water rushes from a tap and stops. There's the sound of heels, then I hear, Okay, you. Stop, somebody's coming.

Yeah, we better get back, I'm starving like a fucking fat bride.

There's more sounds of heels, probably the gossipers walking away, and I hear a Hi, and then the first voice saying, in English now, in a cheerful tone that does not mean what it says, That's such a gorgeous dress you have on! I pee, wipe, and the toilet flushes itself.

I am washing my hands and admiring my interesting face when a voice says: Are you from Africa too?

I look in the mirror, and this woman in a blue dress is standing there smiling at me. I notice the smell of her sweet perfume is all over, like a living thing. I smile back. It's not exactly a smile-smile, just the brief baring of teeth. That's what you do in America: you smile at people you don't know and you smile at people you don't even like and you smile for no reason. I nod, turn around, and start drying my hands under the noisy dryer. When I turn back, the woman is waiting for me like we're maybe on Main Street at home and she's selling me some cheap eggs.

Can you just say something in your language?

she says. I laugh a small laugh, because what do you say to that? But the woman is fixing me with this expectant stare, which means she is not playing, so I say:

I don't know, what do you want me to say?

Well, anything, really.

I let out an inward sigh because this is so stupid, but I remember to keep my face smiling. I say one word, *sa-li-bo-na-ni*, and I say it slowly so she doesn't ask me to repeat it. She doesn't.

Isn't that beautiful? she says. Now she's looking at me like I'm a wonder, like I just made magic happen.

What language is that? she says. I tell her, and she tells me it's beautiful, again, and I tell her thank you. Then she asks me what country I'm from and I tell her.

It's beautiful over there, isn't it? she says. I nod even though I don't know why I'm nodding. I just do. To this lady, maybe everything is beautiful.

Africa is beautiful, she says, going on with her favorite word. But isn't it terrible what's happening in the Congo? Just awful.

Now she is looking at me with this wounded face. I don't know what to do or say, so I fake a long cough just to fill the silence. My brain is scattering and jumping fences now, trying to remember what exactly is happening in the Congo because I think I am confusing it with another place, but what I can see in the woman's eyes is that it's serious and important and I'm supposed

177

to know it, so in the end I say, Yes, it is terrible, what is happening in the Congo.

I squeeze hand soap into my palm and start washing my hands all over again, my back to the woman. But she is not trying to leave me alone. She has pulled up the chair that was by the door and is sitting now; I don't even know why they have chairs in the bathroom.

Tell me about it. Jesus, the rapes, and all those killings! How can such things even be happening? she says. I can't tell if it's really a question-question or if it's a question I don't need to answer, but in the end I hear myself saying, Yes, I also really don't know. Then I begin drying my hands.

I mean, I can't even – I can't even process it. And all those poor women and children. I was watching CNN last night and there was this little girl who was just – just too cute, she says. Her eyes start to mist and she looks down. I glance at the box of Kleenex at the edge of the counter and wonder if I should pick it up and hold it out to her.

It just broke my heart, you know, the woman says, her voice choking. Then she lifts her head like she has remembered something important.

Now, Lisa, up there, my niece, one of the brides-maids, the tall one, real skinny redhead – she's going to Rwanda to help. She's in the Peace Corps, you know, they are doing great things for Africa, just great, she says. I nod, even though I don't really know what the woman is talking about. But

178

her face is looking much, much better, like the pain from earlier is going away.

And last summer, she went to Khayelitsha in South Africa to teach at an orphanage, and let me tell you, we all donated – clothes and pens and medicines and crayons and candy for those poor African children. Then she puts her hand over her heart and closes her eyes briefly, like maybe she's listening to the throb of her kindness. I'm surprised by the way she says *Khayelitsha*, says it so well, like maybe it's her language even.

And, oh, she took such awesome pictures. You should have seen those faces! she says, and I look at her smiling face tilted upward now, catching the brilliant light, and I can see from it how the children's faces must have looked. They were smiling like she is smiling now. Then I'm seeing myself in this woman's face, back there when we were in Paradise when the NGO people were taking our pictures.

Just lovely, you know, she says. Now we are looking at each other and smiling even wider, like we've become friends for real, here in this restroom with the cream tiles and bright-bright lights and orange chair.

Oh, and listen to this, while she was there she also went and took pictures of Table Mountain and Robben Island. Oh. My. God. Table Mountain is sooooo amazing. Just beautiful. I'm telling you, I saw those pictures and told myself I simply have to visit. I have never seen anything like it. Maybe next year, Christopher and I will go on our wedding anniversary. Oops, speaking of which, I better get my butt up there, she says, and she gets up and starts toward the door, opens it, and disappears like she was never there.

When I get back upstairs people are standing in a circle, listening to Tshaka Zulu sing a traditional song. Even though his body is all wrinkled with age, he looks beautiful and fierce in a knee-length skirt made of colorful animal skins. Around his neck is a necklace of sharpened bones, and hoop earrings dangle from his ears. On his head is a hat made of animal fur. He wears matching armbands around his thin arms. In one hand is a long white shield scattered with little black spots.

I stand next to TK, who is filming the performance with his BlackBerry, maybe so he can share it on Facebook. Around us, other people are doing the same, it's all phones and cameras. Tshaka Zulu has the large booming voice that reminds me of Prophet Revelations Bitchington Mborro, it's like he is singing to someone lost on the highway when the bride is just seated right before him, smiling like this is the best song ever. When the song finishes everybody applauds, and Tshaka Zulu beams with pride. It is his thing to perform at weddings and wherever people from our country are holding events, and looking at him at it you would never think there was something wrong with him, that he was really a patient at Shadybrook.

★　★　★

I am hungry but I don't eat that much food when it's eating time because even after so much practice I still haven't properly learned how to eat with a fork and knife. I always spill my food all over the place, and the meat slips around when I cut it, and I feel like people are watching me, laughing secretly. This is why I get so self-conscious when I eat in public; most times, like now, I'll just pretend I'm not hungry. I'm practicing, though; the only reason it's slow going is that in the house I just eat with my hands, like how you're supposed to eat.

Aunt Fostalina is beside me, eating a salad, and Uncle Kojo and TK have their plates piled high like they've been starving all their lives. Uncle Kojo has moved over to the next table to sit with this other man from his country. Uncle Kojo and the man are not exactly matching but their flowing, colorful, embroidered outfits are almost similar and it makes them look interesting, sitting together like that. Earlier, this other guy stopped by their table and asked to take a picture. I keep watching Uncle Kojo; whenever he is with someone from his country, everything about him is different – his laugh, his talk, his eating – it's like something cuts him open to reveal this other person I don't even know.

Later, Dumi comes over to our table; he is holding in his arms a pretty little boy with flowing hair. I smile a real smile at the boy but he just stares back. He clutches a white ball with spiky rubber thingies. Dumi is tall and looks like he goes to the gym; he is not very handsome, but he is better-looking than Uncle Kojo. I wish he didn't have his dreadlocks, though, they don't suit him.

I'm remembering what Aunt Fostalina said about them dating, so I'm watching to see if there's anything interesting in the way they interact. I listen to them talk about the regular things – When was the last time you saw so-and-so? What kind of work are you doing now? – and about how things are back home, our old president who doesn't want to die so we can get a new leader at last. Dumi's deep voice is a little rugged, like it walked all the way to America and is now worn out from the effort.

He doesn't tell Aunt Fostalina she looks good, like I've heard other people do; he tells her she looks like sunrise. You look like sunrise, Fee, that's what Dumi says, in our language. I have never heard anyone call Aunt Fostalina Fee before. She smiles, and I stare at her because of the way she smiles. Like she is hearing music and she is dancing to it on the inside.

They stay silent for a while, as if they have no more words, as if both our language and English are not enough for them. The silence starts to make me feel awkward so in the end, not knowing what to do, I pick up a fork with my right hand, knife with my left, and brave my plate. I cut a piece of meat. It doesn't dance around, which gives me courage, so I cut another, and another, hoping to kill time. The silence doesn't go away; it's like they are using it to talk. At the other end of the hall, the bride hasn't moved; she is talking to a bridesmaid and a tall man in a yellow shirt.

Uncle Kojo looks over at our table. He has a drumstick in his hand, and when he sees the bridegroom, he nods, raises the drumstick the way you raise a glass to say cheers. Dumi nods back. The boy starts chewing the spike things on the ball.

Hi, cutie, what's your name? Aunt Fostalina says to the little boy, breaking the long silence. The boy giggles, covers his eyes with one hand.

He is shy. His name is Mandla, Dumi says. I am wondering how come an American boy has a name like Mandla, but it's not my conversation and nobody has spoken to me so I stay out of it. I concentrate on my meat; it tastes good, so I eat piece after piece.

Ah, I see, Aunt Fostalina says. It's a nice name.

He is Stephanie's son, Dumi says, like he hears my thoughts. He looks in the direction of the wedding table, at his wife. But I passed along my father's name, Dumi says; he kisses Mandla on the nose, ruffles his hair. I wonder how a white person's hair feels to the touch; I've never touched any before, since up to now I still haven't made any white friends like that. It probably feels silky, like the beard of a maize cob.

But Mandla doesn't like his hair played with because he shakes his head and says, in a high

183

voice, Don't! I am surprised he can talk because he's been quiet all this time. He squirms like a wet fish in Dumi's arms, wanting to be let down. Once on his feet, he throws his ball at Aunt Fostalina's plate and laughs. I pause, my knife in midair. Aunt Fostalina doesn't say anything, but I know she is not pleased.

No, Mandla, stop, don't do that, Dumi says. He apologizes to Aunt Fostalina, leans forward to fish for the ball, dreadlocks falling over his face. Mandla is watching him, eating his hands now. When Dumi finishes wiping the ball with a paper towel, Mandla holds his tiny hands out.

Not now, sonny, I told you you can't throw the ball. We'll play later, at home, okay? At home, Dumi says, looking at Mandla with a serious parent face, but you can just see that Mandla is used to getting what he wants.

Give me my ball, he says, with this strange strength in his voice. When he scrunches his face up and starts to cry, Dumi looks at Aunt Fostalina, frustrated-like. She shrugs.

Okay, but no throwing, okay? There's people, Dumi says.

When Mandla gets the ball, he throws it and it hits an old lady in a pink dress on the breast. I stop breathing, but the old lady just smiles like nothing's happened, picks up the ball from her lap, and holds it out to Mandla.

Isn't he a sweetheart? she says to Dumi with an old lady's pointless smile, and Dumi smiles back.

Mandla snatches the ball, walks back to our table. He is obviously enjoying himself. When he looks at me I give him a serious eye that says, You are just too much and you need to stop that nonsense before something happens. But I know, from Mandla's grin, that he doesn't even get it, that they have not taught him anything about reading eyes.

Here, now you can give me the ball, Dumi says. He is bending down to be level with Mandla, his hands cupped. Mandla takes a few steps back, shakes his head.

Do you want Dad to pick you up? Dumi says.

No! You're not my daddy! Mandla screams, his voice shrill now. I wipe my mouth with a paper towel. A few people turn their heads to look, but then they go on with their talk and eating. Mandla stands there looking at Dumi, as if daring him to do something. Dumi only shakes his head; I can tell from his face that he is embarrassed and doesn't really know what to do anymore.

He had too much candy earlier, he says, his voice explaining-like, and I want to laugh because what has candy really got to do with a spoiled kid?

That's when Mandla throws the ball at me, and by the time I see it, it has already hit my right eye, one of the spike thingies jabbing the inside. The pain is something else. Before I know it, I have forgotten that I'm at a wedding, in a hall full of people, forgotten that I'm in America. Just before Aunt Fostalina sharply tells me to sit down,

185

I grab the little brat, go *pha-pha-pha* with three quick slaps, and rap his head with my knuckles, twice.

It's only when I sit back down and look around that I realize what I have done. The white people have already gasped, and a shocked voice has already said, Oh my God. Heads have been shaken and eyes have widened in disbelief. A few hands have already flown over mouths, and the silence has already descended. It stays in the air like a stain, until this booming voice, which I quickly recognize as Tshaka Zulu's, shouts from near the door, where he is seated:

Do not to fear. This is just how we handle unruly children in our culture, it's nothing, you must relax, please, he says with a laugh. Nobody laughs with him; there is this hot fire of silence. If looks could burn, I would be on the floor lying in a pile of ashes. I can just tell that I have done something that is not done, something taboo. I know that I will never forget those faces, and I know, looking at them, that I will never hit a kid again, no matter how bad he is.

Dumi is carrying Mandla off, and now that he knows he is the center of attention, he is screaming like he will get paid for it. The mother is looking from the wedding table, wiggling her mountain and craning her neck to see what is wrong with her son. I'm grateful to her fatness because I'm thinking if it wasn't for that, she would have maybe gotten up and rushed over. I pick up the knife and make like I'm just focusing on my plate.

Is he going to be okay? a boy's voice yells after Dumi, and I want to give him a look but I dare not turn around. I am relieved when Dumi carries Mandla out through the door that leads to the restrooms. When his screams eventually die down people go back to their eating, but I can tell they are still disturbed. To my left, an old man keeps giving me this severe stare like I've eaten his cake. The children who had been running around now sit by their mothers like they have seen a terrorist.

Don't do it again, I always tell you, you are in America now, Aunt Fostalina says, without a sign of irritation in her voice, and I am relieved. If the bride had been beautiful, then Aunt Fostalina would have been in one of her moods; if she were in one of her moods, then I would be worse off than Mandla, worse off than an injured deer. I nod, put the knife back on my plate, and reach for a glass of Coke, which doesn't even taste real.

CHAPTER 13

ANGEL

So I tell Aunt Fostalina that I want to go home and visit just for a little while, to see how my friends and Mother and Mother of Bones and people and things are. At first there is silence, like Aunt Fostalina didn't even hear me speak. We're sitting in the living room and I'm drinking a Capri Sun from a straw. Aunt Fostalina is on the couch, looking at pictures of women wearing nice Victoria's Secret underwear. Surrounding her are stacks of magazines, and there are stacks on the glass coffee table in front of her, more stacks by her feet.

I finish my Capri Sun, reach onto the shelf behind me, and get a guava. I look at it like I've never seen a guava before, then hold it under my nose. The smell hits me where it matters, and I feel like my heart and insides are being gently pried open. I shake my head, rub the guava in both hands, take a bite, and laugh.

We'll see if you'll still be laughing when you get constipated, Aunt Fostalina says, turning a page. I just keep chewing; how can she understand that each time I take a bite, I leave the house,

188

Kalamazoo, and Michigan, leave the country altogether and find myself back in my Paradise, in Budapest?

Last week, Messenger came to America seeking asylum and brought me a surprise package. Because I got it just a few days before my birthday, I held off opening it. It was wrapped in kaka wrapping, and I giggled when I finally cut the black string with a scissors, peeled off the clear plastic and then the layers and layers of a Chinese magazine. Bringing fresh foods and stuff from home is not allowed; if the border people find them, they throw them away, so I was just glad my guavas survived. Even before I finished unwrapping, the smell of guava was all over, delicious and dizzying. I closed my eyes and inhaled like I hadn't breathed in ages.

I had lost contact with Bastard, Stina, Godknows, Chipo, and Sbho for a long while, even though when I left I'd promised to always stay in touch.

I'll write, there's plenty of paper and pens there so I'll be writing every time, I remember saying, just before Aunt Fostalina and I got on that car on Mzilikazi.

Promise? Chipo said.

Yes, I promise, I said.

Cross your heart, Sbho said.

Cross my heart and hope to die, I said.

What if you don't write? Godknows said.

Why wouldn't I write? I said.

Because you'll have found some pretty white friends and forgotten us, he said.

189

I'll have some pretty white friends but that doesn't mean I'll forget you, I said.

Out of sight out of mind, Stina said.

That's kaka, you know I'll never forget you, I said.

We'll see, Bastard said, with this look like he knew something I didn't. When I was in the car and pulling off I kissed my hand and waved like I'd seen an NGO lady do one time and shouted, I'll write, always, always, always!

In the beginning, during the first few of months of my arrival, I did write. In those letters I told them about America, the kinds of things I was eating, the clothes I wore, the music I was listening to, the celebrities and stuff. But I was careful to leave out some things as well, like how the weather was the worst because there was almost always something wrong with it, either too hot or too cold, the hurricanes and stuff. That the house we lived in wasn't even like the ones we'd seen on TV when we were little, how it wasn't made of bricks but planks, a house made of planks in America, and how when it rained those planks got mold and smelled.

I didn't tell them how in the summer nights there sometimes was the bang-bang-bang of gunshots in the neighborhood and I had to stay indoors, afraid to go out, and how one time a woman a few houses from ours drowned her children in a bathtub, all four of them, how there were poor people who lived on the streets, holding up signs to beg for money. I left out these things, and a lot more, because they embarrassed me, because they made America not feel like My America, the one I had always dreamed of back in Paradise.

With time I stopped writing altogether. I just started putting it off, telling myself I'd write tomorrow, next week, in a couple of weeks, I'd write in a month, I'd write soon, and that was it, before I knew it I'd lost touch. But it didn't mean I'd forgotten about them; I missed them, missed them very much, and there were these times when I'd be doing something and get this terrible feeling of guilt for not keeping in touch. I also missed Budapest, missed Fambeki, missed Paradise, missed Mother and Mother of Bones and MotherLove, all those people, even Prophet Revelations Bitchington Mborro, with his craziness, I missed them all. And when I got the guavas the gang sent with Messenger, these years later, it felt good knowing they remembered me as well.

Aunt Fostalina, I say, trying to get her attention, but her head stays glued to the magazine. These days the magazines have replaced working out because Aunt Fostalina doesn't have the energy since she is so busy with her two jobs, one at the hospital and one at the nursing home. The reason she is working hard like this is so she can finish paying for the house she just bought for Mother and Mother of Bones in Budapest. I've seen the pictures; it's a nice big house with a pool, just like the other houses we used to hit for guavas.

The house is even nicer than this one we live in here in America, which I find strange because when I was at home I heard that everything in America was better.

Every once in a while Aunt Fostalina glances up from her magazine at the TV, at that woman whose pretty face looks like something is wrong with it, talking about how to lose ten pounds in ten days and telling people to call now and change their lives.

I'll just go maybe for two weeks and then I'll come back, I say, even though Aunt Fostalina is still ignoring me.

Darling, it's not time yet. When that time comes, you'll go, she finally says, and flips another page.

But you said once that when I turned fourtee—

Child, it's not like your father is Obama and he has the Air Force One; home costs money. Besides, you came on a visitor's visa, and that's expired; you get out, you kiss this America bye-bye, Aunt Fostalina says.

But why can't I come back? I can just renew my visa, I say.

Darling, leave me alone, do I look like the Immigration to you? she says. She is speaking in our language now, which means the conversation is over. When Aunt Fostalina switches languages like that, you know whatever was being talked about is finished.

Now the TV screen has split into two, and there's two pictures of the woman, a before one, when she was bigger and looked like a real person, and

192

an after one, where she is thin and looks like a beautiful thing.

Give me that phone, then go to my room and bring me my blue purse; I need to order this push-up, Aunt Fostalina says.

Upstairs, I look out the window of Aunt Fostalina's bedroom at the cemetery across the road. The first thing you notice is all those decorations, like they are maybe trying to tell you that death is beautiful. At the entrance is a large concrete thingy with letters in a language I don't know, on top of which lies a big sculpture of a reclining woman, her head resting to the side. She is covering her face with one hand as if to say there's too much sun in life, as if to say she doesn't want to be disturbed.

All over the cemetery are beautiful sculptures of angels: an angel looking at the sky, an angel asleep on a stone slab, an angel carrying a dove, an angel with a hand on the heart, an angel kneeling in front of a fountain. Looking at them like that, you would think that angels are common things that run around the place in real life, like cats and dogs and cockroaches and cars. The graveyard itself is covered in green grass, and all over are trees that cast long shadows in the day. And then there are the tombstones; some look like little houses, some look like castles, some just look strange, but they are all interesting.

Whenever I look at the cemetery I always think of Father lying at Heavenway, where they buried

193

him, his grave nothing but a mound of red earth, and I almost wish that he too were buried somewhere beautiful, where you can see why it is that when they bury the dead they say, Rest in peace. When we moved here from Detroit and I first saw the cemetery, I didn't even know it was a place of the dead; I thought it was just a museum of something, another interesting place where interesting things happened. The road that divides our house from the cemetery is a smooth belt, and I always wonder where exactly it would end if I followed it. In America, roads are like the devil's hands, like God's love, reaching all over, just the sad thing is, they won't really take me home.

There are two homes inside my head: home before Paradise, and home in Paradise; home one and home two. Home one was best. A real house. Father and Mother having good jobs. Plenty of food to eat. Clothes to wear. Radios blaring every Saturday and everybody dancing because there was nothing to do but party and be happy. And then home two – Paradise, with its tin tin tin.

There are three homes inside Mother's and Aunt Fostalina's heads: home before independence, before I was born, when black people and white people were fighting over the country. Home after independence, when black people won the country. And then the home of things falling apart, which made Aunt Fostalina leave and come here. Home one, home two, and home three. There are four homes inside Mother of Bones's head: home before the white people came to steal the country, and a king ruled; home when the white people came to steal the country and then there was war; home when black people got our stolen country back after independence; and then the home of now. Home one, home two, home three, home four. When somebody talks about home, you have to listen carefully so you know exactly which one the person is referring to.

Two days ago, the president of our country came on TV during the BBC news. He was raising his fists and speaking, saying how our country is a black man's home and would never be a colony again and what-what. Aunt Fostalina snatched the remote control from the coffee table, pointed it at the TV like it was a gun, and shot. We all turned to look at her, sitting there, shaking, her face suddenly ugly like she was chewing some thorns. TK, who is no longer a fat boy because he has started lifting weights and now looks like Will Smith in *Ali*, started to laugh but then he stopped himself, maybe because of the look on Aunt Fostalina's face.

Uncle Kojo grabbed the remote and changed the channel back. Aunt Fostalina glared at him for a while, then got up and left the room without saying anything. On TV, the president said, just after Aunt Fostalina left, as if he were telling a secret and he had been waiting for Aunt Fostalina to leave before he could say it: We don't mind sanctions banning us from Europe; we are not

Europeans, and Uncle Kojo threw his fists in the air and pumped them real hard. Then he saluted the TV and shouted, Tell them, Mr President, tell these bloody colonists. Then he was grinning, looking first at TK, and then at me.

That there, boys, is the only motherfucker with balls on our continent. Africa's leading statesman! he said. Me and TK looked at each other, puzzled, and then we smiled, and then we exploded in laughter because it was the first time we heard Uncle Kojo using that word, *motherfucker*, and so it sounded interesting and beautiful. TK was still laughing when he left the living room and went up the stairs. Later, when I got onto Facebook, he had told the story there and there were so many likes and LOLs on his wall.

I'm on my third Capri Sun now, and my stomach is so full of guava and liquid it could burst. I just ate the last of the guavas and already I have this sadness thinking about the length of time, maybe years, before I will taste guava again. Aunt Fostalina is busy trying to order her push-up bra on the phone, and you can hear that she and whoever she is speaking to are having issues. The problem with English is this: You usually can't open your mouth and it comes out just like that – first you have to think what you want to say. Then you have to find the words. Then you have to carefully arrange those words in your head. Then you have to say the words quietly to yourself, to make sure you got them okay.

And finally, the last step, which is to say the words out loud and have them sound just right.

But then because you have to do all this, when you get to the final step, something strange has happened to you and you speak the way a drunk walks. And because you are speaking like falling, it's as if you are an idiot, when the truth is that it's the language and the whole process that's messed up. And then the problem with those who speak only English is this: they don't know how to listen; they are busy looking at your falling instead of paying attention to what you are saying.

I have decided the best way to deal with it all is to sound American, and the TV has taught me just how to do it. It's pretty easy; all you have to do is watch *Dora the Explorer, The Simpsons, SpongeBob, Scooby-Doo*, and then you move on to *That's So Raven, Glee, Friends, Golden Girls*, and so on, just listening and imitating the accents. If you do it well, then before you know it, nobody will ask you to repeat what you said. I also have my list of American words that I keep under the tongue like talismans, ready to use: *pretty good, pain in the ass, for real, awesome, totally, skinny, dude, freaking, bizarre, psyched, messed up, like, tripping, motherfucker, clearance, allowance, douche bag, you're welcome, acting up, yikes*. The TV has also taught me that if I'm talking to someone, I have to look him in the eye, even if it is an adult, even if it's rude.

I don't know why Aunt Fostalina doesn't think

to learn American speech like this, seeing how it would make her life easier so she wouldn't have to have a hard time like she is right now.

I said the Angel Collection, Aunt Fostalina is saying. She has muted the TV and raised the volume on the handset so I can hear the other person as well; she sounds like a bored young girl.

I'm sorry, what? I mean, I didn't quite hear that, maybe it's my line. I can picture her head cocked, the young girl, a frown of concentration on her face.

Angel, angel, angel, Aunt Fostalina says, raising her voice even louder.

There is silence, like maybe the girl is getting ready to pray.

Ah-ngeh-1, Aunt Fostalina adds helpfully, dragging out the word like she is raking gravel. I silently mouth – *enjel. Enjel.* I hear the girl make a small sigh.

I'm sorry, I don't know what you mean, ma'am, she says finally. You can tell from her voice that she is getting tired from trying to understand.

What do you mean, you don't know what I mean? You don't understand what I'm saying? Such a simple word! Aunt Fostalina says. She is speaking with her hands and head now, and I can tell from her knotted face that if the girl doesn't get it soon, it's not going to be good. I clear my throat to remind Aunt Fostalina that I'm in the room so maybe she will ask me to speak for her, but she doesn't. Now she has scribbled the word *angel* all over the magazine, and the naked woman

198

with the bra and underwear is all clothed in black ink, the letters like tiny angry insects.

Ma'am, I'm terribly sorry we're having these – difficulties. But we have a website that you can ord— the girl on the phone starts, her voice suddenly lifting. You can tell that she is pleased with the fact that she has thought of the website, that things are going to work out after all. I am relieved as well, and I start thinking maybe I should run upstairs and grab my MacBook for Aunt Fostalina to use. I get up from the couch.

No, I am not. Ordering. Online, Aunt Fostalina says firmly, separating her words now, which is never a good sign. I sit back down. She pokes the Victoria's Secret woman's face with a pen as she says each word.

I am not ordering online. I am speaking in English, so as far as I'm concer—

Maybe you can spell it? Now the girl sounds like she is getting annoyed, like maybe she is saying some serious insults inside her head that she can't say out loud.

Mnncccc, now you want me to spell it? Aunt Fostalina says. She looks at me like she can't believe what she is hearing, but I look away at the TV; the woman is gone, there's a new one sitting on an exercise ball. I'm waiting for Aunt Fostalina to tell the girl on the phone off because that's what she sounds like she's getting ready to do, but something changes her mind and she sits up and starts to spell.

It's *A*, Aunt Fostalina says. Her voice is a bit

calmer. She has written the letter on the magazine, as if to be sure.

Okay, *A* as in *apple*—

Not *apple*. *A* as in *annus*, it's a different sound. *N* as in *no*. *G* as in *God*. *E* as in *eat*. *L* as in *Libya*. There, you go, *angel. Angel. Angel*, Aunt Fostalina says.

There is a brief silence, like maybe the girl is considering what she has written, and then she says, Oh! You mean enjel!

Yes, angel, that's what I was trying to tell you all this time. I want a red one, Aunt Fostalina says, rolling her *r*, the sound of it like something is vibrating inside her mouth, and I promise myself I'll never ever sound like that.

When Aunt Fostalina gets off the phone with the Victoria's Secret lady, she dials a number that must be busy because she quickly hangs up. She immediately dials another, and she has to hold for a little while before I hear her leave a message, in our language, for the other person to call her back. I know the reason Aunt Fostalina is calling is that she needs to tell the Victoria's Secret story to someone in our language, because this is what you must do in America whenever something like this happens. You have to tell it to someone who knows what you mean, who will understand exactly what you say, and that it is not your fault but the other person's, someone who knows that English is like a huge iron door and you are always losing the keys.

After leaving her message, Aunt Fostalina just sits there as if something important is happening inside her and she is waiting for it to come out, kneel in front of her, and announce that it's finished and can it please go attend to other business. She also has this look – I have seen it many times before but I still don't know whether to call it pain or anger or sadness, or whether it has a name. I am careful not to meet her eyes as she puts her card back in her purse, and then gets up, walk downstairs to the basement, and slams the door shut behind her.

I know that she will turn on the lights as she descends the creaking stairway, that she will take small measured steps like there is something down there that she dreads, that when she gets to the bottom, she will stand in front of the mirror that covers one wall and look at her reflection. I know that she won't be looking at her thinness but at her mouth. I know that she will stand there and start the conversation all over and say out loud, in careful English, all the things that she meant to say, that she should have said to the girl on the phone but did not because she could not find the words at the time. I know that in front of that mirror, Aunt Fostalina will be articulate, that English will come alive on her tongue and she will spit it like it's burning her mouth, like it's poison, like it's the only language she has ever known.

CHAPTER 14

THIS FILM CONTAINS SOME DISTURBING IMAGES

Marina is from Nigeria and thinks she is the princess of Africa just because her grandfather was a chief or something over there and she wears all these colorful traditional outfits, never mind they are ugly and make her look like an old woman. Kristal thinks that since she taught us to wear makeup and has a weave, she is better than Marina and myself, but the truth is she can't even write a sentence correctly in English to show that she is indeed American. They are my friends mostly because we live on the same street, and we're all finishing eighth grade at Washington Academy. Right now the three of us are hanging out at the basement of my house.

These days, when we get off school we hurry home to watch flicks. We always do it at my house because there's nobody there in the afternoons since Aunt Fostalina and Uncle Kojo are always at work, and TK comes home only to sleep, like this is a hotel. When we come in from school we fling our book bags by the door and head straight to the downstairs computer. Before, we used to watch XTube, but now we have discovered RedTube, which is way classier and doesn't have many viruses.

We've been watching the flicks in alphabetic order so we're not all over the place. So far, we've seen amateur; we've seen anal, which was plain disgusting; we've seen Asian, which was respectful; we've seen big tits and blond and blow job; we've seen bondage, which was creepy; we've seen creampie and cumshot, which were both nasty; we've seen double penetration, which was scary; we've seen ebony, which made us embarrassed; we've seen facials, which was dirty; we've seen fetish, which was strange; we've seen gangbang, which was like a crime; we haven't seen gay, since we were afraid of it, so we skipped it; we've seen group, which was nasty; we've seen *hentai*, which was exciting; we've seen Japanese, which was quiet; and we've seen lesbian, which was interesting. Today we are watching MILF, and since it's Kristal's turn, she makes a pick and clicks on Play.

The flick begins with this dude in a ski mask breaking into a home, and immediately I start wondering if I locked the door upstairs, which is something Aunt Fostalina always insists I do when I get back from school. I can't remember if I did, but I don't want to go and check so I just tell myself that I locked it. The break-in guy in the flick is wasting time, just fooling around, peeking through a window and then taking a tool out of his pocket to pry the window open. After a while, he is hoisting himself up, taking his time still. When he has half his body in, Marina says, Fuck this, and reaches for the computer to fast-forward.

When Marina starts the film again, the man is already inside the woman, so she rewinds a little bit, stops it when the woman is getting up from her knees, licking her lips like she has just kissed some sugar. Now we can see that the man is really a young guy, but still, his thing is like a man's. The woman looks much older, like she could be his mother or something. We see her walk toward the railing that divides the large living room into two, her oiled skin glimmering in the light. She has a tattoo of a red and green flower growing all over her drooping left buttock and finally curling around her thigh.

The woman gets to the rails, hikes up her long leg on one of the metal thingies, and grips a pole with both hands for support, her nails looking bloody against the white metal. I'm looking at her purple high-heeled shoes and wondering how anyone can stand on those things. The boy comes up behind her, his thing like a snake in front of him. I reach forward and click on Mute because when the real action starts we always like to be the soundtrack of the flicks.

We have learned to do the noises, so when the boy starts working the woman we moan and we moan and we groan, our noise growing fiercer with each hard thrust like we have become the woman in the flick and are feeling the boy's thing inside us, tearing us up. We stop briefly when the woman takes her leg down from the railing and bends over, still grasping the pole. Now the boy is pumping grinding digging. We imagine he is fire and we scream as if we are burning in hell. Usually Kristal is the loudest because she has a high-pitched voice, but today Marina surpasses us all.

I'm finna play it again, Kristal says after we get to the end of the short clip and we're sitting there staring at the screen. Kristal's voice is low, like she is maybe dying of thirst. She is already leaning toward the computer.

What happens to the thing when men sit on the toilet to do a number two? Marina says.

It looks like it would dangle and dip into the water, I say.

Don't you think they would have to bring their legs together like this, Marina says, drawing her knees together like she's getting ready to sit a baby on her thighs. Then she cradles her hand on top of where the thighs meet, making like it's a man's thing.

There, like that, it makes more sense that way, she says.

Upstairs, the phone is screaming; I've been ignoring it ever since the flick started and I don't want to go and get it.

Answer the phone and git it over with, damn, Kristal says, and I want to tell her that she shouldn't forget whose house it is, but instead I say, Be right back, don't start without me.

When I see the 011–263 on the caller ID I know it's somebody from home and I start to get worried. These days, with all that's happening, whenever you see a number from home you start freaking out because the call could be about anything. Like last week, Aunt Fostalina's friend MaDumane called to say her husband, who works for the newspaper, had been taken by the police in the middle of the night for the things he had written. The police banged on the door, and the husband had gone to look and they seized him like that, wearing nothing but shorts. He has not been seen or heard from since.

And then, in another phone call, Aunt Fostalina's cousin NaSandi called to say her son, Tsepang, who was my age, had been eaten by a crocodile as he tried to cross the Limpopo River to South Africa. I still remember playing with Tsepang one Christmas when we were little. That was also the Christmas Father bought me a yellow BMX bike, and me and Tsepang took turns riding it around the neighborhood until he rode straight into a nest of thorns. He cried until no sound came out of his throat.

If people are not calling with stories like that, then they are calling to ask for U.S. dollars to buy food because things are now being paid for in U.S. dollars and South African rands. These are the phone calls Aunt Fostalina dreads the most, so much so that she almost doesn't even want to answer the phone anymore. The calls just keep

206

coming and coming like maybe they've heard Aunt Fostalina is married to the Bank of America.

Today, it's Mother on the phone. I am glad to hear her voice so I start smiling. I miss her so much sometimes it makes me dizzy but then there is nothing I can do about it. I can tell from how she sounds that everything is all right, so I relax.

How was it falling? Mother says.

Falling? I say, racking my brain to figure out what she means.

Falling from where? I say.

Falling from the sky because I apparently did not give birth to you. Maybe an angel did because otherwise you'd know you actually had a mother and you'd maybe call her every once in a while to see how she's doing, Mother says. I don't say anything because I'm not sure what's the right thing to say. The last time I spoke to her was maybe two, three weeks ago. Four weeks; I don't remember.

Darling, am I not talking to you?

I've been pretty busy, I say.

Yes, you've been busy because I hear now you have a job and a wife and children to take care of. And I see that America has taught you to speak English to your mother, and with that accent. He-he-he, so you are trying to sound white now! she says, then she is laughing hysterically and it's hard to tell if she is serious or not. I start to call her crazy but I hold it and tell myself that it is one of the American things I don't want to do, so I just roll my eyes instead. On TV, on the

Maury show and Jerry Springer and stuff, I've seen these kids calling their mothers crazy and bitches and whores. I've practiced the words, but I know I'll never say them aloud to my mother or any other adult.

Did you give Aunt Fostalina my message? she says.

Yes, I say. My heart skips a beat but I keep my voice level so she can't tell I'm lying. I chose not to tell Aunt Fostalina that Mother had said to see about sending money to buy a satellite dish from her neighbor's son who was importing the dishes from China.

I had meant to give Aunt Fostalina the message, but then when she came in from her second job later that night, her body looking like a sack, and threw herself on the La-Z-Boy and let out a tired sigh, I just didn't have the courage.

Well, make sure you tell her again. We need the dish, why do you want to enjoy the fine things all by yourselves in that America? Mother says. Anyway, your friends are here.

My friends? I say.

Yes, I saw them just wandering about and invited them in, who knows what they were up to. Stay right there.

Now I am aware of the chatter of familiar voices in the background. Godknows's and Sbho's voices stand out and I get goose bumps just from hearing them talk. There is a strange feeling coming over me and I feel this dizziness and I have to sit down.

Time dissolves like we are in a movie scene and I have maybe entered the telephone and traveled through the lines to go home. I've never left, and I'm ten again and we are playing country-game and Find bin Laden and Andy-over. We're teasing Godknows for his peeking buttocks, we're watching a fight, we're imitating the church people, we're watching somebody get buried. We're hungry but we're together and we're at home and everything is sweeter than dessert.

Are you there? I said, what are you doing? It's Sbho's voice.

Nothing, I say.

Nothing? You mean nothing-nothing?

Well—

How can she do nothing in America? That doesn't even make sense! I hear Godknows say in the background.

I'm coming from school, I say, trying not to be irritated.

You're coming from school? She says she is coming from school, and here it's early evening, ha-ha, Sbho says, half to me and half to the others. I hear them laugh, but I can't figure out why they are laughing. Time difference? Please.

Have you seen Victoria Beckham? Kim Kardashian? Lady Gaga? Oprah? Have you been to New York? Hollywood? What are you wearing now? Do you have white friends? What are their names? Sbho is speaking in questions and I don't know how to respond because everything is coming

209

out all at once, like a rap song. Then Godknows saves the day by snatching the phone because I hear Sbho protest and beg him to give the phone back. Then I hear Mother's voice announcing that her phone is not a toy.

Wassup, Darling, how you doing, boo? Are you pretty good? Godknows says. I start to respond but then he is already talking over me: I heard all that talk from your mother's TV. That's how you talk over there in America, you know wha'm saying, my nigga, wassup with all the whores and motherfuckers over there? How's New York? How's my man Obama? he says, and I laugh a small laugh because I don't really know how to respond. Then there is an awkward silence, the silence of waiting.

Well, so, in just a few months I'm going to live in Dubai. My uncle finally left London and is now working over there, he's coming to get me and I'll leave this kaka country too, Godknows says, as if this is something he's just remembered. I know from his voice that he is smiling his wide smile.

That's nice, Godknows, I say.

Yes, it is nice, he says.

There is silence again, but it's broken by a long scream coming from the basement, followed by giggles. I have almost forgotten Kristal and Marina are still down there. Now I know they went on to watch flicks without me and this pisses me off. I don't know when Godknows gets off the phone but I suddenly find myself talking to Bastard.

210

How is Destroyedmichygen? Bastard says. His voice has broken and it sounds strange; it's like I'm talking to somebody I don't know.

Destroyed what? Oh, Detroit! It's good, but I don't live there anymore. I live in Kalamazoo now, we moved not too long after I got there.

Did they make you leave?

No, not really. We just left.

You know you are lucky, Darling, he says after a while. His voice sounds tired and I don't know what to say to him so I just keep quiet.

Can you send me a Lady Gaga shirt and an iPod? I hear Sbho shout in the background.

What is happening over there? Chipo says when she comes on the phone.

What's happening? I say. I hear another scream from downstairs. A fat fly flies across the living room and sits on a pizza that somebody left lying around. I pick up a newspaper to kill it but when I look up it is gone.

Yes, outside. What do you see when you look outside? Are there people and what are they doing? Chipo says.

I look outside, through the lace curtain. The street is empty, like maybe Martha Stewart was here and cleaned everything up. When I start to tell Chipo that nothing is happening, a bunch of police cars zip down the street, lights flashing, sirens screaming. I count seven of them.

Just some police cars going down the street, I say.

Where are they going? Are they going to arrest somebody? Are there criminals over there? What did they do? Are you going to go outside and see? she says. In the background I hear Godknows ask, What's happenin', what are the motherfuckers doin' in America?

I move the phone from one ear to the other, cradling it between my head and shoulder. I'm feeling a little spent; I just don't know how to deal with all these crazy questions. I lean toward the glass table and start to play with the mail. A card addressed to TK that says *Join the U.S. Army*, a pink Victoria's Secret envelope, a red JCPenney envelope, a thing from Pizza Hut, an envelope with a plastic key taped outside, a Bank of America envelope, a Discover Card envelope.

Well, what is happening over here is that your mother is finishing cooking istshwala and macimbis, and Sbho is standing there watching her and eating a guava. When Chipo announces this I get a strange ache in my heart. My throat goes dry; my tongue salivates. I am remembering the taste of all these things, but remembering is not tasting, and it is painful. I feel tears start to come to my eyes and I don't wipe them off. Chipo is still going on.

—And outside, a woman in a yellow dress and white hat is walking down the street. She is walking like a caterpillar because she is big. Now she is stopping a vendor on a bike to buy some fat maize from him. Now, now, oh Jesus, there is a whirlwind. It is not a big whirlwind, but it is a whirlwind all the same and it has whipped up dust and debris. The clothes are dancing on the clothesline. Ha-ha-ha, the woman's dress is lifting and she is trying to hold it down with both hands. We can see big brown thighs and green parachute underwear. My daughter is trying to fly in the wind, I am going outside to get her, bye.

When we were little we used to play in the wind whenever it came. We would run outside to meet it, hands outstretched like wings, bodies balanced on tiptoe and reaching toward the sky. We wanted the wind to pick us up, and when it didn't we spun around in dizzying circles singing, *Take me to London, baby. To see my uncle, baby. Who has a baby, baby. A baby girl, baby. Oo-uh-huh, baby!* This is the song I am singing when Stina asks me what I am doing. His voice sounds far away, like he's speaking from up a tree.

That is strange; that's exactly the song Chipo was singing on her way to get Darling just now, Stina says after we have greeted each other. Darling is Chipo's daughter; they claimed they decided to name her after me so there would be another Darling in case something happened to me in America. It's kind of cute, but I don't know how to feel about it, somebody being named after me like I'm dead or something.

When are you coming back? Stina says after a long silence. I open my mouth and hear Aunt Fostalina's voice inside my head. I don't know

213

how to tell Stina that I don't know when I'm coming home. Through the window, I can see the tall mailman walking up the driveway, toward the house. I wait for him to ring the door before I put the phone down after telling Stina to hold on, knowing I will not be picking up the phone. It's hard to explain, this feeling; it's like there's two of me. One part is yearning for my friends; the other doesn't know how to connect with them anymore, as if they are people I've never met. I feel a little guilty but I brush the feeling away.

After getting the package I close the door and watch the mailman walk back to his truck. He is tall and strong, and I'm thinking of how when he was making me sign for the package I couldn't look him in the eye. But I was aware of him towering over me, big hairs covering his arms and legs. I was also thinking of what his thing would look like if he were to take off his uniform. When I see the mail truck pull away, I set the package on the kitchen table. It is from Victoria's Secret and is addressed to Aunt Fostalina and I know it's the push-up bra. They have spelled her name *Fosterline*.

When I get back to the basement, Kristal and Marina are watching something else.

What the hell is that? I say.

She-male, Kristal says.

What's she-male? And why did you jump all the way to *S*? I say.

It don't matter, Kristal says. It's still people

fuckin', ain't it? She scoots over to make room for me but I remain on my feet, both hands on my waist, thinking of whether I should sit or turn around and stomp up the stairs to let them know I'm upset.

On the screen is a tall, beautiful girl who has a penis. It's not like those fake ones the lesbians were wearing when we were on *L*; no. It is real. Of all the flicks we have seen, this one stuns, and I can feel my head start to spin in confusion. The sight of long hair and a pretty face and an Adam's apple and big breasts and a big penis all on one body makes me feel that on top of the badness we are doing, this is added badness, so I say, You shouldn't have skipped.

Fine, let's go back, then, Marina says quickly, and I know from the sound of her voice that she, too, is not ready to watch a she-male. I breathe a sigh of relief and sit down when she leans forward and clicks the Back button.

Yo, so my girl Alexis hooked me up with this cool link. Wanna check it out? Kristal says.

What's on it? I say.

How the hell am I s'posed to know? Our computer just be so slow, like it's trynna download Jesus.

Well, you just said it's a cool link, I thought you'd seen it, Marina says.

So? Scoot over, Kristal says, and she reaches for the keyboard.

The first thing we see is the caption *This film*

contains some disturbing images. I look at Kristal and then at Marina to see what they think about this because it reminds me of like a horror movie and I'm not trying to see any horror. Kristal is running her hands in her weave, and Marina starts to do a drumroll on her thighs, so in the end I shrug and start making sounds to accompany the drumroll, but then this crazy scream just explodes and we all stop what we are doing.

The scream sounds like it has devoured all the pain there is and is now choking on it. It hangs in the air like something alive. I'm thinking of how it sounds so familiar, like I've heard it before, but I can't really figure out where, and from whom. I badly want to click the Mute button, I know we all want to because it is such a terrible sound, but nobody touches the mouse. Then the camera does a long shot and we see her lying on the floor, hands in fists, head thrown back, mouth open and all teeth. She is in this yellow dress with white flowers on, and she has these country-game legs, long legs that would make enormous counts and run far.

Then this woman comes in the picture and goes for the girl's legs, and the girl starts kicking like there's a devil inside her. Then this gang of women comes in and pounces on the girl, pinning her down. I am reminded, from the way they are doing it, of how men back home would hold down a goat during slaughter, or how Prophet Revelations Bitchington Mborro and the Evangelists held down the pretty woman on the mountain to exorcise her demon. Now the women are busy shouting things at the girl, and even though I don't understand the language, I know from their hot voices they are telling her to stop the screaming and kicking and behave.

Only one woman is not taking part in the holding down, and it's because she is the one with the long knife. Tall, big-bodied woman, large arms, giraffe neck. Round face. Almost pretty. Oval eyes. Big breasts. Long skirt the color of leaves in the fall, red blouse. Yellow hoop earrings, colorful bangles on the wrists, rings on the fingers. Dirty rag in hand, and in the other, the knife; I want to ask what she is going to do with the knife but I know that if I open my mouth there will be no words. And then to the side there is this old, old woman with skin like worn leather. She is watching everything through squinted eyes. She keeps nodding and nodding, her wilted hands clasped over a walking stick.

The knife woman starts to clean the knife with the rag and I get this shiver. She is doing it slow and deliberate, like maybe she knows we are watching, a frown of concentration on her face. She spits on the knife, wipes, spits, wipes, and, satisfied, flings the rag away. By now I have my legs pressed together tight. I glance at Kristal and Marina and they have the same posture.

Then the knife woman bends toward the girl, teeth digging into the bottom lip, fat fingers wound

217

tight around the knife. When the knife reaches the girl, Marina gets up, and we hear her running up the stairs. I want to get up and run myself but my thighs just feel heavy so I sink back into the couch and just cover my eyes with my arm and listen to the girl's screams, cutting now like somebody doused her voice with paraffin and lit it.

When I look again there is a lot of blood on the floor. The girl has been moved to a corner. Her dress has been straightened out over her legs; you could not tell what had happened just a few minutes before. The screaming and kicking is gone, like whatever was raging inside the girl has grown wings and flown away, leaving her looking like a flower pulled from wet earth, roots and all. Kristal and I sit there, not moving, just staring, and I know, from how we are not looking at each other, that we will never talk about what we have seen.

CHAPTER 15

HITTING CROSSROADS

Kristal isn't old enough to have a license but that doesn't mean she can't drive, which is how come right now we are on our way to the Crossroads Mall. It's Marina's mother's car – we took it because she works nights at Borgess Hospital and sleeps during the day, like an owl, waking up at five in the afternoon, which gives us enough time to go to the mall and back. Marina says her mother sleeps like she's dead but if she happens to wake to go to the bathroom, she keeps her eyes shut, staggering and bumping into stuff like a chicken with its head cut off; if she were to go outside, she wouldn't see nothing.

We have never done this before and we almost didn't because Marina and I weren't so sure at first, but after watching Kristal reverse the car from the driveway and put it back in its spot using just one hand we got a little brave and jumped in, fastened our seat belts, and giggled. When we were getting ready to leave, though, we saw Mr Harris. Mr Harris is Marina's neighbor, and he was driving back home in his crawling car, so we had to duck in our seats and stay low until we heard the car park next door and the door bang shut. We lifted our heads just enough to watch Mr Harris shuffle to the mailbox and then the house like he'd been told he'd get a prize if it took him no less than ten years to do it.

Marina is in the front seat since this is her mother's car, and I'm in the back behind Kristal, which is fine by me in case we do a head-on collision or something. For the first few minutes I'm leaning forward and looking at Kristal's thin hands on the wheel. My own hands are clutching at the back of Kristal's seat like I'm driving it. Marina is quiet, which means she too is scared and maybe she's even thinking of telling us that she was just playing, that we should take the car back and forget Crossroads. It's Kristal who is busy talking but I'm not even listening to her; I'm looking to see where all this is going, and how.

At one point the car swerves to the left and I inhale sharply and get ready to scream but I catch myself since nobody else is screaming. We drive in silence for a bit, but after Kristal gets us down Paterson and takes a left on Cobb without any problems, I start to feel better and put all of my butt properly on the seat. By the time we hit Westnedge we have all rolled down our windows, have our elbows out as if we'd bought the car with our own money as well as paid for the road.

This morning, on our very last day of middle school, a boy brought a loaded gun to class, so they shut Washington down and sent everybody home with a letter. Those who saw it said the boy had a list of people he wanted to shoot. They said the loaded gun accidentally fell out of his backpack and went off; the janitor wrestled him for it before he could kill anybody.

I didn't see anything, but I heard the *bang-bang-bang* of the discharging gun from the cafeteria, and by then kids and teachers were screaming and scattering all over like chickens, clogging the corridors and trying to get out all at once. It reminded me of the stampedes back home when things started to fall apart and the stores were empty, how people would pour out onto the street and run like they were dying, chasing after trucks loaded with mealie-meal, sugar, cooking oil, bread, soap, and just about anything.

We pass the churches and liquor store on the right, the Chinese hair store on the left, the car garage; pass the Shell gas station on the left and the Speedway one on the right, pass the tattoo place, the bank, the Holiday Inn, the Starbucks, the fancy private high school that Marina will attend in the fall while Kristal and I go to Central; we pass the Chinese restaurant and the Indian restaurant and Walgreens and the McDonald's and the Burger King. Today, because we are going where we want and we are in charge, it feels different driving through the city, like maybe everything we see is ours, like we built it all. I have spread my fingers in the wind and every once in a while I grab it and fling it back at itself.

We are cruising like that, and I'm being forced to listen to this stupid Rihanna song that everybody at school used to play like it was an anthem or something. Well, maybe the song isn't stupid, it's only that I just got generally sick of that whole Rihanna business, the way she was on the news and everything. I know her crazy boyfriend beat her up but I don't think she had to be all over, like her face was a humanitarian crisis, like it was the Sudan or something. We cruise and she croons and I want to grab the radio and throw it out of the window. We are just passing the adult store on our right when we hear the wailing sound, and we know that the police are chasing us. All the fun comes to a sudden end, like it was water in a bucket and somebody just tipped it over.

The last time we were stopped by the police, I was in a car with Uncle Kojo and Aunt Fostalina, and we were on the highway, I don't remember coming from where. The policeman wanted to take Uncle Kojo in but then he didn't because Aunt Fostalina begged and begged and in the end he just let them pay for the ticket there, on the spot. Marina is saying something about her mother killing her, and Kristal is saying something else, but I'm not even following because I'm busy thinking about what will happen to us; in America, jails are not for just adults and real criminals.

Kristal pulls over and parks. I turn to look behind us and it's all flashing blue and sirens. I think about opening the door and running, just running, but then I remember that the police will shoot you for doing a little thing like that if you are black, so I sit in the car and say, We shouldn't have come, now what are we going to do, what will Aunt Fostalina say?

Long after the police cars have thundered past and disappeared, we are still looking at one another as if we've been sitting in the dark and somebody just flicked on the lights. We are realizing that the police were not chasing after us but just rushing somewhere, and we were in the way. The fear leaves our faces, and we sit there and laugh, reluctantly and nervously at first, and then our courage comes back and our voices pick up and we are proper laughing now, laughing like we mean it, like we want to drive the car with just the sound of our voices.

We get on the road again and when we stop at the red light next to the statue of that soldier on a horse, I am so happy about not being arrested, so happy, I hear myself singing this song we used to sing at school back home when we were little:

Who discovered the way to India?
Vasco da Gama! Vasco da Gama!
Vasco da Gama! Vasco da Gama!

Because I am no longer in a stolen car with Kristal and Marina, because I'm no longer in America on my way to the mall, I lift and lift and lift my voice better than Rihanna. I am

223

home-home now, with my friends at school, and we are each wearing a brown uniform with a yellow collar and a badge that says Queen Elizabeth Primary School, a picture of a rising sun and the words *Knowledge Is Power* written in red cursive at the bottom. We're going to India, marching in Vasco da Gama's footsteps, and we're wearing white socks and black shoes. Because this is where I am now, and because it is a place where you sing like something is burning inside you, I sing until Marina is yelling my name and Kristal has turned off the radio and is saying, The fuck? You need to calm down, damn.

What, you had the volume on full blast when you were listening to your stupid songs, did you hear me complain? I say.

Well, least we wasn't listenin' to no tribal stuff, Kristal says, and turns a corner. I don't know if she's kidding or not, but these days, ever since Kristal got this chest like she's going to breastfeed the whole of America, she has this thing about bossing people around, like maybe somebody made her queen.

Whatever, leave me alone, I say. And FYI, I am singing in English.

No, you ain't, Kristal says, and Marina giggles. We are passing through a construction site, so the two lanes have merged into one. On our left are rows of drums.

How would you know? You can't even speak English, I say.

224

Say what? Kristal says. I know, even though she hasn't turned around, how her face is looking. You can see it all in her voice. A curled lip. Narrowed eyes. A frown. Say what?

Well, it's true, everybody knows you can't speak proper English. Like right now: Say what? What on earth is that? I say. Marina coughs a fake cough. And what is *naamean? Naamsayin? I'm finna go?* All that nonsense you speak. Is it hard for you to just say *I beg your pardon?* Or simply, *What did you say? You know what I mean? You know what I'm saying? I am going to go?*

Whatchu tombout? Kristal says, and her voice tells me her face is all scrunched up now but I am not backing off.

It's true. You know, when I first met you, I couldn't understand anything coming out of your mouth, not a single word, nada, and you sit here and say you are American and that you speak English!

I am starting to talk fast now, and I have to remember to slow down because when I get excited I start to sound like myself, and my American accent goes away. But I know I have told Kristal because she is quiet for a while, just staring at the road ahead and saying nothing. Marina turns around and gives me a high-five. Suddenly we can smell tar or something burning coming from outside; it is a terrible stench.

Eww, Marina says, and covers her nose with her hands like maybe it'll help the smell.

You don't know nothin', Kristal says after a while, turning to give me a look like I'm the one that's stinking up the car.

First of all, it's called Ebonics and it be a language system, but it be our own, naamean, 'coz we ain't trynna front.

I beg your pardon? I say.

Uh-huh, I beg your pardon, my ass, trynna sound like stupid white folk, she says.

What did you say? I say.

You heard me, shit, Kristal says. The car slows down a little bit.

No, that's not true. It's just the way we talk, Marina says.

Is anybody talkin' to you, fool? Kristal says, turning to Marina. 'Sides, you better not start nothin'. I've seen them Nigerian movies and y'all can't talk, period; why you think you have them subtitles? Kristal says. I don't mean to laugh but then I'm laughing.

Well, it's kind of true, in a way. I mean, when I watch your movies I have to read the subtitles myself, even if they're supposed to be in English.

That's 'cause you are not smart. And what do you mean *my movies*, have you ever seen me in them, huh? Marina says, knives in her voice. Kristal laughs and I look out the window at a dog that's sitting in the back seat of another car and staring straight ahead like it's looking to make sure the driver doesn't take a wrong turn, like it's in charge of directions. The construction

226

has just ended and we're getting back into two lanes.

And talking about being smart, I must say y'alls are mad smart 'coz otherwise you wouldn't be able to pull that 419 shit, Kristal says to Marina. The car changes lanes.

What 419 shit? Marina says.

She means the scam e-mails; don't act like you don't know, I say. Like, Dear Miss Darling, We need your help to wash this black money and you'll get a million bucks. Or, I'm the manager of this bank and this rich client has died in a plane crash and has no next of kin so can we give the twenty million to you? You know, those kind of crazy e-mails, I have dozens of them in my junk-mail folder right now, all of them from Nigerians, I say.

I don't know what you're talking about. I've never seen them, Marina says.

Well, that's 'coz y'all be the ones sendin' them, Kristal says, and I clap my hands and we both laugh.

That's not funny, Marina says. She has a crack in her voice so we stop since we are in her mother's car, after all.

Anybody know what be the speed limit? Kristal says.

How does one know that? Do they put up signs for it or something? I say.

We get to the railroad tracks when the lights are flashing and that bar thingy is descending. Kristal tries to beat the train but she is not fast enough, so, in the end, she slams the brakes, and we're jolted forward; I have to grab the back of Kristal's seat to stop myself from crashing into it.

My bad, my bad, Kristal says.

You need to watch it, it's my mother's car, Marina says.

Take it easy, big head, didn't I just say my bad? Kristal says.

We sit there and watch the train. With the blue ones, you have to wait for only maybe like three minutes and you go, but this is one of those long brown ones so it takes forever; even God didn't take that long to create stuff.

Look, look, Marina says, and we look to our left and the dude who's driving the red car is leaned out and looking into our car like maybe he knows us. When he sticks out his long tongue and wiggles it, Marina squeals.

That's nasty, don't look at his stupid ass, Kristal says, but I steal a glance anyway. When boys do the tongue thing I find it terrifying and interesting. Ahead, the train roars and roars, car after car after car after car. There is graffiti on some of the cars, but I can't really read it. Then the last of the train passes and the bar thing lifts and we are moving again.

We park by Borders and we are walking out of the parking lot when right there, next to a black van, I see my car. I don't even hesitate, I run to it, yelling, My Lamborghini, Lamborghini,

Lamborghini Reventón! Maybe I start freaking out, I don't know, but Marina is pulling me away and asking what's wrong with me.

Do you know how much that car costs? she says when we're out of the parking lot.

How much? I say.

Almost a couple of million dollars, she says.

You're lying. Millions? For that little car? I say.

Duh, Kristal says.

You can Google it; that little car is actually one of the most expensive cars out there, Marina says.

Well, I say, and leave it there. I stop to let a car pass before I cross over to the entrance of the mall. The thing is, I don't want to say with my own mouth that if the car costs that much then it means I'll never own it, and if I can't own it, does that mean I'm poor, and if so, what is America for, then?

I look back at the parking lot but I can't see the Lamborghini among the mass of cars. I crane my neck this way and that but it's gone, just like a dream that you dream and you know you dreamed it but you can't even remember what it was. I'm walking a little behind Kristal and Marina now so I can keep glancing back and glancing back. If Bastard and Stina and Chipo and Godknows and Sbho were here, they'd be screaming and teasing and howling with laughter and dying now.

Inside Borders, an old woman in a red vest with badges all over meets us at the door with a bleached smile and says, How can I help you

229

today, ladies? but we just breeze by like she is air. Kristal is at the front, Marina behind her, and then me. The smell of new books is all around us but we don't stop to look at anything even though I kind of want to because I don't hate books. I haven't read any interesting ones in a while, though, since I'm always busy with the computer and TV. The last book I read was that *Jane Eyre* one, where the long, meandering sentences and everything just bored me and that Jane just kept irritating me with her stupid decisions and the whole lame story made me want to throw the book away. I had to force myself to keep reading because I had to write a report for English class.

It's early in the morning so the mall is a little dead. If this was at home, the place would be throbbing with life already: little kids riding that escalator over there like it would take them to heaven, their screams rising like skyscrapers – you would hear them all the way at Victoria's Secret on the third floor; the mothers gossiping and laughing on the first floor, taking turns to look up and shout warnings at their children, bodies constantly shuffling about because women never stand still since there is always something to do, always something; the men doing their thing maybe around those benches outside Payless, maybe passing around a Kingsgate cigarette or huddled around a newspaper and maybe talking about football scores in the European League, or the war in Iraq, their voices deep but never rising above those of the women and children because a man's voice needs to stay low always; and then, in the open space where that Indian girl does threading, the older kids would be dancing to house music, to DJ Sbu and DJ Zinhle and Bojo Mujo, being reckless with their contorting bodies like they know they don't own them and therefore they don't care if they break; and in the massage chairs near the elevator, toothless old people sprawled out like lizards basking in the sun, making groaning noises as the massage thingies worked their wilted bodies; and at the telephone near the candle shop, an impatient line queuing to make calls to relatives in places like Chicago and Cape Town and Paris and Amsterdam and Lilongwe and Jamaica and Tunis; in the air, the dizzying aromas of morning foods cutting those perfumed smells from Macy's to shreds; and maybe, on that little square outside Foot Locker, under the fake tree, someone preaching from a Bible, a small crowd gathered around him, maybe wondering whether to believe or not, litter at their feet and around the mall to show there are people living there.

A strange feeling is coming over me, and Marina is shouting my name from upstairs, and then I realize I've just been lost in thought and they have gone up and left me standing outside the piercing store. I jump on the escalator and head upstairs. On the other escalator, going down, a small man with slicked-back hair is holding on to two large bags of trash. His name tag reads JESUS. We both smile grins because this is what we must do; when we pass, he says, Buenos días, señorita, and I smile even more and say, Buenos días.

Inside Best Buy, Kristal has headphones over her ears and is nodding hard. Marina is staring at the iPods like she'll buy one. I stop in front of the posters but then decide to pass when I see the DVDs. I pick up one that says *Salt* and has Angelina Jolie on the cover. I haven't really watched any Angelina Jolie movies, but I know that she can go anywhere in the world and get a baby wherever she wants. When I saw that she got that pretty little girl from Ethiopia, I was jealous; I wished she had come to my country when I was little and got me too. I could be Darling Jolie-Pitt right now and living in a mansion and flying around in jets and everything. But then again, she might have picked Sbho, the pretty one.

When I see a DVD with a guy who's trying to look like Nelson Mandela, I pick it up, put the Jolie one back. It says *Invictus*. I haven't seen the film, but I have heard about it; maybe I'll ask Aunt Fostalina to pick it up from Blockbuster or ask TK if he can get it from Netflix.

Whatchu doin'? Kristal says, leaving the music section. She is unwrapping some gum; I hold out my hand and she rolls her eyes, drops it into my palm, and starts unwrapping a second one.

Can't you see I'm looking at *Invictus*? I say, making like I've seen the movie. I pop the gum into my mouth; it's a spearmint.

Do you know who this guy is? I say, holding the DVD up so Kristal can see the cover.

Pssshh, who don't know Morgan Freeman? she says.

I know that, I mean who is he playing in the movie?

Who?

Nelson Mandela, I say, and I am surprised by the pride in my voice, like maybe I am talking about someone I know, like we used to play country-game together or something.

Oh yeah, he be that old guy in them printed shirts. I'm finna go to JCPenney, y'all, Kristal says, and she's already getting out of Best Buy.

Outside, Marina halts by the jewelry store, where there are the watches. I stop, but Kristal keeps walking toward JCPenney. The watches are both beautiful and important-looking. I put both hands on my waist and laugh.

What are you laughing at? Marina says.

Like, the prices are funny. Who would buy a three-thousand-dollar watch? I say.

Well, if I had the money and could afford it, I totally would. There's nothing wrong with wanting nice things, Marina says.

Whatever, I say, and pop my gum in Marina's ear just to irritate her, then I move on and look at the diamond rings in the next display. They too are expensive, but I know that even if I had all the money in the world, I wouldn't buy them. Then I see this one ring that looks kind of different from the rest. The ring part is twisted, and the head is made of diamonds that form a cluster like

233

tiny seeds. The price tag says $22,050, and I start to tell Marina that her store is crazy when my teeth miss the gum and I bite the inside of my lip. The pain stings so much I close my eyes and clamp a hand over my mouth, the salty, metallic taste of blood spreading all over my tongue.

At JCPenney we head straight to the Juniors section. We pick out jeans, T-shirts, dresses, sweaters, just pick and pick whatever we want. We don't talk that much because we don't want anybody following us or asking why we're not in school and where our mothers are and that kind of stuff. Sometimes we lose one another for minutes but then we run into one another again because we're circling and circling. When our arms are full we go to the fitting rooms. There are some stores where they'll tell you to take just five or maybe six things to try at a time, but JCPenney is not like that; here, you can take even a mountain to the fitting rooms if you want and nobody will bother you.

Let's dress for a party, Marina shouts from her room.

Shhhh, don't be so loud, fool, Kristal says.

What kind of party? I say.

Sweet sixteen, Marina says, keeping her voice low.

When we come out, Marina is in a strapless black dress with sparkling thingies at the bust going all the way down to the stomach. A lace-like thing covers the skirt part. Kristal is in a red dress

234

with frills; it's sleeveless and has a deep cut that leaves her big boobs in your face, just the way she likes, and right now she has her chest pushing out to exaggerate the boobs. And me, I'm in a long cream one that sweeps the ground. We stand there like models, staring at our reflections.

You need boobs to wear a strapless like that, Kristal says, looking at Marina in the mirror. I giggle, but not too much, since my boobs, too, are small-small; sometimes I don't know why I even wear a bra.

Whatever, Marina says, and rolls her eyes.

After we agree that Kristal has the best dress, we go back to the dressing room to change for a dance party. When we come out we are looking like whores: skimpy skirts where you can't even bend without showing your panties, and tight tops we almost cannot breathe in. We don't spend that much time in front of the mirror, maybe because we are a little embarrassed. We hurry back to change for a girls' night out. When we look at one another we laugh because we are all wearing the same skinny jeans, and Marina and Kristal are even wearing the same sleeveless lace shirt. Since I am the one wearing something different, a V-neck with a French flag on my stomach, I win the round, but when I turn around to go back to my fitting room, Marina says, You could have at least wore something with an African flag.

We change for prom, for church, for the red carpet, for a blind date; we just change and change, meeting for every round to admire and compare. We have just changed for a football game when this small woman comes into the fitting rooms wearing scrubs and carrying a couple of dresses. She doesn't say anything to us, just passes and heads for the handicapped fitting room at the end of the row. Kristal laughs for no reason in particular, but after the woman shuts her door, Marina says, I'm changing, I'm going home now, and I say, Why? right at the time Kristal says, Are you for real?

We change and leave everything in messy piles.

Let's see who gets to the car first without running, I say, and we take off. We power-walk out of JCPenney like we're trying to lose weight, past the jewelers and the diamonds, down the escalator, past the booths, the old men sitting in the massage chairs. I am at the front and when I glance behind me Marina is dangerously close so I pump my hands and count four-five-six, and walk, and walk. We tear through Borders, and by the time we get to the doors I can't bear it so I push them open and break into a run. Kristal overtakes me and gets to the car first, and I hear Marina screaming behind me, Not fair, guys, it's not fair, you broke the rules.

Inside the car, it feels like the devil is grilling sinners; we roll down our windows and fling our arms out. Then we see her; in the car directly facing us, a woman in a black hijab sitting behind the wheel and rummaging in her purse, maybe looking for keys. She looks at us, smiles briefly, then goes back to her purse, but we just keep staring at her like we are maybe at the zoo. We don't say anything, but we know it's because of her dress and the things we see on TV that we stare – if she were wearing jeans or anything else we wouldn't even look at her.

Kristal starts the car but then just keeps sitting there like she's forgotten how to drive.

What's wrong with my mother's car? Marina says. I lean forward, put my head between the front seats to see what is going on.

You know George, right? Kristal says.

Who's George? Marina says.

The little motherfucker who brought the gun to school, Kristal says.

What about him? I say, and start waving because the woman is now waving, maybe because we are still staring. Then Marina waves, and we are still waving when the woman's car starts pulling away.

Never mind, Kristal says, and she starts reversing the car.

When I get home, Aunt Fostalina's car is pulling out of the driveway. She rolls down the window and tells me she is on her way to Shadybrook, so I get into the car, throw my book bag in the back seat. Every so often, Aunt Fostalina is summoned to Shadybrook nursing home to pacify Tshaka Zulu. When his craziness starts, Tshaka Zulu will threaten the other residents and staff with the assegai he claims is hidden somewhere inside his room. I have seen the short stabbing spear; it is not real, but nobody knows this. Tshaka Zulu showed it to me one day; it's just a drawing of a spear that he keeps folded and hidden away among the pictures of himself when he was a young boy, back in our country.

The thing with Tshaka Zulu's madness is that when it comes, when the medicines they keep him on stop working, he refuses to speak in English, and then Claudine, the quiet, pretty lady who runs the nursing home, will call Aunt Fostalina to talk to Tshaka Zulu in our language. This seems to be the only medicine that works, but what Aunt Fostalina has discovered is that when Tshaka Zulu is supposedly crazy, he doesn't really need calming but listening to. His appears to be the madness that makes him talk, and Aunt Fostalina brings me along because she gets bored listening.

Today we park the car on the quiet street, rush through the boiling blanket of air and into Shadybrook. The door is opened before we ring the bell by a grinning crazy with blond hair. His name is Andrew. Something is wrong in his head but he is also very smart. Two months ago, for example, the police came to get him because he was said to have hacked into some websites and posted bad pictures of himself. Aunt Fostalina breezes past him toward the basement, which is where Tshaka Zulu's room is.

Hi, I say to Andrew, because I have a hard time

238

just pushing past the guy like he doesn't exist, even though he is a crazy. Shadybrook always smells like a hospital, and already I can feel my stomach clenching.

Hi, Peter, Andrew says to me. Do you have a cigarette? Which is the question he always asks, and I shake my head no, like I always do. I have stopped correcting him when he calls me Peter. In the common room I wave at a woman I have never seen before. She is seated next to a walker, staring listlessly into the air like she is waiting for something, for an angel to come and bless her, while the TV is on. I quickly look away; I always feel guilty around sick people because there is nothing I can do for them.

Tshaka Zulu is wearing his traditional dress and standing on the bed. Claudine is pacing up and down the basement, crossing and uncrossing her arms.

Thank God you're here, she whispers to Aunt Fostalina. I don't know how long I can do this, she says.

It's okay, I came as soon as I could, why don't you get some rest, Aunt Fostalina says.

Tshaka Zulu picks up his shield, raises it above his graying head, and shouts, Bayethe, I welcome you to my kraal, do you want to see my spear? And I have to try hard to suppress a laugh. I know he is not himself and all, but this is something else. The good thing, though, is that he is not really dangerous. He gets down from the bed and proceeds toward his wooden stool, the kind that old men used at home, and sits under the poster of a topless Masai girl, crazy beads all over her body.

Being in Tshaka Zulu's room is like being in a museum of remembrance or something – the walls are choking with things: newspaper clippings of Nelson Mandela when he came out of jail and stuff, pictures of our country's president when he first became president and he had all his hair, a picture of Kwame Nkrumah, Kofi Annan, a big picture of Desmond Tutu, pictures of Miriam Makeba, Brenda Fassie, Hugh Masekela, Lucky Dube, a newspaper clipping of Credo Mutwa, framed pictures of Bébé Manga, Leleti Khumalo, Wangari Maathai, and so on.

The family pictures are put separate and they take up an entire wall. On days that he is himself, Tshaka Zulu will go over the pictures, point out his sons and daughters and nieces and nephews and grandchildren. He will tell you the jobs they do, the kinds of things they like, where they live, who they are married to, and I am always surprised by how he remembers every detail, like he lives with all these people. He has named all his children and grandchildren, given them names like Gezephi, Sisa, Nokuthula, Nene, Nicholas, Makhosi, Ophelia, Douglas, Sakhile, Eden, Davie, Ian, each name carefully thought out and finally given over the phone.

It's how I get to touch them, Tshaka Zulu said

to me one day when we were going over the names.

You see, every time they are called by name and they answer, I am the invisible hand touching them and calling them my own, he said.

I don't know exactly what kind of craziness Tshaka Zulu suffers from; Aunt Fostalina told me the name one time but I have forgotten it because it was a complicated name, but I think it's far much better than some kinds I have seen. Once, when we were coming from hitting Budapest, a crazy man chased us all the way home, half naked. And at one wedding, before we moved to Paradise, a groom just upped and picked up a log and started clobbering people, including his own bride. He never got better; wherever he went, people were always fleeing for their lives.

CHAPTER 16

HOW THEY LIVED

And when they asked us where we were from, we exchanged glances and smiled with the shyness of child brides. They said, Africa? We nodded yes. What part of Africa? We smiled. Is it that part where vultures wait for famished children to die? We smiled. Where the life expectancy is thirty-five years? We smiled. Is it there where dissidents shove AK-47s between women's legs? We smiled. Where people run about naked? We smiled. That part where they massacred each other? We smiled. Is it where the old president rigged the election and people were tortured and killed and a whole bunch of them put in prison and all, there where they are dying of cholera – oh my God, yes, we've seen your country; it's been on the news.

And when these words tumbled from their lips like crushed bricks, we exchanged glances again and the water in our eyes broke. Our smiles melted like dying shadows and we wept; wept for our blessed, wretched country. We wept and wept and they pitied us and said, It's okay – it's okay, you are in America now, and still we wept and wept and wept and they gave us soft little thingies and said, Here is some Kleenex, here, and we took the soft thingies and put them in our pockets to look at later and we wept still, wept like widows, wept like orphans.

In America we saw more food than we had seen in all our lives and we were so happy we rummaged through the dustbins of our souls to retrieve the stained, broken pieces of God. We had flung him in there way back when we were still in our own country, flung him during desperate, desperate moments when we were dizzy with hunger and we thought, How come he will not pity us, how come? Thought, Why does he not hear us, why? Thought, How come we ask and ask and ask and still are not given even a morsel, how come? And blind with rage we flung him away and said, Better no God, better no God than live like this, praying like this for things that will never come. Better no God.

But then when we got to America and saw all that food, we held our breath and thought, Wait, there must be a God. So happy and grateful, we found his discarded pieces and put them together with Krazy Glue bought at the dollar store for only ninety-nine cents and said, In God We Trust too now, In God We Trust for real, and began praying again. At McDonald's we devoured Big Macs and wolfed down fries and guzzled super-sized Cokes. At Burger King we worshipped Whoppers. At KFC we mauled bucket chicken.

We went to Chinese buffets and ate all we could inhale – fried rice, chicken, beef, shrimp, and as for the things whose names we could not read, we simply pointed and said, We want *that*.

We ate like pigs, like wolves, like dignitaries; we ate like vultures, like stray dogs, like monsters; we ate like kings. We ate for all our past hunger, for our parents and brothers and sisters and relatives and friends who were still back there. We uttered their names between mouthfuls, conjured up their hungry faces and chapped lips – eating for those who could not be with us to eat for themselves. And when we were full we carried our dense bodies with the dignity of elephants – if only our country could see us in America, see us eat like kings in a land that was not ours.

How America surprised us at first. If you were not happy with your body you could go to a doctor and say, for instance, Doctor, I was born in the wrong body, just make me right; Doctor, I don't like this nose, these breasts, these lips. We looked at people sending their aging parents away to be taken care of by strangers. We looked at parents not being allowed to beat their own children. We looked at strange things like these, things we had never seen in our lives, and said, What kind of land is this, just what kind of land?

Because we were not in our country, we could not use our own languages, and so when we spoke our voices came out bruised. When we talked, our tongues thrashed madly in our mouths, staggered like drunken men. Because we were not using our languages we said things we did not mean; what we really wanted to say remained folded inside, trapped. In America we did not always have the words. It was only when we were by ourselves that we spoke in our real voices. When we were alone we summoned the horses of our languages and mounted their backs and galloped past skyscrapers. Always, we were reluctant to come back down.

How hard it was to get to America – harder than crawling through the anus of a needle. For the visas and passports, we begged, despaired, lied, groveled, promised, charmed, bribed – anything to get us out of the country. For his passport and travel, Tshaka Zulu sold all of his father's cows, against the old man's wishes. Perseverance had to take his sister Netsai out of school. Nqo worked the fields of Botswana for nine months. Nozipho, like Primrose and Sicelokuhle and Maidei, slept with that fat black pig Banyile Khoza from the passport office. Girls flat on their backs, Banyile between their legs, America on their minds.

To send us off properly, our elders spilled tobacco on the dry earth to summon the spirits of the ancestors for our protection. Unlike in years long gone, the spirits did not come dancing from the land beneath. They crawled. They stalled. They were hungry. They wanted blood and meat and millet beer, they wanted sacrifices, they wanted gifts. And, save for a few grains of tobacco, we had nothing to give, absolutely nothing. And so the spirits just gazed at us with eyes milked dry of care. Between themselves they whispered: How will these ones ever be whole in that 'Melika, as far away from the graves of the ancestors as it is?

Do people not live in fear in 'Melika, fear of evil?

Do they not say it is like a grave in that 'Melika, that going there is like burying yourself because your people may never see you again?

Is not 'Melika also that wretched place where they took looted black sons and daughters those many, many years ago?

We heard all this but we let it enter in one ear and leave through the other, pretended we did not hear. We would not be moved, we would not listen; we were going to America. In the footsteps of those looted black sons and daughters, we were going, yes, we were going. And when we got to America we took our dreams, looked at them tenderly as if they were newly born children, and put them away; we would not be pursuing them. We would never be the things we had wanted to be: doctors, lawyers, teachers, engineers. No school for us, even though our visas were school visas. We knew we did not have the money for school to begin with, but we had applied for school visas because that was the only way out.

Instead of going to school, we worked. Our Social Security cards said *Valid for work only with INS authorization*, but we gritted our teeth and broke the law and worked; what else could we do? What could we have done? What could anybody have done? And because we were breaking the law, we dropped our heads in shame; we had never broken any laws before. We dropped our heads because we were no longer people; we were now illegals.

When they debated what to do with illegals, we stopped breathing, stopped laughing, stopped everything, and listened. We heard: exporting America, broken borders, war on the middle class, invasion, deportation, illegals, illegals, illegals. We bit our tongues till we tasted blood, sat tensely on one butt cheek, afraid to sit on both because how can you sit properly when you don't know about your tomorrow?

And because we were illegal and afraid to be discovered we mostly kept to ourselves, stuck to our kind and shied away from those who were not like us. We did not know what they would think of us, what they would do about us. We did not want their wrath, we did not want their curiosity, we did not want any attention. We did not meet stares and we avoided gazes. We hid our real names, gave false ones when asked. We built mountains between us and them, we dug rivers, we planted thorns – we had paid so much to be in America and we did not want to lose it all.

When they talked about employers checking on workers, our hearts sank. We recalled the tatters of our country left behind, barely held together by American dollars, by monies from other countries, and our blood went cold. And when at work they asked for our papers, we scurried like startled hens and flocked to unwanted jobs, where we met the others, many others. Others with names like myths, names like puzzles, names we had never heard before: Virgilio, Balamugunthan, Faheem, Abdulrahman, Aziz, Baako, Dae-Hyun, Ousmane, Kimatsu. When it was hard to say the many strange names, we called them by their countries.

So how on earth do you do this, Sri Lanka?

Mexico, are you coming or what?

Is it really true you sold a kidney to come to America, India?

Guys, just give Tshaka Zulu a break, the guy is old, I'm just saying.

We know you despise this job, Sudan, but deal with it, man.

Come, Ethiopia, move, move, move; Israel, Kazakhstan, Niger, brothers, let's go!

The others spoke languages we did not know, worshipped different gods, ate what we would not dare touch. But like us, they had left their homelands behind. They flipped open their wallets to show us faded photographs of mothers whose faces bore the same creases of worry as our very own mothers, siblings bleak-eyed with dreams unfulfilled like those of our own, fathers forlorn and defeated like ours. We had never seen their countries but we knew about everything in those pictures; we were not altogether strangers.

And the jobs we worked, Jesus – Jesus – Jesus, the jobs we worked. Low-paying jobs. Backbreaking jobs. Jobs that gnawed at the bones of our dignity, devoured the meat, tongued the marrow. We took scalding irons and ironed our pride flat. We cleaned toilets. We picked tobacco and fruit under the boiling sun until we hung our tongues and panted like lost hounds. We butchered animals, slit throats, drained blood.

We worked with dangerous machines, holding our breath like crocodiles underwater, our minds on the money and never on our lives. Adamou got murdered by that beast of a machine that also ate three fingers of Sudan's left hand. We cut ourselves working on meat; we got skin diseases. We inhaled bad smells until our lungs thundered. Ecuador fell from forty stories working on a roof and shattered his spine, screaming, *¡Mis hijos! ¡Mis hijos!* on his way down. We got sick but did not go to hospitals, could not go to hospitals. We swallowed every pain like a bitter pill, drank every fear like a love potion, and we worked and worked.

Every two weeks we got our paychecks and sent monies back home by Western Union and MoneyGram. We bought food and clothes for the families left behind; we paid school fees for the little ones. We got messages that said *Hunger*, that said *Help*, that said *Kunzima*, and we sent money. When we were asked, You guys work so hard, why do y'all work so hard? we smiled.

And every so often we listened over the phone to the voices of our parents and elders, shy voices telling us what was needed. They had long since ceased to be providers for us; we were now their parents. Our extended families sent requests and we worked, worked like donkeys, worked like slaves, worked like madmen. When we hesitated, they said, You are in America where everybody has money, we see it all on TV, please don't deny us. Madoda, vakomana, how we worked!

We had never seen such a big monster of a country – it was like there were many countries in it: Michigan, Texas, New York, Atlanta, Ohio, Kansas, DC, California, and so many others. We went to places and took lots of pictures and sent them home so they could see us in America. We took pictures outside the White House; we took pictures leaning against the Lady Liberty as if she were our grandmother; we took pictures at the Niagara Falls, at the Times Square; we took pictures with dolphins in Florida, took pictures at the Grand Canyon – we went everywhere and took and took and took pictures and sent them home, showing off a country that would never be ours.

And when those at home saw the pictures and

wanted to come and see America for themselves, we said, Sure, buyanini, chiuyayi, you are welcome to come. We sent them monies for visas and tickets and they came. It was mostly the youth who came, leaving behind old people and children. They came in droves, abandoning the tatters that were our country. We did not think about mending the tatters, all we thought was: *Leave, abandon, flee, run – anything. Escape.*

And when they came to join us in America, hungry and hollow and hopeful, we held them tight and welcomed them to a home that was not ours. We smelled their hair and clothes, we begged them for news of our land – big news, small news, any news. We asked them to describe how the earth smelled right before it rained, to describe how after the rain, flying ants exploded from the ground like fireworks.

We asked, Is the City Hall still the same? The Tredgold Building? And Renkini? The jacaranda trees that line the streets in town – do they still bloom that dizzying purple? Is that crazy Prophet Revelations Bitchington Mborro still there? He prayed for me to get my visa, can you believe it? What about Main Street, does it still flow like a river, and does that blind beggar still sit outside Spar supermarket and sing *Thabath' isiphambano ulandele?* We asked the arrivals all these questions and watched them as they spoke; we wanted to put our heads in their mouths to catch every precious word, every feeling.

251

And then came the times we called home, and young strangers answered the phone, and we said, Who are you? and they said, I'm Thabani's son, Lungile; I'm Nyarai's daughter, Tricia; I'm Prayer's second child, Garikayi. We listened to these strangers and said, Jesus, Thabani is a parent now? Nyarai has a daughter now? Prayer is a parent now? When did it happen, when did all these children have their own children? That is how time went. It flew and we did not see it flying. We did not go back home to visit because we did not have the papers for our return, and so we just stayed, knowing that if we went we would not be able to reenter America. We stayed, like prisoners, only we chose to be prisoners and we loved our prison; it was not a bad prison. And when things only got worse in our country, we pulled our shackles even tighter and said, We are not leaving America, no, we are not leaving.

And then our own children were born. We held their American birth certificates tight. We did not name our children after our parents, after ourselves; we feared if we did they would not be able to say their own names, that their friends and teachers would not know how to call them. We gave them names that would make them belong in America, names that did not mean anything to us: Aaron, Josh, Dana, Corey, Jack, Kathleen. When our children were born, we did not bury their umbilical cords under the earth to bind them to the land because we had no land to call ours. We did not hold their heads over smoking herbs to make them strong, did not tie fetishes around their waists to protect them from evil spirits, did not brew beer and spill tobacco on the earth to announce their arrivals to the ancestors. Instead, we smiled.

And when our parents reminded us over the phone that it had been a long, long time, and that they were getting old and needed to see us, needed to meet their grandchildren, we said, We are coming, Mama, Siyabuya Baba; we are coming, Gogo, Tirikuuya Sekuru. We did not want to tell them we still had no papers. And when they grew restless and cursed America for being the greedy monster that swallowed their children, swallowed the sons and daughters of other lands and refused to spit them out, we said, We are coming very soon, we are coming next year. And next year came and we said, Next year. When next year came we said, Next year for sure. And when next year for sure came we said, Next year for real. And when next year for real came we said, We are coming, you'll see, just wait. And our parents waited and they saw, saw that we did not come.

They died waiting, clutching in their dried hands pictures of us leaning against the Lady Liberty, graves of lost sons and daughters in their hearts, old eyes glued to the sky for fulamatshinaz to bring forth lost sons and daughters. We could not attend their funerals because we still had no papers, and so we mourned from afar. We shut ourselves up and turned on the music so we did not raise alarm, writhed on the floor and wailed and wailed and wailed.

And with our parents gone, we told ourselves, We have no home anymore, who would we go to see in that land we left behind? We convinced ourselves that we now belonged only with our children. And those children – they grew and we had to squint to see ourselves in them. They did not speak our language, they did not sound like us. When they misbehaved, we said only, No, Don't do that, Stop, Time-out. But that is not what we wanted to do. What we wanted to do was get switches and karabha and karabha and karabha. We wanted to draw blood and teach red, raw lessons to last them lifetimes, but we feared being arrested for bringing up our own children like our parents had brought us up.

When our children were old enough and we told them about our country, they did not beg us for stories of the land we had left behind. They went to their computers and Googled and Googled and Googled. When they got off, they looked at us with something between pity and horror and said, Jeez, you really come from there? They did not want to hear the stories our grandmothers had told to us around village fires, stories of Buhlalusebenkosi, how the rabbit lost its tail, Tsuro na Gudo. They would not be part of the horror we had fled.

We accepted many things as our children grew, things that baffled us because we had been raised differently. But we took it all and said, There is no journey without a price, and this is the price of the long journey we made those many years ago. When our children became young adults they did not ask for our approval to marry. We did not get bride prices; we did not get gifts. At their weddings we did not spill beer and tobacco on the earth, did not beat drums to thank our ancestors – we smiled.

Our children raised their families and we did not tell them what to do, how to bring up their children. They hardly came to see us; they were busy with jobs and their new lives. They did not send us monies like we had sent our parents. When we grew old, they did not beg us to stay with them. When we grew very old, they put us here in these nursing homes where we are taken care of by strangers, strangers who have left their countries just like we left ours those many years ago.

Here our own parents come to us in dreams. They do not touch us, they do not speak to us; they only behold us with looks we cannot remember. When we approach them, we find ourselves surrounded by oceans we cannot cross. We reach out, we yell, we beg, we plead; it's no use. Always, we wake from these dreams groping for mirrors, wounds in our eyes; we see ourselves through searing pain.

When we die, our children will not know how

to wail, how to mourn us the right way. They will not go mad with grief, they will not pin black cloth on their arms, they will not spill beer and tobacco on the earth, they will not sing till their voices are hoarse. They will not put our plates and cups on our graves; they will not send us away with mphafa trees. We will leave for the land of the dead naked, without the things we need to enter the castle of our ancestors. Because we will not be proper, the spirits will not come running to meet us, and so we will wait and wait and wait – forever waiting in the air like flags of unsung countries.

CHAPTER 17

MY AMERICA

When I'm not cleaning the toilets or bagging groceries, I'm bent over a big cart like this, sorting out bottles and cans with names like Faygo, Pepsi, Dr Pepper, 7-Up, root beer, Miller, Budweiser, Heineken. They are collected over at the front, where they have been returned for deposit, and then wheeled back here, where I have to separate the cans and put them in the rows of tall boxes lining the wall. When the boxes fill up, I pull out the giant plastic bags that hold the cans, tie their mouths, and pile them into a colorful mountain. The glass bottles go into small carton boxes that are supposed to be stacked separately.

You're getting pretty good at this; I bet if we blind-folded you, you'd still net all them cans. I glance up from the cart to see Jim, the short, hairy manager, grinning from the door of his office. He has a cigarette in one hand, a phone cradled between shoulder and ear. I don't smile at Jim, which is what he expects me to do, and just keep on with my business. I can shoot a can of Pepsi into a box on one end of the wall, land a Faygo somewhere in the middle, and finish with a Natural Light on the other end, all without pausing, without having to check the labels.

I am done with the cans and just getting started on the bottles when the woman comes from behind me, which is where the other entrance is. I watch her walk by without even giving me a glance, like she's passing a rock. The way she twists, you would think she was maybe Beyoncé or Kim Kardashian, but she's nothing but green eyes and a tanned plank walking on black heels. When she gets to Jim's office he raises the phone cord and she slides under it and disappears inside before Jim slams the door shut. She is not even his wife; I know because I have seen the wife, always with their red-haired kid, who looks like a mosquito in tights.

It comes out of the bottle of Miller in my hands; I'm still standing there looking at Jim's door thinking about what they are doing when I feel something crawling up my arm. One glance, and the Miller bottles are shattering at my feet, shards of glass dancing all over the dirty floor. By the time Jim rushes out of the office to see what's happening, I'm standing on the table near the box-crusher thingy, screaming, my feet next to the microwave.

It's just a cockroach, Jim says, turning around to give me a look, his voice sounding like he is really talking about just a cockroach.

Now it has parked itself next to a can of Heineken

like it's trying to hear what's being said. It's the most gigantic thing, coat a deep, shining brown, like maybe it's coming from a spa. I cover my eyes when Jim lifts his foot to crush it. When I look again, he is sweeping it into a pan and carrying it to the big Dumpster near the entrance.

Come on, now, back to work, he says when he reappears. You don't have cockroaches in Africa? Jim does this thing that gets on my nerves: he always speaks as if Africa is just one country, even though I've told him that it is a continent with fifty-some countries, that other than my own country, I haven't really been to the rest of it to say what is what.

You're just acting up, I know you've seen all sorts of crazy shit over there, he says, speaking over his shoulder. I open my mouth to tell him to leave Africa out of it, but he disappears back in his office and slams the door, so I just hold up my middle finger and then get down from the table.

The beer bottles are the worst. They will come with all sorts of nasty things. Bloodstains. Pieces of trash. Cigarette stubs drowning in stale beer the color of urine, and one time, a used condom. When I started working here, back in tenth grade, I used to vomit on every shift.

'Darling to the front; Darling to the front, please,' says the voice bleeding from the crackling intercom. I don't need to be called twice; I'll take bagging groceries or sweeping the store, anything that will get me away from the nasty bottles. I

259

dump the Budweisers I'm holding back into the cart and head for the sink to wash my hands. I use tons of soap and extra-hot water because of the dirty bottles. When I pass the meat room with its terrible cold, I smile at the meat guy, who shouts something in his language and waves hi with a bloodied knife. I pause at the blue swinging doors with the sign Employees Only, fasten my apron tighter around my back, then I'm in the brightly lit store, the cold air licking me all over.

Hours later, I'm punched out and waiting in the hot parking lot for Uncle Kojo to pick me up. Megan, the talkative cashier, is sitting on the curb just to the side of the main entrance, texting her boyfriend and muttering about he should have been there ten minutes ago and how she is going to dump his trifling ass and this and that. Two police cars boil down the street, sirens wailing; now when I see a police car in this neighborhood, I don't even look surprised. Across the street, at the park with the two-cents grass, the Occupy people are holding up their signs, Occupying. When I first saw their pretty little tents and food piled on tables, I laughed at how they were trying to pretend they knew what suffering was.

The parking lot is almost deserted save for Jim's big blue van, a couple of cars, and a red bike. The old Jamaican guy with the fierce dreadlocks is rummaging through the Dumpster for bottles, a black trash bag slung over his shoulder, the golden head of a lion half visible on the back of his shirt. When he comes into the store all cleaned up and saying Rastafari this, Rastafari that, in his soft-spoken voice, his smile a brilliant, brilliant white, you wouldn't know he fishes for bottles in the trash; here, you don't even have to be a crazy to do that kind of thing.

I can't believe that skinny bitch was whining about me being let off early today, Megan says, putting her cell phone inside her purse. I can tell from her brief silence that she wants me to say something, so I say, even though I know who she's talking about, What skinny bitch?

That Teresa.

Hmmn, I say.

Did you hear her? Talking about she needs to pick her sick son up and stuff, like hello, I want to go home as well.

Hmmn, I say.

And I know that clown Jim was gonna let her go too because he's trynna get into her panties, she says.

Hmmn, I say.

I mean, she only just started working here and already she's asking for favors. Who does that?

Hmmn, I say. Sometimes I don't even bother coming up with proper words for conversation. It's not necessary; some people are content to just talk by themselves. Now the two police cars head back up the street; the sirens are off, and there's a black guy in the rear of each car.

It's fourteen years I've been here and no newbie is gonna be going home before I do. Vicky can go first, 'coz she's been here twenty years, so I'm real cool with her. But other than that, it's not gonna happen, hell to the no. I have seniority, you know what I'm saying? I don't know what Megan is saying but I still nod. Her phone beeps and she rummages inside her purse and fishes it out. A red card falls onto the ground. She doesn't notice, and I don't feel like opening my mouth to tell her; she just makes me feel tired with all her talk-talk-talk. I watch her read the text, eyebrows raised.

Son of a bitch, Megan mutters under her breath. I can tell from her knotted face and the vicious way she is punching her keypad that it is an angry message she's sending. Then time flips inside my head and I'm picturing Megan all old and gray, bending over a cash register to punch at the keys, stopping now and then to shuffle to the back of the main counter to get lottery tickets and cigarettes for customers. Inside me, I have this strange feeling that I can't explain, but it's almost like I want to lie down and cry for Megan.

Then I'm not seeing Megan anymore but myself, bent over a bottle cart. My face, wrinkled with age, is now shaped like a can of pop, and my head is a lump of snow. I have to drag myself to the can boxes because I am so old I cannot throw anymore. When I feel a hand on my shoulder, I jump. Then I turn around and Jim is standing there grinning. He has this thing of just touching

262

my body, like maybe he knows me like that, and I don't like it.

I scared you, didn't I? he says, his smile making like it will chase his ears away. I don't tell him that what scared me was my own daydreaming.

Do you want to work this weekend? Brian just called and canceled, no explanation whatsoever, Jim says. I am still thinking of my old self doing bottles so I say no inside my head, but then I hear my mouth say yes. It's summer, so I have to pick up as many hours as I can; next fall I start at the community college and Aunt Fostalina is having me save for it. I don't know, the way she talks about how expensive college is for foreign students and stuff, it's like maybe you're trying to buy a country or something.

Great, I'm gonna go ahead and put you on the schedule, he says, already walking back to the store. Then he pauses by the door.

You know what, Darling? You are a great kid. You are not like rest of them; you're different, Jim says. The double doors open and close like a mouth, swallowing him.

Yeah, he's right, Megan says. She has put the phone away again and is now just sitting there with legs crossed at the ankles, smoking and looking at the passing cars.

I mean, you're like all the other kids and all but then you're still different. You're not full of shit. It's an African thing, ain't it? My cousin is dating this guy from one of them little islands in Africa and he is the sweetest guy I ever seen. Nothing like this son of a bitch, who can't even keep a damn appointment, she says, kicking her purse.

Hmmn, I say. I'm not even listening to Megan; I'm thinking about how if I had a choice, I too would refuse to work on the nasty bottles. When Aunt Fostalina first talked to me about getting a job, I laughed.

You think it's funny? she said.

I'm not even an adult, what will I be working for? I said. I remember she didn't answer, how she just sat at the kitchen table sipping rooibos tea and poring over her bills, brows perpetually furrowed like Frida Kahlo had painted the frown there before she died.

I know we won't be going straight home and I don't ask where we are going. After TK was sent to Afghanistan, Uncle Kojo was fine at first, and then he wasn't. Now he has this thing about traveling, about being on the road; whenever he gets behind the wheel, it's like he wants to discover America. He went to the doctor and was told to take some time off, which he did, and to go home, which he couldn't do; even though he went to college and has been here for thirty-two years and works and his son, TK, was born here and everything, Uncle Kojo still has no papers. So the best he can do is drive around, sometimes short distances, sometimes long ones, which is why we now call him Vasco da Gama behind his back.

We pull out of the parking lot, get onto Main Street. We stay on it for a while, drive past people sitting on their porches and staring expressionlessly at the road the way adults used to wait for the NGO people back in Paradise; past groups of kids who stand in the middle of the street as if they are goats looking for water, the boys shirtless and all shades of black and brown, jeans pulled so low you can see the brilliant colors of their boxers; past girls strutting up and down like they are walking somewhere better than these hard, hot streets; past older-looking kids standing under fierce green trees that never bear fruit.

Instead of proceeding to turn onto Third Street, which would take us home, Vasco da Gama gets on Lincoln. I watch the neighborhood recede in the rearview mirror, the plank houses looking like they are planning to slam themselves onto the ground and howl once we are out of sight. Now the car slows down because of all the potholes. We keep going down Lincoln, down Lincoln, and in my head I'm singing, *Who discovered the way to India? Vasco da Gama! Vasco da Gama! Vasco da Gama!* And when Vasco da Gama tells me to keep quiet, I realize I have started to sing out loud. I stop the singing just as he swerves to avoid hitting a pit bull wandering around on its own.

We move slowly now, past the old apartment buildings on our left, weeds growing all around. On our right is a baseball field, and these white kids with striped blue uniforms are running all over the place, throwing and catching the ball. The adults are standing in clusters, looking on, rows of cars surrounding the little ballpark like teeth. Now I'm watching it in the rearview mirror, and when it disappears, I realize that around us it's become all jungle, carcasses of old cars drowning in tall grasses, abandoned old buildings with bashed windows and caved-in roofs and peeling walls. If these walls could talk, the buildings would stutter, wouldn't remember their names.

I'm not even expecting to see a person in this jungle when the woman emerges. Vasco da Gama is surprised too because he brakes sharply, jerking us forward. We watch her, a tall, thin woman crowded into this tiny black leather skirt and this red tank top. Her hips are yo-yos and she's walking toward us like she knew all along we were coming. Vasco da Gama has rolled down the windows, and outside, the heat is a steaming blanket; it is engulfing.

She peeks inside the driver's window and somehow it feels like she has entered the car and filled it with even more heat. When she says, Hi, sugar, I don't know if she's saying it to me or Vasco da Gama. Her large eyes look like she could drop to sleep at any moment. I cannot decide if she's beautiful or not, but she is nicely made up – eyebrows done, lips a light red, fingers painted to match her top.

You got a quarter? she says to nobody in particular, and I wonder what she's going to do with a quarter in a place like this, what that quarter is going to buy for her. Her voice is hoarse, like she's been singing at the top of Fambeki.

Then she looks at me and says, You're so cute, what's your name, sweetie? When I tell her, she smiles, and it's when she's smiling that I notice how beautiful she is, how really, really beautiful. Then the strangest thing happens – she just starts muttering my name like she's praying it. When Vasco da Gama holds out a twenty-dollar bill, she doesn't even take it – she's just standing there saying Darling and Darling and Darling over and over like she's crazy. It starts freaking me out and I am relieved when Uncle Kojo drives away. In the rearview mirror she looks like a chicken with the feathers plucked off.

When we get home Aunt Fostalina doesn't ask us where we were. She gets up from the couch and goes to the kitchen, where she has rice and beans and fish waiting. These days she cooks, because of Vasco da Gama's issue. What happened is that after TK left, Uncle Kojo stopped eating, and at first Aunt Fostalina laughed and said, in our language, Indoda izwa ngebhatshi layo, but when Vasco da Gama just kept on without eating and started losing weight, Aunt Fostalina went online and got recipes from his country because that's the only food she could get him to eat.

I pick up my Mac and get online; Vasco da Gama picks up the remote and starts flipping through the channels. The good thing is he doesn't watch that awful football anymore, with those giant men running and smashing into one another over a tiny ball. The bad thing, though, is that now Vasco da Gama watches nothing but the war – soldiers bombing things, soldiers walking streets carrying big guns, soldiers crawling on the ground, soldiers making things explode, soldiers smashing buildings, soldiers in big ol' cars crawling all over, children trying to dodge the soldiers to play on the street like they are supposed to.

But I know that Vasco da Gama doesn't really see all this, that he is busy scanning all those faces for TK, even the pretty faces of the Afghan kids. In the meantime TK just smiles his lopsided smile from the picture on the mantelpiece as if he is enjoying Vasco da Gama's anxiety, as if he will burst out laughing and get out of the army uniform that doesn't even suit him.

When TK said he was joining the army, I didn't even think he was for real. He just came one day when we were all eating spaghetti and said, I'm joining the army. I remember Vasco da Gama saying, What did you say? I remember TK looking at him like somebody had told him he was a man or something and saying, I said, I'm joining the army. I remember Vasco da Gama standing up calmly like he was going to the restroom and, instead, slapping TK real hard. I remember the cracking of it, like Vasco da Gama had dynamite in his hands.

★　★　★

The dusting takes me too long because there are just so many things to dust and only one of me. Not only that, this house is such a monster; there is the ground floor, then the second floor, then the third floor. My problem is that instead of cleaning like I'm supposed to, all I ever really want to do is check things out – the large piano, the strange fish tank with the colored fish to match the furniture, the tall bookcases filled with rows and rows of unread books, the Buddhas, the masks, all the queer statues on the ground floor, the paintings and art thingies, the long couches, the fireplace.

Then there is the kitchen with the many counters, the interesting fridge and stove and all the gadgets. The winding staircases, more couches upstairs, long TVs and more gadgets, the many bedrooms with interesting furniture and built-in bathrooms, the dog's bedroom, complete with a wardrobe full of dog clothes and things, the rooms stacked with shoes and shoes, the rooms that are just full of clothes, the gym with the many machines. I don't know how many rooms are here, how many people live in this house, but if I had a house like this, I wouldn't ever go out.

The woman who used to work here, Esperanza, left to see her sick mother in Mexico and did not return when she was supposed to, so that's how I'm here, doing her job while they find somebody else. The owner of the house, Eliot, is Aunt Fostalina's former boss. Aunt Fostalina says when she first came to America she went to school during the day and worked nights at Eliot's hotels, cleaning hotel rooms together with people from countries like Senegal, Cameroon, Tibet, the Philippines, Ethiopia, and so on. It was like the damn United Nations there, she likes to say.

Two weeks ago, when Eliot called Aunt Fostalina looking for someone trustworthy, she said she had someone, meaning me, and afterward, she told me not to even think about touching anything because there were hidden cameras all over. When I'm not working at the store, I have to come here, even though I don't like the idea of cleaning somebody's house, of picking up after someone else, because in my head this is not what I came to America for.

After I have dusted the obvious things, picked up socks and T-shirts and underwear and towels and magazines left all over the floors, cleaned all the bathrooms and counters and made the beds and vacuumed, I go to the kitchen, load the dirty dishes in the dishwasher. A couple of hours later, when I have done almost everything I need to do and am doing the kitchen counters, the door opens and Eliot walks in with a skinny girl I've never seen before but who I think must be his daughter, Kate. Titi, the weird little dog, trots in after them, wearing a pink leather jacket and a yellow bandanna around the neck.

Other times I would have lied and said, Awww, that is so cute, which is the right thing to say in a situation like this, but today I don't even try because this is too big for lies so I just do exactly what I am supposed to do, which is to shake my head. I mean, this is something else. Next time, I think to myself, this little dog will be wearing earrings and carrying a purse with an iPod and lip gloss inside. I watch it do rounds around the house like it is possessed. Finally, it circles around my legs, sniffing me, tail wagging and looking at my face like we speak the same language, but I just give it a talking eye and say, inside my head, *No, dog, you don't even know me like that.*

The dog stands there, and I look at it coolly, to show it that no matter what it does, I will never be friends with an animal, even though that animal has its own bedroom and pink bed and a closet and drawers full of expensive clothes and leashes. Finally it takes off, and I am pleased with myself because I'm thinking it's gotten the message, but before long it's back again, this time with a yellow rubber duck in its mouth. It drops the thing at my feet and looks up to me with pleading eyes. When I refuse to budge, it nudges my left leg with its little head; I flinch and tighten my leg muscles to stop myself from kicking the dog. *I'm not dealing with you*, I say inside my head, and I busy myself with the counters even though I've already cleaned them.

Hey, there, the place looks great, Eliot says, coming into the kitchen. When he says *the*, it sounds like *zee* – Zee place looks good. Zee pizza

271

is in zee fridge. He throws his keys on the counter, opens the fridge and fishes out an orange bottle of VitaminWater, unscrews the cap and aims it at the trash can at the opposite wall. When he misses, he shrugs, gulps down all the water, his Adam's apple dancing with each gulp. He belches and sets the bottle on the counter; this man is not even ashamed of not picking up the top.

So how is it going back there? Eliot says. He means my country. He likes this stupid phrase, *Back there*, and I hate the way he says it, as if my country is a place where the sun never rises. Before I respond he says, Have you met my daughter, Kate? She just came from college. Kate, this is Darling, Fostalina's niece. You remember Fostalina, don't you? Used to work at the hotel, babysat you and Joey sometimes, he says. Eliot turns to look at Kate, who is standing timidly just outside the kitchen like she needs a visa to come in.

Hi, she says. I nod and watch her. She doesn't know this but I already know all there is to know about her, know that two weeks ago she tried to kill herself at college after her boyfriend broke up with her because he said she was not sexy enough, but this is the part her parents don't know. I know that when she looks in the mirror she sees an ugly fat cow and that she hates her body because it's not what it's supposed to look like.

This is why she is starving herself, which again her parents don't know. I also know that if she cannot get out of eating she goes to the bathroom and vomits it all. It was all in her diary that I found hidden under the bed while I was cleaning her room; I read it because hidden things are meant to be discovered. I wonder how she lives, how she deals with the hunger, those long, terrible claws that dig and dig in your stomach until you can barely see, barely walk upright, barely think, and you would do anything, anything, for even just a crumb.

Kate is glistening with sweat, her long blackish hair sticking to her face. She is not ugly; in fact, I think she is very, very pretty, so I don't know what her issue is. From her looks, I don't think she can be that much older than me. She remains just standing there, looking like she needs my permission to move. The dog is now bothering Eliot, jumping around him and stuff, so he opens a cupboard, pulls out a bag of treats, holds one out in his palm. The dog picks it up and storms off.

Are you gonna get something to eat? Eliot says, heading for the stairs.

Yes, but I'm just gonna take a shower first, Kate says. Her voice sounds far away, like maybe it was detained at the border or something. She follows the father upstairs; I wonder where the mother is, but it's not my place to ask. I watch Kate head up, her Invisible Children T-shirt sticking to her body, bones screaming through the fabric. I pause briefly and wonder what exactly she will do when she gets upstairs, whether she will indeed take a shower or perhaps go to the toilet and do

273

something crazy. And if, before or after that, she will reach under the bed and write expensive nonsense in her expensive diary.

A little while later, I turn around from cleaning the doors of the fridge and she is standing behind me like a ghost. I wonder how long she's been there. Her hair is wet now and she is wearing Bastard's Cornell shirt.

You go to Cornell? I say. When I was thinking of applying to college, I was going to apply to Cornell because I felt like I already knew the place, like we had a connection, but then later I saw the tuition and almost died; if you are an international student like me, it is very hard to get scholarships. But still I am excited by the shirt, and I'm hoping Bastard will appear out of the air, that the whole gang will just appear. I start thinking of the things we would do in this neighborhood whose name I keep forgetting. I open my mouth, maybe to tell Kate about Bastard and the others and Paradise, but then I close it; there is nothing to say.

I watch her move around the kitchen like a cat, opening the fridge, opening cabinets and drawers. I busy myself with cleaning the sink, which I've actually already done; really, I'm looking to see what she is going to eat. When, at last, she has her breakfast arranged on her plate – five raisins, one little round thing, and a glass of water – I burst out laughing.

She turns to me with this confused look and I double over. I mean, I can't help it; I just kill myself with laughter. Because, Miss I Want to Be Sexy, there is this: You have a fridge bloated with food so no matter how much you starve yourself, you'll never know real, true hunger. Look around you, and you have all these riches that you don't even need; upstairs, your bed is fit for a king; you go to Cornell, where you can be anything you want; you don't even have to clean up after yourself because I'm doing it for you, right now; you have a dog whose wardrobe I couldn't afford; and, what's more, you're here, living in your own country of birth, so just exactly what is your real problem?

Later, Vasco da Gama comes to pick me up and I say good-bye to Kate, but she doesn't respond, which is how come I know that she is mad at me, but I don't really care because it's not like I stole her guavas. And besides, I don't work for her, I work for her father, and I doubt I'll get fired if she told – next week, I'm supposed to start teaching him my language because he says he and his brother are going to my country so he can shoot an elephant, something he has dreamed of doing ever since he was a boy. I don't know where my language comes in – like, does he want to ask the elephant if it wants to be killed or something? Anyway, I know I'll get paid well. Eliot always pays me well, and ever since that Kony video came out, he's been nice to me like I'm from Uganda, like I'm one of the heartbreaking kids in the film. He has traveled all over Africa but all he can ever tell you about the countries he has visited are the animals and parks he has seen.

We are going down West Main, headed toward the highway, and I'm wondering where Vasco da Gama is taking me when his phone starts to ring. He fishes it out of his shirt pocket, glances at the screen, and hands it to me, which means it's Aunt Fostalina on the phone.

You have to go to Shadybrook right away, she says.

We're on the road, I don't know where Vasco da Gama is headed, I say in my language so he doesn't understand.

Well, tell him to turn around.

But—

Darling, just put him on the phone, she says, and I know from the sound of her voice that it's serious. I do, and when Vasco da Gama makes a right at the light before the Walgreens, I suck the insides of my mouth, look out the window, and smile because I've been saved from another crazy trip.

At Shadybrook, Tshaka Zulu meets us at the door like he is the one who called us here; he steps out, pushes Uncle Kojo aside, hands me a real spear, and says, Be armed, warrior, those white vultures, wretched beaks dripping with blood, must not be allowed to settle on this black land. There is anxiety in his voice. Not knowing what to do or say, I just look at the spear in my hand, then at Uncle Kojo, and smile.

What did he say? What is he actually saying? Uncle Kojo asks, and I start translating Tshaka Zulu's words inside my head but it's hard to concentrate because now he is tilting his face toward the sky and uttering this terrible cry that is like nothing I have heard before; long after he has closed his mouth, the air is still ringing. In addition to wearing his dress, Tshaka Zulu has painted his body a bright red color, and his head is all red and black and white feathers. Today, he is awesome – even I have to agree that he looks like something else, which is maybe why I am also feeling this strange stirring inside me, this thing without a name that makes me want to clap my hands and jump and shout and just get crazy with it like I have swallowed electricity.

Where is it, the rest of my impi? We must do a cow horn right now, hurry, Tshaka Zulu says, looking this way and that.

This man is crazy. What is he saying? Uncle Kojo says, standing there like he doesn't know what to do.

The impi? I say. I am not smiling anymore because I am realizing that I have never seen Tshaka Zulu like this. There is a strange look in his eyes, like they are not eyes but maybe a pit and something fierce is raging inside. I don't need anyone to tell me that this is proper craziness. He has been getting worse lately – last week, for instance, he walked out of the nursing home when no one was looking and somehow convinced a stranger to take him to the airport. There, he demanded a jet to fly him to Buckingham Palace so he could go and talk to the queen about the things she owes him.

I look at the door and wonder where Claudine is, why she is not trying to do anything.

Tshaka Zulu turns and points in the distance, sweeping the air with his spear. Then I'm aware of the one I'm carrying. It's slightly heavy, the wood is old, the metal part a little rusty; where did he even get these things?

You see? You see what I'm seeing? he says, turning to look at me.

Yes, I see them, I say, but really all that's there are houses and trees and mailboxes and cars.

What are you talking about? Uncle Kojo says. He is ringing the bell now and banging the door and peering through the window. I nod vigorously, following where Tshaka Zulu is pointing. At the end of the street, three kids ride their bikes.

Are you seeing them as I am seeing them? What are you seeing? Tshaka Zulu says.

What is happening with this man? And why is that woman in there not doing anything? Uncle Kojo says. You can tell from his voice he is getting frustrated but I'm too worried to answer him so he just looks like another crazy talking to himself.

I said, what do you see, warrior? Tshaka Zulu says.

Vultures, I say with this slight quiver in my voice. I don't even know what I'm talking about.

If we ever let them settle, then the whole mother-land will fall, and we will be ruled by strangers. We will be forced to speak tongues from white lands, worship their wretched gods. They will enslave us on our own soil; we will be their dogs. But no, he says, and here he pauses and laughs. It is a big, big laugh, like it will swallow the sky.

I say no, by my father's black cow, today it will be death or victory.

When Tshaka Zulu says *death or victory*, my heart skips. It is the way he says it, says it through gritted teeth like he is hurting, the tendons at the sides of his neck popping. According to him, the white vultures are hovering close; some, he says, are on horseback, and some are crouching in bushes with their evil sticks that spit fire. His language is deepening now and I'm having a hard time understanding everything; it's like listening to a skipping record.

When he starts down the driveway, I follow at a distance, Uncle Kojo behind me. He is saying things but I'm not listening. Tshaka Zulu is rushing, his animal-skin skirt swooshing, the colorful feathers on his head dancing. Then he breaks into a run, and I notice, with horror, that he is running toward this pizza guy who has just parked at the neighbor's house and is getting out of his car, a pizza in hand. I'm already seeing a spear ripping the guy's guts, blood all over. I drop my own spear and look at Uncle Kojo, who is yelling and flailing his arms. The pizza guy looks

279

up just as the sound of sirens fills the air. I don't know who called the police, or when.

The pizza guy stands frozen for a second, then maybe something clicks in him and he quickly gets in the car and fumbles around. Tshaka Zulu's spear sails in the air, but it doesn't go far before falling on the pavement. By the time he bends to pick it up, the police cars have descended. Doors open and bang and I'm seeing guns all over, which is why I turn around and sprint back past Uncle Kojo toward the nursing home, where a face is looking out the window. Behind me I'm hearing: Drop your weapon! Stop! Get on the ground! Show your hands! Drop your weapon. Drop your weapon! Drop your weapon! And I know that Tshaka Zulu will not drop his weapon. When I look over my shoulder, he is lunging skyward like some crazy plane trying to take off.

CHAPTER 18

WRITING ON THE WALL

The night I mess up the wallpaper in my room, I am supposed to be studying wounds for my bio test. I don't really care a thing about the material I'm reading, or even about bio itself, and besides, I think wounds are just disgusting. Flipping through pages and pages of sickening pics, I feel my heart lurch. I know wounds are not flowers, but this is just too much. When I get to a discolored open mass oozing pus and blood on the side of this girl's face, I am done. I shut the book, slide it under the bed, and hear it connect with the wall.

I know already that this sciences thing that Aunt Fostalina is pushing me to focus on is just not for me. Now that I'm almost finished with high school, her thing is to go on and on about how I have to get into medicine or some kind of nursing or whatnot when I start college next year, or if that fails, at least do law. These, she says, are the careers that count, and I didn't come all the way to America to do meaningless stuff and be nothing. What I know, though, is that none of it sounds inspiring to me; I mean, I haven't figured out exactly what

I want to get into, but I have zero passion for what Aunt Fostalina wants me to do.

I am sitting on my bed and staring at the wall, just thinking about how I will begin to tell Aunt Fostalina this, when my new BlackBerry starts to vibrate. I find it under the covers, flip it open, and read Marina's text.

wt u doin?

nuthin. trynna study stupid bio, I text.

lol, y is it stupid? i kinda lykit, she texts.

thts coz u wanna be a doc. nt feelin it, I text.

wl u know my dad wants me to. n-e- ways, wt u gonn do? she texts.

dunno, I text. Marina doesn't respond for a while, and I'm not surprised. Ever since she moved to her fancy high school, we don't communicate like we used to. When she finally responds, I have taken a red marker and written *iBio iyirabishi* on the wall above my clothes hamper, and I'm drawing a circle around it. I pause to look at the vibrating phone, finish the circle, then pick it up.

sowwy, Kyle. hd 2 talk 2 him 4 a min, the text reads.

k, I text. On the wall, my letters are large, like how I used to write in grade one. The red looks like blood, and I realize, for the first time, that it will be hard to clean off.

I put on slippers and leave my room. The kitchen is bright from the streetlamps so I don't bother to turn on the lights. I get a sponge, squeeze a drop of dish soap on it, add a little water. On my way back I hit the side of my pelvic bone against the edge of the kitchen table. I double over in the half dark and quietly cuss. After the pain passes, I proceed to my room.

When I'm done cleaning the wall, it looks worse than before. The red has bled all over, leaving an ugly stain, and the letters have refused to fade. Once, when we hit Budapest, we took with us a bag of black markers we had gotten from the NGO people and we went crazy on the Durawalls. We drew penises, big penises, rows and rows of them, since we didn't know what vaginas looked like, then we complemented the penises with words like *golo, beche, mboro, mhata, svira, ntshompi, bolo, zeka,* and every other obscenity we could think of. I guess they tried to clean the mess later, but it wouldn't come off. There were stains on the walls for days until they painted them over.

When I look at my phone again, Marina has sent another text.

umn, **so we did it last night**, the text reads.

OMG! I text. Before she responds, I add, **did it hurt?**

thr ws no blood, she texts.

thn u didn't (rme), I text. When we gave up watching flicks, because Aunt Fostalina found us at it one day and whupped me and Marina, sparing Kristal because she said she didn't want to get into trouble since Americans call whupping child abuse, we made a bet to see who would do it first. Kristal is now pregnant, so the bet to see who will be next is between Marina and myself. I reach for the Juicy Fruit gum pack on the nightstand, take two pieces, peel the wrappers. I pop the gum in my mouth and chew slowly, the sweet taste exploding on my tongue.

u weren't thr, Marina texts.

wtevr. guess wht? I text.

wht? she texts.

i made up w. Tony, I text.

wht? she texts.

out. made out w. Tony, I text.

OMG! she texts, and before I respond, she adds, whr? hw ws it? wait, he's not gay? I hear voices talking outside my window; it sounds like the people are standing there, so I turn off the light, part the curtain, and look outside. In the dark, I can see the clustered silhouettes near the big tree by the road. My window is pulled up so I can hear the voices, but after listening for a bit, I realize they are talking in a foreign language. I don't recognize it, maybe a European language or something. I stand there for a while, my face pressing against the screen. When I turn the lights back on and look at the phone Marina has texted, ?????

lol, no. @chick, on wed., I text. On Wednesday, I arranged with Amma to come and pick me up. Aunt Fostalina was working nights. Amma rang the bell and I met her at the door with my book bag in one hand, a big bottle of water in my other. When Uncle Kojo looked at us with bloodshot eyes, because he was already halfway through his bottle of Jack Daniel's, I said, We're going to study for a test tomorrow, even though Uncle Kojo's drunken eyes said *You are actually not going anywhere decent dressed like that.*

Amma and I were on the dance floor at Chick when Tony and this other dude with dreadlocks came to join us. Amma was busy dancing, because that's who she is; me, I was just standing around because I think R & B and hiphop are kaka. Most of it doesn't make sense; I mean, it's all about insults – fuck this, bitch this, pussy this, whores that. But when the boys started grinding against us I began swaying to the music so I wasn't just standing there looking stupid. Tony's body was pressed tight behind mine like it would take a saw to separate us, his hands up and down my sides, groping my stomach. He was breathing hot air on my neck and I could feel his hard thing on my butt.

I remember the music changing to dancehall, which also has insults but at least its beat is danceable. Once, we had to stop dancing so we could watch this girl with a big weave standing on her head, her legs spread in the air, her yellow skimpy skirt bundled around her butt, white panties showing. Then this skinny boy with green hair just pounced on the girl like they were in a fight or something and grabbed her by the ankles, spread her legs even farther apart like he wanted to split her in half, started gyrating against her before flipping her around so she was bent over, after which he continuously slammed and pounded and just smashed into her like she was a piece of meat.

It was all weird, but everyone just went wild with cheers. I guess it was supposed to be this crazy new dance, daggering is the name of it. I thought it strange and wrong, but after a while I found myself clapping because that's what everyone was doing. When a new, quieter song came on, Tony turned me around and started kissing me out of nowhere but I thought maybe that's how it went. I was surprised by how it felt, his cold, awkward tongue like a slab of flesh in my mouth.

so hw ws it lyk? Marina texts.

dunno, cool, I text. I can picture her rolling her large eyes, her round face impatient for details. I toss the phone on the bed, pick up the marker, and start drawing dangling tongues on the wall, and before I know it, the tongues are turning into snakes – short snakes, long snakes, two-headed snakes. The phone vibrates, but I don't pick it up. When I'd gotten home that night, I went straight to the bathroom, took a brand-new toothbrush from under the sink, squeezed the biggest glob of toothpaste on it, and brushed with hot water and scraped my tongue before getting into the shower.

When I hear the main door opening downstairs I can tell, by how long it takes to close and by how hard it slams, that it's Vasco da Gama coming back from his travels. I picture him taking measured steps like he is jumping the border, almost tripping on the rows of shoes occupying half of the walkway before plopping on the large couch opposite the TV. I picture him tilting his head to the left and holding still, so still it's almost as if he is listening to God speak, and then, like one waking up from a brief sleep, jolting to life and reaching out for the remote on the glass coffee table in front of him. I picture him pressing buttons with his large, clumsy fingers, pressing and pressing, leaning forward now, fingers moving faster because he must find a war channel in case he is able to pick out his son from among the other American boys dressed like soldiers.

What is happening is that Vasco da Gama is getting worse. Now his travels are actually out of hand; each time, he goes farther and farther, like maybe he is practicing for driving to Afghanistan to get TK. At first he would stay away for hours, then it was one night, then it was a couple. He would return looking unkempt and fierce, like he'd been to war, murdered bugs and insects caking the hood of his car, the windshield, the grille, and the license plate. Aunt Fostalina, who is always busy with her jobs, isn't really doing anything about Vasco da Gama's issue. Maybe she hopes he will get tired of traveling; maybe she thinks it's the only thing that keeps him going; maybe she doesn't want to deal with it or just doesn't know what to do.

But that's not all: the beer and liquor bottles have begun to show up like they're produced by a magician. At first they were hidden under the car seat, in the trunk, under the kitchen sink, in the basement, just random places like that. Since I was always home if I wasn't at school or work, I would gather the bottles and throw them away because I knew it wouldn't be a good thing if Aunt Fostalina found them. In the end she did; you can't hide a thing like that forever. She was cleaning the basement one weekend and discovered the stashes and stashes of bottles. They talked about it but then it kept going on. That meant her and Uncle Kojo were done; now they are just living together, like neighboring countries.

Last week, I came home and caught Aunt Fostalina with Eliot. At first I had no idea he was in the house; I came in, made a sandwich, parked on the couch, and started texting Kristal when Eliot just appeared in the living room wearing these white boxers with red kisses, hairy stomach spilling all over the place, his thing sticking out against his boxers. He took me by surprise and I screamed. A little while later, Aunt Fostalina rushed in to see what was happening, wrapped in her favorite wrap cloth, the one with the little fading flags of our country.

Downstairs, I stand at the entrance of the living room and peek inside. Uncle Kojo sits in half darkness; the living room is lit by the TV, where exhausted-looking soldiers are walking through clouds of smoke, a couple of bombed-out cars burning behind them. It's afternoon on the TV, but the smoke is painting the day and making it look like night. There is just too much smoke. I think I'm beginning to smell it, beginning to see it seeping through the screen into our living room, covering Uncle Kojo. I leave him like that and go to the kitchen to microwave food for him because otherwise he will forget to eat.

When I get back I clear the bottles of gin from the table, replace them with Uncle Kojo's jollof rice and curry. He is leaning back on the couch now, his eyes closed; I don't know if he is sleeping or thinking or what. I watch his face for a while, then without knowing why I do it, I grab one of the gin bottles, take a sip. It's nasty and it burns; I swallow it only because there is nowhere to spit. It has started to rain on the TV, and a lone soldier is standing under a tree, smoking. I kneel at Uncle Kojo's feet, untie his shoes, and remove them. I think about shaking him to see if he is awake, but in the end I sit on the sofa and watch the soldier in the rain just standing there like his mother forgot him, like he is Syria and has been counted out of country-game.

The first thing I notice when I wake up in the morning is the mess on my wall. At first I don't know what happened, but then my thoughts quickly come together and I remember how I went crazy with the marker the night before. The clock on my bedside stand reads 7:15, which means I have less than half an hour to fix the wall before

Aunt Fostalina gets back from work. I fly out of bed and rush for the basement.

I head for the corner with the large storage boxes and quickly find one labeled HOMELAND DECORATIONS, ETC. I toss the lid aside and just start rummaging. Before long, I find this batik the size of a beach towel. It's a painting of a market scene and it's crazy with life and color, people selling things – fruits, vegetables, foodstuffs, colorful beads and cloth, handbags, belts, animal carvings, just anything you can think of. There's children, women, men, women with babies on their backs, old people, a couple of dogs, a bicycle, everybody and everything alive under a bright blue sky.

Looking at the cloth I'm remembering how beautiful it felt to be in a real scene like that, everybody just there together, mingling together, living together, before things fell apart. I begin to feel this ache in my heart that always comes when I think of home these days, so I put the batik aside and do some more digging. I find a medium-sized copper clock in the shape of the map of our country. There is a drawing of a giraffe in the center, reaching above some trees where the hands of the clock meet. The time is stuck at six o'clock, and the long hand is broken. And last, I find this weird mask; it's split in the center, one half white, the other black. The black half is split further in numerous crazy patterns that I can't figure out, but it looks interesting to me so I take it and the other stuff upstairs to my room.

When I have finished covering the wall, the mask

290

is looking at me with the puzzling face; it's like it's trying to tell me something that will take years for me to understand. Next to it, the clock telling a broken time. And finally, on the other side of the dresser, the batik market is mad busy. I imagine I can hear all sorts of things – vendors singing their wares, some calling out to me to buy things at reduced prices; boys whistling sweet tunes to girls; babies crying out for sweets: the voices of children singing Who discovered the way to India? and playing Andy-over; the mothers' laughter rising above everything else.

I stand there looking at the decorations like that, and then I remember this artifact that I found at Eliot's place when I was cleaning the other day. I get on my knees and reach under the bed, where I hid it. It's an ivory slab the shape of the African map, and right in the center of it is carved an eye. The rest of the slab is these intricate designs of various patterns.

When I saw the slab at Eliot's, sitting there with the other artifacts he'd bought on his world trips, it felt like the eye was looking at me so the right thing to do was to steal the ivory map. I hang it right above my bed and look around my room; it looks complete, but I feel like I'm not because I'm busy thinking about home and I feel like I can't breathe from missing it. It's a heavy feeling that I know will not go away so I pull out my Mac and get on Skype to call Mother.

It's Chipo who answers the phone. At first I

can't even tell it's Chipo; I think I'm speaking to a grown woman. When she tells me who she is, I am surprised to find her at my mother's house because surely she is too old for guavas now. Still, I think it'd be rude to ask what she is doing there so I don't bring it up.

Where are the others? I say, after we greet each other.

Bastard finally went to South Africa. Godknows is in Dubai. Sbho joined this theater group and I hear they'll be traveling and performing all over the world soon, she says.

And Stina? I say.

Oh, Stina? Stina is around but I'm not quite sure what his deal is. Sometimes he is here, sometimes he disappears for long spells at a time.

So it's just you all alone? I say.

I'm not alone, I have Darling here, she says.

Darling?

Yes, Darling, my daughter. You forget?

Oh, I say. We wait in silence, maybe because neither of us can think of anything to say. I'm picturing Chipo there all by herself, and I can't help but feel sorry for her, feel bad for her. Then something shifts inside me and I start to feel disappointed, and then angry at our leaders for making it all happen, for ruining everything.

I know it's bad, Chipo, I'm so sorry. It pains me to think about it, I say.

What is so bad? Why are you feeling pain? she says.

What they have done to our country. All the suffering, I say.

Well, everywhere where people live, there is suffering, she says.

I know. But last week I saw on BBC—

But you are not the one suffering. You think watching on BBC means you know what is going on? No, you don't, my friend, it's the wound that knows the texture of the pain; it's us who stayed here feeling the real suffering, so it's us who have a right to even say anything about that or anything and anybody, she says. Her flippant tone totally comes out of nowhere and slaps me in the face, just taking me by surprise. I am so shocked I don't know what to say.

What? I can't – well, it's my country too. It's our country too, I say. Here, Chipo laughs this crazy womanly laugh and I shake my head and think to myself, *What the fuck? Where is this even coming from?*

It's your country, Darling? Really, it's your country, are you sure? she says, and I can feel myself starting to get mad. I hover the mouse cursor over the red phone thingy, wondering if I should just click it and hang up because really, I have no time for this shit. When I look up, my eyes meet the eye above my bed; I let go of the mouse.

Where is my mother? Put my mother or grand-mother on the phone, I say.

Just tell me one thing. What are you doing *not*

in your country right now? Why did you run off to America, Darling Nonkululeko Nkala, huh? Why did you just leave? If it's your country, you have to love it to live in it and not leave it. You have to fight for it no matter what, to make it right. Tell me, do you abandon your house because it's burning or do you find water to put out the fire? And if you leave it burning, do you expect the flames to turn into water and put themselves out? You left it, Darling, my dear, you left the house burning and you have the guts to tell me, in that stupid accent that you were not even born with, that doesn't even suit you, that this is your country?

My head is buzzing. I throw the computer, and when I realize what I've done, it is sailing toward the wall. I gasp as it connects to the mask, cover my ears when they both crash onto the floor. I don't look to check the damage, I just get out of my room like the air has been sucked out. I find myself standing in TK's room, right in front of his bed. On the opposite wall is a blown-up poster of TK and his friend Boby doing the Azonto dance, limbs in these crazy postures, grins on their faces. I imagine TK making fun of me with that face so I turn away and look at the dartboard on the other wall. My heart is beating fast, and my throat is tight.

When I start feeling calm again I move around the room. It is spotless because Uncle Kojo keeps it dusted and clean; if you didn't know different, you'd think it was lived in. On the large desk, next to the TV, is an Xbox, a couple of DVDs, a box of Kleenex, a plastic cup filled with pen and pencils, a *Playboy*. Everything looks like TK will just walk in and use his things like he never left. I reach up to the big wooden shelf by the window, push the miniature drums to the side, reach my hand farther among the lions and leopards and elephants, and touch Tshaka Zulu.

Always, I do not expect the dead silence in this room, and to fill it, I will greet Tshaka Zulu and maybe go on to tell him about the weather. Or, if there is interesting stuff to report, I will tell him, things like: Aunt Fostalina is sleeping with that white man; there was a terrible earthquake in Japan; they are arresting people again at home. In his will, Tshaka Zulu said he wanted Aunt Fostalina to fly his ashes home and have them buried in his father's village, inside a kraal, like how it is supposed to be, but for now Aunt Fostalina cannot go back, none of us can.

Today, though, I have nothing to say to Tshaka Zulu; I just keep my hand on the wooden urn that's shaped like a calabash and stand there like I'm blessing it. I don't even move when Uncle Kojo comes in looking like he just emerged from a donkey's mouth.

They have actually killed bin Laden, he says, shouting, even though it's just the two of us in the quiet room. His breath reeks of alcohol and the smell hits me right in the stomach.

Oh, I say. I walk away from the shelf and stand by the window.

You know who he actually is?

That terrorist dude, I say. I catch myself too late, but today Uncle Kojo doesn't say anything to me for using the word *dude*. He is just standing there, his body filling the doorway, car keys in his hands. I notice the bandage above his wrist and wonder what happened to him, if he got wounded on one of his trips.

He was in Pakistan, hiding. Soon, the president will come out and make a statement. Yes, bin Laden is actually dead, isn't that something? he says, jiggling the keys.

When America put up the big reward for bin Laden, we made spears out of branches and went hunting for him. We had just appeared in Paradise and we needed new games while we waited for our parents to take us back to our real homes. At first we banged on the tin shacks yelling for bin Laden to come out, and when he didn't, we ran to the bushes at the end of the shanty. We looked in the tall khaki grass, in the thickets; climbed trees, looked under rocks. We searched everywhere. Then we went and climbed Fambeki, but by the time we got to the top, we were hot and bored. It was like looking for air; there was just no bin Laden.

Why are we even looking for him? Sbho said.

I don't know, this game is boring, we need better games, Chipo said.

Maybe we should look for Jesus, he is more important than bin Laden, Godknows said.

Jesus is worse, nobody can find Jesus, not even the Americans, Bastard said.

That's not true. Mother of Bones found him, I said. We were quiet for a while, standing there, tall because the mountain made us tall. We looked down. At the shanty. At the red earth. At Mzilikazi. At the Budapest houses in the distance. Bin Laden could have been anywhere.

We stood there. Above, the sun was busy frying us. Then Stina threw his spear down the mountain and we threw ours after his and watched them fly. Then Bastard went to the edge and started urinating, and Godknows and Stina joined him. Chipo and Sbho and myself stayed behind, watching the boys thrust their hips forward and shoot in the air, each wanting his pee to go the farthest.

We had given up on bin Laden and were just walking along Mzilikazi when we saw Ncuncu. Ncuncu had been Bornfree's dog for a good while before she just decided one day, for reasons that we would never know, to simply stop being his dog. Now she roamed Paradise and all over like a madman, scavenging for food and not even responding when you called her name or whistled to her. When we saw her there on Mzilikazi, we ran toward her, shouting, Bin Laden! Bin Laden!

Maybe Ncuncu heard us. Maybe she didn't. She remained there, right in the middle of the road, head bent toward something we couldn't see; you would have thought she was praying for the country. The big Lobels lorry came out of nowhere. Now we were flailing our arms like mad and screaming real hard to warn Ncuncu, but it was no use. The next thing we knew, there was a sickening *khu!* and the big lorry came to a halt. Then, while we were standing there stunned, it just took off and thundered away.

There was red on the road. Two gaping furrows where the tires had plowed into the earth. An unsounded yelp drowned in the hollow of a twisted throat. White fur, red streaks in some places, like somebody clumsy had tried to decorate. Big, bared teeth. Crushed meat. Long pink tongue licking the earth. A lone paw raised in a perfect high-five. Bones jutting from the side of the stomach. One eye popped out (I could not see the other). And the delicious, delicious smell of Lobels bread.